To

Nigel

DARK RIVER MELODY

All best wishes,

Happy Birthday!

Mick (M. D. Murphy)

DARK RIVER MELODY

M.D. Murphy

Cutting
Edge
Press

A Cutting Edge Press Paperback Original

Published in 2015 by Cutting Edge Press

www.cuttingedgepress.co.uk

Printed and bound in Great Britain

ISBN: 978-1-908122-63-6
E-PUB ISBN: 978-1-908122-64-3

As Ovid has sweetly in parable told,
We harden like trees, and like rivers grow cold.

Lady Mary Wortley Montagu, *Town Eclogues* (1747)

LONDON, DECEMBER 1799

CHAPTER 1

On the fluke of a tide, on the fate of the wind, a ship lurched down the river. The sailcloth was spanking in the breeze; a mile inland you could hear it coming. The fishermen caught it with the wind, heads tilted they listened to its slow heaving progression. The boards creaked and were never for a-ceasing. For nine months the waves had rocked this vessel, buggered its stern. Now it arrived in a slump upon the shores of the city.

Tom Gobey paced on deck in the greying light. The wind was in his ears and blustering through the bankside trees. From the shoreline a cacophony of voices filtered through the mist – sudden whoops, deafening cries, raucous laughter, women sobbing, men in song. Here was a city hell-bent on noise, dedicated to the art of hullabaloo. When one person shouted, another person roared – even the rats squealed louder than those in Botany Bay.

The ship shuddered along the dockside and ran aground against the wall. Gobey came down the gangplank with his left knee in pain. The black smoke drifted from the foundries, a metallic gas wafted in the air. The doxies wandered in their flimsy dresses, seeking out business in the way of all cities, on the whims of base men.

Gobey's legs were still rubbery from the sea voyage. He leaned on a railing and watched the river – it slipped the hips of the city, out towards the Tower, towards those grave dungeons from where he'd been transported. Driftwood, tangled nets, bobbing barrels and old mashed corks dragged with the tide.

His kin were of the river. River people. Mudlarks, they called them – those who worked the foreshores foraging among the waste. They lived in the squalid courts and alleys close to the Thames. Any day, every day, you would find them waiting on the steps for the tide to recede. When the river had departed, they'd wade out in search of coins, coal, metal – anything that might be sold. At the end of the day, their clothes were grimed rigid. They stood stiff when they removed them, like dismembered men. Gobey's father used to say. 'The river is in your blood. One way or another it will call to you.'

But Gobey wasn't called. He pleaded to be apprenticed as a printer for a publishing house, and eventually his father let him go. Of his known ancestry, he was the only person who had learned to read and write – it was that small accomplishment that led to his transportation. On that foul voyage he was shackled to an old purse thief, who had said, 'What ya done, what crime is yours?'

And Gobey had snapped back at him, 'I wrote a pamphlet that told the truth.'

'What truth is that?'

'All men are born equal. There's no God. The King is a parasite, the Government a taxing scourge on the poor.'

The old man had stared for some time. Then he spoke, as if a bollock was lodged in his throat. 'You call that truth.'

'I do.'

'I've never met a truth worth dying for.'

Long gone now, those folks who brought him up. His mother died with her boots on, they say – except she didn't have any boots. She left this world keeled against a riverboat, her feet stuck in the mud. A year to the day, his father died of natural causes. That is, the causes deemed natural from a life of ceaseless toil and squalor. One morning, in a life of forty years, he failed to rise. The sun came up without him, the tide swished out alone. If Gobey would live as long as his father, he had twelve years left – twelve years to build a life, to carve out an existence. Most of his friends were now scattered, and there were no surviving kin he could visit. All his love was now centred on his sweetheart, Eileen Dineen. He would cross Hades to find her, on hands and knees over scorching coals.

Gobey turned from the river to find a man staring at him – short, broad and muscled, something vicious in his look. He had a thick, stunted neck, a jaundiced wash to his eyes and complexion. He thought the man was smiling, but came to see he was showing his teeth – a snarl, or some spiteful gesture. Slowly and somewhat strangely, the man stepped backwards into a smoky warehouse and was lost in the mist.

Gobey moved uneasily from that place. He couldn't say he knew the man, but felt the man knew him. Whatever the case, there was little warmth in his demeanour. As he turned the corner, he had a strong impulse to watch his back. Before moving on, he turned to the smoky entrance of the warehouse. He caught another glimpse of that buttery face among the shadows, then all was lost in a cloud of steam.

Gobey wandered past the moored boats and stacked crates. A group of four slave traders stood colluding against the wall. Their collective breath washed in and out before them. He watched them, spitting and crushing the spit beneath their feet in the gravel. That vile old traffic had long ceased on these shores, but here was a band of rogue traders, running against history and contemptuous of any law. They were trying to hurry a lone slave through the docks.

One of the slavers was chewing tobacco, talking with the mash visible in his mouth His comrade was a big man, bursting out of his clothes. Breathless, the sweat steamed from him like a cooked dinner. The jacket could not contain his stomach, the breeches were pinched on his legs. He stepped forward and lashed the slave with a cat-o'-nine-tails. Swinging high and round, the whip-knots fizzed like blowflies, the cords cracked on impact.

Gobey made a slow approach, studying their actions. Though he had no stomach for a quarrel, it seemed he had no means of avoiding one. Trouble had followed him all his life, and to a large degree he had courted it – for he was forever trying to squeeze justice from unjust men. And he never could rely on his loose mouth to stay closed, even when he willed it to do so.

Gobey stood in the line of their spit. An impediment to the flow, he pointed to the beaten slave. 'Won't you let the gentleman be?'

'He ain't a gentleman.'

'Well let him be, whatever he is.'

'I'll do what I likes with him.'

'You don't have to beat him.'

'You ain't listening.'

'I am.'

'Then you ain't hearing.'

'I hear.'

The man raised the whip to strike the slave, but Gobey stood in front of him. They tussled, the slaver's belly vast and squashing against him. Pulling back, Gobey snatched the whip and hurled it into the river, trotting away from the men. As he passed, the cowering African called up to him. 'Okoye, my name is Okoye.'

Some way along the docks, Gobey turned and roared at the slavers. He cupped his hands to channel the sentiment – 'Liberty! Equality! Fraternity!' He trotted a few steps and turned once more, 'Freedom!' He could not say if he was endorsing the cause of the slaves, the French Revolutionaries, or his own free self. Free again, and already in trouble – more than he could ever know.

The slaver cursed and spat, wiped his mouth and spat again. He worked a hand into his coat and jerked out a snuffbox. After snorting a large pinch, his eyes went teary, two brown sticks shot out of his nose. He picked up a club and gathered some men. Someone handed him a leashed dog; he slapped its snout to make it wild. Then the men departed, with the dog half-crazed and ready for murder.

Gobey rode on the back of a passing cart along the docks. He felt something weighty on his lap, and found the slaver's money belt had somehow attached to him in the struggle. The belt buckle had got snagged on his shirt. Impoverished as he was, he didn't want their blood money, no part in their filthy trade. He thought about returning it, but thought again, for fear of his life. With a heavy heart, he tied the belt around his waist and tried not to dwell on the consequences.

Far from the docks, he was surprised to come across the vicious looking stranger again, standing on a box at the roadside. As the cart trundled past, the man mimicked the slicing of his throat, a chilling gesture of intent. Passing that man was like passing into the future, into the foretold vision of one's own demise. Gobey could not help wonder if he had stumbled upon some warped prophet of doom.

Some miles down the road, he hopped off the cart and made his way along the crowded streets. There were hawkers pacing on every corner, shouting over each other and over the street music that filtered from all directions. He walked headlong into the screeching pipes and fiddles, a monkey pounding a drum by the roadside. An aeolian harp was moaning in a window, the breeze passed through its strings. A woman with a large basket drifted into him. He stepped aside to let her pass. 'Get your cockles, fresh cockles, sir. All alive-o. All alive-o. Cockles for everyone, all alive-o.'

There was never so much noise on the colony – all he could hear was insects, birdsong, or prisoners working the land. In London, a man could barely hear his own voice, and everything was washed away in the disorientating commotion. There was nothing to do but enter that movement, join the throng.

He wandered through the coal fumes that choked his throat and stung his eyes. An old barrow man stood wheezing against the wall. He was standing on the squashed heads of two cauliflowers and rocking from side to side. He called out blindly, 'Any old veg, any old veg?'

Gobey passed the man and glanced down a tight passage. A band of fiddlers were playing merrily in that confinement. He laughed that anyone could make music in that restricted space. There was barely room to work their elbows without scraping the walls.

At Charing Cross, a wave of black fumes swept along the road. Gobey stepped into an alley, crouching on his haunches, his back against the wall. The carriage traffic fell silent and a strange singing voice rose in the distance – it seemed to pass along the alley walls into the rookeries, then drift down to river.

He sat crouched for some time to fathom that song, that singer. Never had he heard such a voice, nor could he call it human – not man, not woman, but some oddity in between.

Gobey stood and the pain struck his knee, shooting through the tendons on the back of his leg. When the fumes cleared, he went back onto the street. The air had a malodorous property that stained the shop fronts brown. He could taste the city smoke, as if it were emanating from his stomach, rising from his bowels.

On Charing Cross road a figure was slumped in the pillory. He approached that familiar face, those dangling grazed hands. Although the beard was longer, more ragged and now plaited to his belly, there could be no mistake – it was his old pamphleteer comrade, Johnny Steadman. 'Well, well, who's this then?'

Steadman looked up with a wary squint, then a broad grin swept his face. 'Holy Christ, if it's not Tom Gobey. The noble seditionist back on English shores. On English shores, my son.'

'Back I am.'

'That's never seven years.'

Gobey rustled Steadman's hair and peered behind the pillory at the wooden pole of his leg. 'Methinks it is.'

'A citizen again.'

'Sentence served, punishment done.'

'God bless you, son. God bless you.'

Steadman stood with his arms looped through the apparatus, the damp wood clamping his neck. He made a long open study of Gobey – tall and wiry in his ragged breeches, his hole-riddled boots, with the saddened eyes of a newfound yearning, thinner than he had ever been and ever should be. And what a mop of dark hair, a sprawling mass of crow wings and black tangles.

Steadman would have gone on staring, probing his soul and noting his state, but Gobey couldn't stand it, couldn't bear the scrutiny. 'What has you pilloried?' he said, laughing and making light of his mate's predicament. 'You look right at home.'

'Drunk in a tavern, singing on the top of me voice. I had the King, Church and Government guillotined in the verse, their heads rolled in the chorus.'

'A merry old song.'

'Not to the magistrate, not to him.'

'What's happened to all the old friends of freedom?'

'Fled, given up the fight, retired to the country or overseas. Beaten down or driven out. Prosecuted or persecuted, gone all the same.'

'Hey-ho, Johnny – back in the land of the dangerous.'

'A dangerous land for pamphleteers, my son.'

'I'm done with pamphleteering. I'm only here for Eileen, that's all. All me world is with Eileen.'

Steadman puffed his cheeks and wearily expelled the air. He hopped on his tatty leg pole and gritted his black teeth. He gestured with his hand, all the fingernails missing. 'She's not there, Gobey. I wish I could say she was. She's moved on, her rooms are empty.'

'Not there?'

'No, son.'

'Where is she?'

'They say she's abandoned the republic, gone to the other side.'

'Who says?'

'Everybody.'

'I can't believe it.'

'I met her a while back, dressed like an aristocrat, she was.'

'Are you making merry with me?'

'No, son, I ain't.'

'You sure?'

'Yes, son.'

'Where did you see her?'

'She was coming from the bone-setter, Mrs Shapp.'

'Did she talk about me?'

'She did.'

'What did she say?'

'She said never a day goes by when she doesn't think of you.'

'Yeah?'

'Yeah.'

Gobey closed his eyes and opened them – one of his lids fluttered and stilled. He thought he could detect that strange songster keening in the wind, but it was lost in a great flood of screeching carts and trundling barrows. 'Then why did she stop writing?'

'I don't know, son. I don't know these things.

'Where can I find the bone-setter?'

'Covent Garden, above Will's Coffee House. She's one of us, a republican.'

'She is?'

'Oh yeah.'

'Thanks, matey.'

Steadman looked him up and down again, a smile striking his face. 'What's wrong with your breeches? Methinks your arse is hanging out.'

'You're no gent yourself, look at the cut of you.'

They laughed for a moment and allowed the grace of it to linger. It was a long time since they had larked in this way. If much else had changed, their laughter remained, and laughter in all ages is the same – it masks a multitude and staves off the long march to the grave. 'Hey,' said Gobey, waving his hand. 'Was that you I heard singing in the mist?'

'Never heard a voice like it. There's some queer old hogs in this old town.'

'So it was you, singing in the mist, then?'

'Hey-ho, Tom Gobey, you freedom-loving bastard. Don't become a stranger. Come and see me down at the old place, we'll take a sup or two.'

'I'd say there's a good chance of me doing that.'

Gobey turned from Steadman and continued on his way. The wind rolled in from the Strand, rounding corners and lifting hats – it rattled the signs above the shops and taverns on its journey. The morning wore its winter coat of times remembered, and the city seemed as bleak and inhospitable as it had ever been. He stood like a post with the people tramping round him – the dribbling opium casualties wandering from den to den, the dissolute aristocrats coughing into their hands. On the corner, a gin-flushed doxy spat on her feet to clean them. In every direction there were filthy children wandering in the road.

Here was the city of all nations, built on the river and expanding with each year. And somewhere in this vast sprawling metropolis moved his sweetheart – green eyes, dark hair, cherry lips. He could sense her breath, the lilt of her words, the medicine cure of her laughter.

CHAPTER 2

There was nothing in Gobey's sphere that mattered more than Eileen. He had given no thought to where he might live, or how he might sustain himself when the slaver's money was spent. Nor could he envisage a life without her, a desolate existence of solitary striving. Believing his world to start and end with his sweetheart, there was nothing to do but find her. Find her in whatever state she might be in – married, in love, indifferent. In the months of sea travel, he had thought of little else – how she might have aged, progressed, altered. Day and night he had wrestled, agonized, tortured himself with thoughts of rejection. Seven years was a long time for an old love to grow cold, a new love to flourish – a candle blows out here, a flame ignites there. He would take her for better or worse, whatever way her life had taken her.

On a cold afternoon he hired some lodgings in Newgate. Weary from the long voyage, he climbed the stairs and entered a bright room. The window overlooked the prison, and the cries of the inmates echoed against the wall of a shadowy courtyard. Their voices left a chilling ring – men half-dead, and men gone so wrong you could never correct them. He knew all too well the ravages of prison life. On the colony he had known men to crawl the walls, eat dirt, pluck their own eyes out.

With no baggage and only the clothes he stood in, Gobey stretched on the bed. Every bone of his thin frame seemed to be aching, and yet, for all that fatigue, he couldn't rest. He rolled over and stood up, dizzy with the floor rocking like the sea. On the table there was a jug of cloudy water that he drank from. He wet his hands and ran them through his long dark hair. He was glad there was no mirror in the room, for he had no desire to witness the state of his pale face.

He came outside and merged with the street crowds. The drums had started for a public execution. The jeering followed the condemned man's cart and he turned away from the scaffold, the noosed rope swaying in the wind. The streets rocked with drunks, hundreds upon hundreds of unruly people. Blowing horns and waving flags, they had travelled from near and far, from every corner of the city – men, women and children, and with no shortage of dogs and livestock in tow.

He stepped into an alley and steered around the strewn bricks and discarded lumber. A dog followed him in, stopping and sniffing his breeches. No handsome hound, it had a flat snout, a head to crack kneecaps. He couldn't be sure if it had come in war or peace – its black-leathered bollocks were as big as fists and swinging. 'Halloa, Mr Dog, halloa.'

Someone was calling on the street. He looked to the mouth of the alley, a large man was staring down at him. It was the slave trader whose whip he'd thrown in the river, whose money belt he was now wearing. A party of men gathered around the man. Gobey started running, the dog chasing and tearing at his ankles. He vaulted a wall and jolted his knee on landing. Squeezing through a passage, he climbed a fence and slid down the other side. At the end of a winding track, he stopped to rest. His knee throbbed against his hand and the tremor ran the length of his arm.

In a scrubby field, there were drunks staggering half-naked, men squabbling with twiggy girls. Through the bushes, he could see flashes of naked flesh, some outdoor brothel, he presumed. He limped on, travelling along a muddy footpath that looped into a labyrinth of cramped alleyways. The hollow chirping of winter birds carried from the trees – winter birds in mournful chorus, with nothing to sing about and nothing to stop them singing.

He left the alleyways and came onto the street. Holborn was busy, full of hawkers and passing carriages. The tang of frying meat drifted from the chop houses. He turned to find the slave traders approaching, but they hadn't seen him. The big fellow was carrying the dog under his arm, and one was no more ugly than the other.

Gobey slipped into the hovel of a crowded tavern. Men stood drinking in front of a crackling fire, and most of the benches were taken. He made his way to a table and sat down. At the same table, a drunk who was too drunk to speak stared at him – stared and supped to break the monotony of his staring. He had a sickly, philosophical expression, but was too far gone to impart his wisdom.

Gobey made no attempt to speak to him. He consumed a pie without looking up, drank staring into his ale pot. His knee ached and he was glad to rest it. He gazed around the bustling room – people shouting, people gesticulating. The laughter was explosive, a terrible racket in the name of society. He had no desire to belong to any group – not unless, not until, not without his sweetheart.

In the heat of that room he grew sleepy, resting his elbows on the table, placing his chin on his hands. If he closed his eyes, he would surely fall face down. At times, it seemed he was back on the boat, the deck shifting and the waves rocking beneath his feet. The strange cackle of gulls still inhabited his mind, as if there were a pocket of sound in his head reserved for their callings.

He supped the ale and felt a wave of energy surge through him. In one corner of the tavern, coils of blue smoke were weaving haloes above the heads of the customers. A drunken man and his drunken wife had looped arms and were whirling in some jig of their own making. Heavy and swaying, they cleared the centre of the room, flailing with their arms and kicking their legs like wild combatants. He watched them with great amusement, reeling across the boards and back again. They were soon breathless, scrambling to a bench to slump down.

Gobey sat for a while, examining his own hands. They were rough and swollen from labouring in the prison camp, from wielding the pickaxe and sledgehammer. They had started to look like his father's hands, thick and hardened by the river. This brought to mind his mother's feet, thin and bony, never in her short life to grace a pair of shoes. He hadn't for some years wept for the loss of his parents, but now, back in the town of his birth, he yearned to belong to that lost tribe of mudlarks.

With the back of his fists he dried his eyes, pressing into the sockets and trying to stem the flow. Lost in memories of his family he gazed nonchalantly over to the window – a face was squashed against the pane, smudged and distorted. It was the face of that short, muscular man from the dock, once again making the chilling gesture of the slit throat.

Gobey bolted from the chair, knocking a pot of ale over the table. He made his way to the counter and gazed back at the window. The man was gone, but had left a slobbering impression of his face against the glass. At the back of the inn, beyond a long corridor, a door was left open and emitting daylight. He shifted towards the exit and the voice of one of the serving girls hollered at him. 'Hey! You can't go down there!'

'Just passing,' he called over his shoulder. He came into an alley and crossed into another, running the best he could with his knee throbbing. He passed beneath a bricked archway and down some steps that were strewn with damp newspapers and potato peelings. The cobbles were wet from the mist, shiny and slippery as he crossed them. He weaved in and out of the backstreets and stood at a narrow gap between two houses. He began to make his way through, but saw in the distant alley, the small chunky man was progressing towards him.

Gobey returned the way he had come, keeping precisely to the route, for he could not take the chance of wandering into a dead-end street. The steps that he had come down took twice as much effort going up. He passed through the back door of the inn and the same serving girl hollered again. 'Hey! What's your game?'

Gobey had no breath to reply, and raised his hand as some sort of apology. He lurched through a group of people and came out onto the street. The sun was concealed behind a bank of cloud, the pale sky had no rays to warm him. He gazed up and down the road for the bulldog pursuer, but could find no trace of him. Merging with the crowds, he shoaled like a fish downstream.

After walking for some miles, he found a shabby barber shop. He sat with a cloth swept over his shoulders. The barber, a plump man, was full of mirth and banter. 'Chop and shave?'

'That will do.'

He lifted Gobey's hair and let it flop on his shoulders. 'Now, young fellow, what will you have? Is it staying long to support the aristocracy, or going short for the French Revolutionaries?'

'Shortish.'

'Is that a French crop, or an English nip?'

'It's whatever you want to call it.'

The barber laughed heartily and rubbed his hands together. His eyes had a polished humour. 'Do you know,' he said, gesturing with the razor, 'in the year of seventeen ninety-nine, a man can't stand on a corner and say blast to the King?'

'I know it well.'

'That's some law.'

'It is.'

'Am I right?'

'You're not wrong.'

'Do you know what happened to a fellow called Kid Wake?'

'I don't.'

'He hollered at the King and got five years hard labour. He had to stand in the pillory for an hour a day – an hour a day for three months.'

Gobey gasped, closed and opened his eyes. He wanted to rant, to blurt it all out – *Do you know what happened to a fellow called Tom Gobey? Do you, do you? He wrote a pamphlet against the authorities and got seven years for telling the truth.* He held his tongue and nodded in agreement.

'Soon they'll be taxing our thoughts, then we'll all be poor as Bedlam beggars.'

'We would at that.'

The barber talked while he worked, and never stopped talking. He covered topics of great injustice but never did he lose his sense of wit, his knowing smile. He paced around Gobey, gesticulating with the scissors, pointing with his wooden comb. When making a point, he stamped his feet, crouched and laughed at his own humour.

When a man swaggered into the shop, the barber fell silent. It was the man who had pursued Gobey from the docks – he had grease smeared on his face, coal fragments on his lips. He seemed unaware that Gobey was seated inside. The barber fell grave on recognizing him 'Oh, it's you.'

The man caught sight of Gobey and backed out of the shop. Walking backwards, he passed the window, something truly odd about his movement like the sun coming up when it should be going down.

Gobey jerked to his feet and turned to the barber, 'Who's that?'

'Mr Sticks.'

'Who's he?'

'You don't want to know who he is.'

Now the barber seemed edgy, he kept looking to the window for the whereabouts of the man. The job was all but finished, and he wiped Gobey's face where he stood.

Gobey paid the bill and bought a cutthroat razor, tucking it into his belt. He shuffled his feet and stood for a dizzy moment, trying to gather his momentum. 'Is there another way out of here?'

'Only the front.'

'The front will have to do, then.'

'Are you in trouble with him?'

'It looks that way.'

'You don't want to be in trouble with Mr Sticks.'

Outside, the cold air clung to his freshly shaven face, the back of his bare neck. The coal fumes made a ticklish descent into his lungs and made him cough. To the left, a group of young chimney sweeps stood blowing into their hands and swigging from a gin bottle. Approaching from the right, two old men in tricorn hats were making merry – one threw up his hands and the other roared with laughter. Across the road some waifish doxies stamped winter from their feet, dancing a little and jostling each other. An ornate carriage stood in the road; the large black horses scraped their hooves, their pink gums glistening through the mist.

Wild and androgynous, it came once again without warning – the voice that had entranced him at Charing Cross. He gazed over to the working girls who had stopped to listen. He thought the song was from Handel's *Rinaldo*, but had never heard it sung like this. The soloist was messing with the rules, spanning octaves, flitting between contralto and alto.

He tracked the dying song to the carriage on the street. Mr Sticks was peering from the window. In honking laughter, he called across the road. 'You're dead, Tom Gobey, dead.' He raised a musket to his shoulder and fired with a terrific boom. The blast caused the horses to rear, driving the carriage through the smoke into the streets beyond.

Backwards rolling, Gobey tumbled into the barber shop with the gun spray in his face. From the ground, he stared at the ceiling – ears scorched, the sulphurous waft of gunpowder filling the room. Ice-cold and death-defiant, he could not move; there was no strength to lift him.

He passed out and came round with, his ears still ringing. He climbed to his feet and gazed around the blood-spattered shop. The musket spray had largely missed him, but the barber was not so lucky. He was slumped against the wall, fizzing through his nose and gurgling at the throat. There was nothing in the world Gobey could say to him, nothing to put things right. His brain was mangled with tufts of hair, it sat on his head in a lumpy heap. The blood ran from beneath him over the boards, where it formed a sticky pool in the corner. He made a loud expulsion of air, then ceased to exist – a final whistle played him out in a minor chord.

Gobey swayed, unable to comprehend the speed of events. He took a cloth from the barber's shelf and dabbed the blood on his forehead. His hands trembled and a chill took hold. He went out to the street, gazing manically at the passing faces and stumbling into an alley. Thinking hard, he could not place Mr Sticks, or establish any plausible reason why that man should want to kill him. It seemed he was back in a new England, an altered land – one where money belts fall on you, and short, muscular men are keen on your demise.

Onwards, with no sense of direction, with no plan in mind he came to a path between two fields, the lungs of the city. The air was clearer, free from coal smoke and waste vapours. He pressed his back against an oak and slid down, and was asleep by the time he hit the ground.

He woke trembling with the damp earth beneath him, the mist rolling over the grass in coils. He climbed unsteadily to his feet, felt his musket-ripped clothes, a gash on his forehead and nicks on his face. The smell of gunpowder was still with him; he kicked through the wet grass and couldn't walk it off. The black smoke rose above the distant houses – lung tickle, throat itch, chest collapse – what hope for a city with all things injurious hanging over its head?

He looped through a narrow passageway with the mist lingering. Rounding a corner, a young doxy stood in his line of breath – an intoxicating drift of gin came over him. There was not room to pass without turning sideways. They stood in hesitation for a moment. He could hear the rustle of her dress, a thin barrier against the elements. She took his hand in the most tender way. 'Something I can do for ya, sir?'

Their hip bones bumped and he released her hand. 'There's nothing I need, darling. Nothing at all.'

She squeezed past him. 'I'm out to find some business,' she said.'

He watched her progress along the narrow passage. She had no shoes and the soles of her feet were dotted with clinging stones. He couldn't see how she would survive – young girl, big city, danger abounding.

On the thoroughfare to Holborn, a group of seafarers jostled outside a tavern. Their tangled hair had tossing oceans, salt-spraying wind in it. They were raw and scabby their wiry beards concealing scurvy sores and blade scars. Hard and rugged, men who drank and fought for the fun of it. They had knives, whaling hooks, heavy cudgels behind their belts. One of them had a shrivelled monkey on his shoulder, eyeing events.

As Gobey passed, the monkey fired a nut into his cheek. He stopped with the sudden sting of it. The ape gibbered and fashioned menace with his mouth – it taunted, snarled and threatened with its wild swinging arms. The laughter of the men spilled around him. A burly seafarer stumbled forward and reached out, 'Hey laddie, no offence. The ape has no manners. He's spent too long at sea. Too long at sea, I say.'

Gobey shook his hand. 'None taken, none at all.'

Then, unbidden the seafarer spoke with a visionary gleam in his eyes. 'The wind is a siren, the albatross a sign of doom. Black clouds harbour black thoughts, barking seals are the devil's own dogs. Keep watch from the crow's nest, keep watch to guard your life, laddie. To guard your life.'

The man trailed off into tales of shanties, whale talk, waves as big as houses. Oblivious to those words, Gobey drifted away – it felt like he'd been threatened – worse still, cursed.

Leaving Holborn, Gobey passed a field scattered with bricks and old ragged clothes. He followed a trail of torn newspaper along the street. A carriage passed, the aristocrats peering at the window. One of them had a small dog on his lap. The dog was wearing a cravat, decorated with red ribbon – it had a sneery look in its eyes, a wet snotty nose that needed wiping. Gobey laughed and stuck out his tongue, and the canine lord seemed to acknowledge that action.

An old woman sidewinded across the street like a crab on migration. She had protruding wooden teeth, a single eye beaded in its socket. She stopped dead and he walked squarely into her. 'Sorry, lady. Sorry.'

'Clear off,' she lisped. 'Get off with ya.' He put a spring in his step, but she continued to holler as he travelled. 'Get out of me way!'

He paced into the thickening mist curling over the carts and shop fronts. The barrow boys roared imprecations at each other. He leaned against a tavern window to rest his knee. Bombarded with thoughts of Eileen, he struggled to recall her face. She was getting harder to conjure on first attempt, and he had to close his eyes to focus. Now he could see the black lashes, the nib of her nose. But she was fading like the river downstream, out to where the gulls cry to the boundless ocean. He wondered how many tides it would take to wash her to extinction.

CHAPTER 3

On a December afternoon, he made his way through the city. The streets were grey in the winter light, the mist gathered in the alleys. He decided he was not fit to meet Eileen in his present state and must shed his clothes. He had purchased a pair of boots, shiny black, slightly tight, that would need some breaking. He came out of the shoemaker's and walked up and down like a dandy. He might have danced a jig, for he had never owned a pair of new boots. Now, to complete the metamorphosis, he must rid himself of his convict attire, and take on a new garb for the winning of hearts.

He entered Donavan's tailor shop – lit with candles and overhead lanterns. Donavan worked by firelight at the back of the shop. He was seated on a stool, dressed in a long nightshirt, a floppy bed cap drooped over his shoulder. An industrious drone emanated from his throat, neither speech nor song, but more constant, more unconscious.

He watched the tailor working, but the old man didn't look up to acknowledge him. His eye was close to the needle, squinting to view his handiwork. He had a machine-like intensity, a repetitive automation of the fingers. He was fastened like a loom to yarn, inseparable from his daily labour. He suddenly jerked to his feet and began pissing into a pot. While completing that action, he continued to work with one hand, the cloth clasped beneath his armpit to keep the strain on the thread.

The clothes racks swished and Mr Sneathen appeared from behind them. 'Does the sir know,' he said, clearing his throat, 'that clothes come highly priced in this part of town?'

Gobey turned to the man with the polished voice – such a fine suit, an objectionable face. Here was a conceited countenance, a purse-pride of great proportions. Sneathen looked like a fellow who had taken a stumble from a high place, but hadn't yet adjusted to where he had fallen. 'The sir does.' Gobey tapped his money belt. 'And this sir will pay like the next sir.'

Sneathen didn't like the way Gobey smirked – the half-smile spoke of impertinence, an audacious spirit. The thing to do was get him dressed, take his money and remove him speedily from the premises – preferably without dirtying his hands. 'What-can-I-do-for-the-sir?' He hardly took a breath. 'Head-to-toe-is-it, a full refurbishment of existing attire?'

'That will do.'

The assistant condescended to take his measurements, but Gobey waved him away. 'I want something off the peg, from the rack. A shirt, a waistcoat, trousers and a long jacket. No frills, puffs or embroidery.'

Sneathen pouted in a disapproving manner. 'Grey or blue will do much to soften the profile. Why not try a dandy cream for the trousers, or a luxurious white for the scarf? We have a fine range of white silks.'

'Black, no scarf, no silk.'

Sneathen ploughed through the rows of stock, lifting the garments to the light. He turned to suggest a suitable jacket and caught sight of a large tattoo on Gobey's back as he removed his shirt. In blue ink, a crucified Christ was splayed there, two supplicant angels stood on either side catching the dripping blood. Beneath, in bold letters, it read, STRIKE ME FAIR, STAND FIRM AND DO YOUR DUTY.

The assistant thought he must be dealing with one of these lunatic prophets, a deranged expression of faith. 'You're a great Christian, I see.'

'I'm no Christian.'

'But you are a believer, yes?'

'I believe in Tom Paine, and no God you could name.'

'Then why,' Sneathen pointed with his nose, 'Why the illustration?'

'To taunt the prison guards that beat me.'

Sneathen fell silent, his distaste increasing with each exchange. He put a finger to his chin and held it – his head tilted at an angle, his mouth began to twist. 'The beatings have taken none of the sauce out of you.'

Gobey slipped into his trousers and squatted to feel the fit. He put on a double-breasted jacket that dropped to the knee. Sneathen hovered around, tugging the sleeves, brushing the shoulders and tweaking the velvet collar. 'There,' he said, 'You'll do very well for a pallbearer.'

'Let's hope it's not your funeral.'

The assistant tried to smile, but his face remained taut, his eyes glazed. He tried to think of a scathing reply, but nothing came to him. Instead, he held out his hand by way of demand, until Gobey paid him. Sneathen turned dismissively, and was soon lost among the clothes rails and mounds of stacked material.

Gobey left the shop and went to cross the road, but a horse and cart came trundling towards him – it was stacked with dead pigs. He waited for it to pass, the earth vibrating beneath his feet. Then, as if he were picturing a vision from a tale or a dream, a house across the road collapsed. In a puff of dust and debris the whole thing came down. It was no small miracle to see a fellow standing, unscathed among the splintered timber and powdered from head to toe in chalk and sawdust.

The crowds gathered and he moved on. Along the road two men were fighting, looping punches and aiming kicks. They grappled and fell to the ground, rolling in the mud and thrashing around with the carts steering around them. Fallen house, fallen men. He walked on in his new suit, the trouser legs brushing with a silky swish. He stood at a shop window and beheld his reflection – his recently shorn hair, his fine tailored suit, and eyes that seemed to be looking out of another man's body. There were two of Tom Gobey – the gentleman in the glass and the pamphleteer within. In another life, one might have turned his back on the other.

Gobey moved from the window into the crush of the city. He wondered if the jolly barber was still slumped against the wall. There would be a loved one waiting for him tonight, someone would miss him – no one with that much good humour could ever live alone. It was a terrible thing to leave him there, not an easy thing to forget. Such things keep men awake at night.

At the corner of Drury Lane, he stopped at some commotion – a man was being flogged at the tail end of a cart. Flogged at the scene of his crime, shirtless and lacerated and squirming like a snail in salt. His wife wept and danced with each lash, as if she were the recipient of the public punishment. Gobey couldn't watch, and wandered on, the sound of the whip following him – it danced around the buildings and returned as a ring of bells. He had been flogged too many times to witness another punishment, and the sound of the blows brought him shuddering back to one such occasion.

One day on the colony, he was shackled by the feet in a line of convicts. Their arms were left free to work, and they were driving in posts along a pathway to the encampment. The sun was high in the sky – it beat down on their scalps, reddened the backs of their necks. In that blistering heat, they were sweating in places a man shouldn't sweat, from the eyes it seemed, beneath their fingernails and in trickles from their ears. Gobey had hammered down a stake and dropped his tool when a shadow came over him. He turned to find Clusky, one of the guards – a big fellow, rounded at the shoulders with a tendency to stoop. When Clusky looked at you, he snarled, as if he stared through his teeth and had to raise his top lip to gain vision. 'I hears you're a supporter of the French Revolution,' he said. 'An English Jacobin.'

He knew better than to speak loosely with Clusky, for he was a man quick at turning words to his own advantage, and that advantage usually resulted in violence. Gobey tried not to play into his hands, making a slight tilt of his head that could not be interpreted as a nod for 'yes', or a shake for 'no'.

'I hears you say down with the King.'

Gobey made a half-shrug.

'I hears you say out with the Government.'

Gobey closed his eyes and opened them. The sweat was dripping off his nose and onto the soil below. The air he breathed was oven-hot, a stifling mass in his throat. All he could do was swallow and remain silent.

'I hears you're an atheist.'

What Gobey did next surprised himself – and to this day, he could not explain what had prompted this act of great foolishness. It was only a mouthful of words, but all of them wrong in the context of Clusky. Gobey shielded his eyes from the sun and boldly said, 'I've never known a poor man to benefit from any King, God or Government.'

Clusky beat him on the spot, making a hammer of his fist. He clubbed Gobey to the ground and stomped down upon his limbs. Then he had the guards tie him to a frame, where they lashed him, striking his back and zipping off his head. The cat-o'-nine-tails hummed and whirred through the air, and there was no ceasing of that sound – not in his mind, in the years to come, not in his dreams, or in the waking hour. In a mass of lacerations, they had left him to fry in the sun. And, if it's true what they say, that each flogging takes years off your life, then Tom Gobey should have been dead and buried long ago.

Resurrected on his feet now, he breathed in the cool London air. He tried to flee those memories of fever and sweat and savagery. Onwards he lurched, blinking and trying to unthink the hunger and the beatings, the death and vile stench – men rotting while alive, men rotting in their sleep. He thought he would be fleeing his whole life from the hum and whistle of that whip – not so much a cat as a vile demon, some snake-headed Medusa with knotted hair.

At Covent Garden, a sombre grey invaded the sky – a pale thickening overhead, something weighty in the atmosphere. Maybe a day away, but the snow was coming. He could feel it in his bones, sense it in the crisp plume of his breath. It had been so long since his last snowfall, but he had not forgotten those past winters when the snow had silenced the city.

At Will's Coffee House, he stopped beneath the sign, BONE-SETTER. He took the creaky stairs, heard the discordant cries of the planks. He rounded the top of the stairs and ducked a beam, the boards gave way under his feet and cracked as he passed. He looked down a narrow passageway where chairs lined the walls, a bearded codger sat leaning over his cane. 'Is this Mrs Shapp's place?'

The old man was having a nap, and the sudden voice stirred him. 'What? What's that you say? Speak up, lad. I can't hear a thing, not a whistle.'

'Mrs Shapp, is this her place?'

'Yes, yes. This is it, best bone-cruncher in the land.'

Gobey sat opposite and gazed at the old man – the ghostly rack of his face, the withered skin. Crooked and inflexible, he was fixed in a bow, his shiny knuckles holding the candlelight. The old man was in an advanced state of arthritis and every joint was stiff and swollen. He talked without pause for reply, and Tom Gobey listened respectfully.

A door opened along the passageway. Mrs Shapp swept out in a flowing gown, eclipsing the candlelight. She was tall and immense, blessed with a large bone structure. She had thick lips, a brick jaw, and would appear colossal compared to most men. She had immaculate glowing skin, her hair was pristine white, flowing to her waist. 'Mr Bobstain?' She spoke softly. 'Step this way.'

The codger struggled from his chair and hobbled towards the bone-setter. She turned calmly to Gobey. 'Do you have an appointment, sir? It's all appointments here, you know.'

'I'm Tom Gobey, a friend of citizen Steadman. I'm here on a matter of urgency.'

The bone-setter dropped an eyelid, or at least he thought she did. 'Let me deal with this gentleman, then we can talk.'

Bent as a horseshoe, the codger creaked his way into the room and closed the door. A few minutes passed and a deafening cry came from within. Then the old man waddled out, upright and at ease, his stick tapping the boards. He left by the staircase and called over his shoulder. 'A fine woman, fine indeed.'

'Hello there,' she called softly to Gobey. 'Come, do come.'

He entered and made a slow sweep of the room – the white bones mounted and framed, resting on stained cabinets; bones leaning against blank walls and dangling from the ceiling on string. They chimed as they knocked together, and every way he looked there was a femur, or a spray of ribs, or some gleaming part of a bleached skeleton. From behind the desk, she beckoned him to a chair. She studied his approach and spoke in a soothing tone. 'Left knee, much pain, some stiffness. No major restructuring.'

He gazed at her large slender hands, rings on all fingers, including the thumbs – an array of green and purple stones. 'I'm not here for a treatment. I'm looking for me sweetheart, Eileen Dineen. Johnny Steadman said she's been to visit you. I need to find her.'

'Does the knee swell?'

'I'm not here for me knee. I'm looking for me girl. Do you know her? Green eyes, dark hair, a mole on her left –'

The bone-setter raised a palm. 'I know her, she visits. Her collarbone has a habit of slipping out.'

'Eileen Dineen?

'Yes.'

'Where I can find her?'

'I don't know that, but she comes here.'

'Do you –'

'I'll say no more until I've seen your knee. You're going to need two strong legs to prop you.'

She led him to a bench by the window and sat him on the edge, his feet dangling off the ground. She rolled up his trouser leg and wrapped a hand over his knee. Gently rocking, the bone clicked with the motion. Using her thumbs, she pressed the swollen area, driving the fluid up towards his thigh. She nodded to the window. 'Can you see the doves on that roof, hear them cooing?' He looked up and the pain struck his knee and was gone. He saw nothing of what she had done to him.

'There,' she turned away. 'That's it. The best is over, the worse to come.' Her long gown trailed as she walked, the sleeves flaring like wings. She returned to the desk and gestured to him to sit. He adjusted his trousers and stepped down. There was no stiffness, no nagging ache as he moved. 'I'm sorry,' she said. 'Truly I am.'

'For what?'

'I take no pleasure in the telling.'

'Telling what?'

'Your sweetheart is with someone else. Another man has entered her life.'

The room swelled and rocked. He couldn't say whether he was standing or sitting, except that the floor had shifted beneath him. He was vaguely aware of her voice, the soft comforting tones. 'No, no,' he shook his head. 'You must be mistaken, you must. We're bound like pearls on a necklace. She's me first love, me last breath. There's nothing in this world, nothing without her.'

'I fix her bones, I mend her injuries. She comes to me when she's been rough-handled.'

'She does?'

Mrs Shapp nodded and studied his face – his eyes were almost black, his hands trembled and he didn't know what to do with them. 'Bones mend easier than hearts, Tom Gobey. But hearts do mend. When time and tide have done their work, they mend. You are young, you may love again on life's passage.'

He could not speak, he gazed at the ground. She continued to placate him, trying to meet his eyes. 'She has spoken of you with such tenderness. Each day she laments your absence. Whatever path her life has travelled, she still thinks of you.'

'And I . . .' he choked on his words and couldn't finish. He stood up and swayed, floating specks darting before his eyes. He tried to pay her, but she declined the offer. He made for the door with her voice behind him. 'Take care, Tom Gobey. There are men in this city more vile than the King, more ruthless than the clergy – men who answer to no one. Mind yourself, tread lightly as you go.'

'I'll come back for her.'

'You do that.'

He stumbled along the passage and went down the rickety stairs. He stood with his mind racing, stood for God knows how long. Then he lurched onto the street like a man half-blind. Outside, he entered a different London, one before dusk when the atmosphere is pitched into dimness – somewhere between the failing light and the illumination of the first candles, a time when the city takes a breath and holds it, holds it, until darkness reigns. He stepped off the street and crouched in an alley. Waylaid by the night he could barely breathe, scarcely envisage the dawning of a new day.

CHAPTER 4

In his hired rooms at Newgate, Gobey rested on the bed. He was thinking about his childhood, the life of a mudlark in the city. He recalled a day when the light was ashen, a mizzle of rain in the air. The tide had receded and he was with his mother, crossing the mud on the Thames. They were raking the soil for dropped coins and lost cargo from the boats that had overturned or sunk. His mother was singing as she worked, a lilting tune that made a comforting blanket around him. They had not been working long when an aristocrat's carriage stopped on the bank above. The window dropped open and a ruddy-faced nobleman appeared. He called out, 'Strumpet! Want some business?' He laughed and hooted, his comments incomprehensible to Gobey. His mother looked up, then immediately down and continued to work. She was a mudlark, not a prostitute, but often had to spurn the advances of rich men.

The carriage pulled away and Gobey was left with a sickening feeling in his stomach. He was no older than six or seven and didn't know what the man had said, but he thought it was something insulting. He remembered how his mother had stopped singing and proudly turned her back on the departing carriage.

Gobey watched his mother working. Her dress was shabby and torn, her feet were bare, as were his. He tugged at her dress to gain her attention and she turned to meet his eyes. Her face softened on seeing him. 'Hello, my petal.' She had a tender way of speaking. 'What is it, sweetheart?'

'What did the man say?'

'I don't know.' She shook her head in thought. 'The breeze must have blocked my ears.'

Gobey scratched his head, his dark eyes growing darker. He shifted his feet in the squelching mud. 'Why?' he said, staring innocently up at her. 'Why do rich men ride in fine carriages, when we have no money and have to work on the river?'

His mother took a deep breath and swept the hair from Gobey's forehead. 'Well,' she said hesitantly, trying to think of a simple way to explain things. 'Rich men have their wealth handed down through their families. They pass it on to their children when they die, and in that way the wealth stays within the bloodline.'

'And what will you hand me down?'

Grace Gobey laughed and cuddled her son, fingering his hair. She gazed at his grubby face. 'Love,' she said. 'I have nothing but love to give you.'

'What's love?'

'Love, my sweetheart, is the workings of the heart, beyond the taint of money.'

'And when will you give it to me?'

'I give it to you now. Now and in every moment that I live, I give you love.'

She gathered him in her arms and kissed the tip of his nose. He giggled and spoke with great joy in his voice, 'Then I am rich, already.'

'Yes, Lord Tom Gobey, you are rich, already.'

That night, Gobey was bedded down on the floor before the fire. They lived in one room off a courtyard on the Thames. There was little in the way of furniture inside – a small table and one chair, both salvaged from the river. There was no bed and the family bedding was arranged on the ground, blankets and old shawls piled in layers to keep them warm. The walls were damp and icy to the touch, even in summer. But this was not summer, it was November, and a draught was creeping beneath the door. The candle flames were flattening and rising in the breeze, and Gobey was dreamily watching them. His mother was seated beside him, stroking his hair. She was petting him and mumbling sweet nothings in his praise. He was blissfully lost in the sensation of surrender, of mutual devotion.

The door pushed open, shunting and shuddering over the stone floor. Gobey's father entered, bringing the damp night air with him. He smelt like a rag that had been stuffed up a chimney – it seemed half of London's coal smoke was clinging to his clothes. His bare feet made a padding sound as he moved about the room. He kissed his wife and ruffled his son's hair. He went to the table and unpacked a sack of potatoes, a loaf of bread and some coal that he'd wrapped in newspaper. He then used the sack to shut out the draft beneath the door. James Gobey crouched at the fire to warm his hands. He spoke over his shoulder, 'There was a hanging today at Newgate.'

Grace Gobey was seated on the makeshift bed with her son. 'Oh dear.' She sighed and shook her head. 'Anyone we know?'

'Methinks not. A young man from Camden Town, they say.'

Though sleepy beneath the blankets, Gobey listened intently to the conversation. He had a vivid image of a man half-throttled by the hang rope and swinging in the wind. To his way of thinking, the man was not yet dead, but waiting for the privilege. Gobey had never witnessed a hanging, but he imagined that the man's feet would dance, twitch and eventually still.

His father joined them on the blankets, aglow in the firelight. The flames made licking shadows over the ceiling and walls. Without lifting his head, Gobey addressed his father, 'Why did they hang the man, Da?'

'He broke the law, son. He committed a crime.'

'What did he do?'

'He stole some apples.'

Gobey took a few moments to consider this. His mind roamed many avenues before he said, 'Just apples? But you can get apples at the back of Thompson's field, for nothing.'

'Yes, son, you can. I think he stole a handkerchief, too.'

'But we can make a handkerchief from an old rag.'

'Yes, we can.'

'It seems a small crime, Da.'

'Well, it is, son. It is. But he stole them from a gentleman, you see.'

'Is that a bigger crime?'

'Yes, I'm afraid it is. But do you know what the biggest crime of all is, son?'

'What, Da?'

'Poverty.'

'What's *poverty*, Da?

'It's living like us son. Living like us.'

Gobey was sleepy and he closed his eyes. The wind spiralled across the river and moaned within the surrounding courtyards. He imagined this to be the voice of a thousand hanged thieves. He was trying to fathom the world in which he lived, a world where aristocrats could insult his mother and hungry men were hanged at Newgate. In some abstract way, he was beginning to see there were different rules for different people, and that the poor were unlikely to receive any favourable treatment under the law.

Gobey carried this sense of injustice into his life. By the time he was apprenticed as a printer, he was already a republican in his thinking. He was now working for the book publisher, Joseph Johnson, who had befriended radicals and religious dissenters, and was happy to publish their works. Gobey read every pamphlet from the press, ever hungry for new theories on political justice. As a boy, his parents had accepted the inequalities of life, as if nothing could be changed in the balance between rich and poor. This assumption was to be proved wrong – for a momentous event across the Channel had made all things seem possible, when the French had embarked on a revolution.

Now, a decade on, transported and released, Gobey was seated at the window of his Newgate rooms. He looked back with much affection on the events that led up to the glorious day . . .

It was a hot day in July, the year 1789. It had rained in London and the streets were wet and glistening. The air was fuggy and it was sweltering inside the print house. Gobey gasped for air and fanned himself with a sheet of paper. The printing press had stopped to alter settings and change the ink. Gobey was working with his old friend Johnny Steadman, whose leg had been crushed in a carriage accident the previous year. Steadman now had a pole instead of a leg and was hopping up and down on the boards. He was halfway through the telling of some past caper when the door pushed open and their employer, Joseph Johnson, breezed into the room.

The boys were embarrassed that they had been caught in an idle moment, laughing and joking – though Johnson had never been a hard taskmaster and was always lenient with them. On this day, they had no need to worry, as Johnson was beaming and apparently delighted with himself. He stood in the doorway with sparkly eyes and flared nostrils. His hair looked much like a wig, with a clipped fringe and two curls on each side of his ears. His arms became animated when he spoke. 'Salutations, salutations. Have you heard, boys? Boys, have you heard?'

Gobey had a deep respect for his employer. He shook his head and smiled. 'Heard what, sir? What news is there to hear?'

'The French,' he said. 'The French have made an assault on the Bastille. The downtrodden are rising up, boys. Rising up.'

'Is it true, sir?'

'It is, young Gobey, it is. And do you know what that means in terms of work, my lad?'

'That we should change the settings on the press for new pamphlets, sir?'

'No, no, not at all, young Gobey. Not at all. It means you are shutting up shop for the day and we are off to celebrate.'

'Very good, sir. Very good.'

Johnson led his young workers out of the premises. They waited for a carriage to pass, then crossed the road, entering a smoky tavern. Johnson ordered pots of ale and was in the most generous of moods. They drank and joked and speculated on the future of France and how this new-found liberty would surely reach home shores.

The day became night in drunken merriment, laughter and song. Johnson was in his early fifties and was more like a benevolent uncle than an employer. The three men spilled onto the street and, before parting, the publisher shook the hands of his workers and stood back to speak. 'Boys,' he said. 'The French have shed their fetters, now the English must do the same.'

After that celebratory night in the tavern, Johnson's affection for Gobey had grown. He began to take an interest in his young printer, especially when he discovered that Gobey had aspirations to become a pamphleteer. Gobey continued to read every pamphlet, tract and bill that he could lay his hands on. He honed his writing skills and was quickly developing his political strategy. In the first year of the French Revolution, he was able to claim with some conviction – *I am a republican, an atheist, against all established religion, monarchies and Government. I am from the poor and will fight for the rights of the poor.*

Johnson took Gobey to his heart and was happy to act as his mentor. Each week Gobey would write a pamphlet for the publisher's perusal. The following week, Johnson would invite Gobey to his home to discuss the piece. This would inevitably result in Johnson making a jovial dissection of his young student's work. The publisher tested Gobey's theories, tweaking his writing style and challenging his youthful boldness. Johnson had used a memorable phrase to end these sessions: 'Tom Gobey, you have it half-right and therefore half-wrong.'

Each night, after a long day in the printing shop, Gobey would write by candlelight, perfecting his diction and working towards a political manifesto to liberate the poor. On some nights, his friend Johnny Steadman would join him. They would drink much rum and set about changing the world in the image of the French Revolution. On these nights, they would pour scorn and mockery on King George and the prime minister, William Pitt. They were young men, electrified by events in France and utterly carried away on a wave of euphoria.

Time after time, Gobey would return to Johnson's house to hear the same jovial mantra: 'You have it half-right and therefore half-wrong.' It was here that Gobey was introduced to the luminaries of the day – a fine band of liberals, radicals and religious dissenters. He met the Swiss artist, Henry Fuseli; the radical writer and orator, John Thelwall; the chemist and radical Unitarian, Joseph Priestley; the political philosopher, William Godwin; the pamphleteer and novelist, Mary Wollstonecraft; the dissenting preacher, Richard Price; the poet, William Blake; and the political author Tom Paine, who was fast growing in reputation and notoriety.

In such distinguished company, Gobey flourished. Inspired and energized he continued to write with great fervour, often working through the night to finish a pamphlet, or to formulate a theory for the redistribution of wealth. His squalid days as a mudlark never left him, and he used these hard times to fuel the justice of his arguments. If he ever doubted the conviction of his quest, he only had to think of his mother spending a lifetime without shoes – and his father, hunched and broken from scavenging on the banks of the dark river.

Following an accustomed invitation to Johnson's house one morning, Gobey arrived to receive a critique of his work. He entered the study to find the publisher not his usual jovial self. He was looking pinched and jowly, tired around the eyes. He did not rise from his chair with the usual greeting and merely looked up at Gobey. Never knowing Johnson as anything other than congenial, Gobey imagined some crisis or bereavement in the publisher's life.

Johnson rose from the chair and took a long time to stand. He moved in weary stages, as if any quick motion might cause him distress. 'Tom Gobey,' he said in a solemn voice. 'I have stayed up most of the night to read your pamphlet.'

'You did, sir?'

'Yes, I had to use candle wax to keep my eyes open.'

This would have normally been a source of amusement between them, but on this occasion, Gobey thought it inappropriate to laugh, or even respond to the comment. It was not usual for Johnson to work through the night and Gobey began to wonder if he had upset the publisher in some way.

Johnson continued. 'This pamphlet you have written – it's all your own work, is it?'

'Developed over many months and written this week.'

'You've had no help from another. Is that true?'

'No help at all – except from yourself, sir.'

'So, you want to become a pamphleteer, do you?'

'I do, sir.'

'And you believe you have the credentials for the calling'

'I hope so.'

'And you will champion the causes of the poor?'

'I will, me heart's in the work.'

'You have no fondness for the monarchy or aristocracy, I take it?'

'None at all.'

'So, young Gobey. What makes you think that anyone would desire to read your work?'

'Well, I . . . I –'

Gobey stammered, and before he had time to finish, Johnson cut in on him. 'Speak up. Tell me, do. Why should anyone wish to read your work?'

'Because . . . because . . . I write the truth, where others remain silent.'

'And this cause of the poor, you say your heart is in it, is that the case?'

'It is, sir. Every scrap of me heart.'

'Then we shall see it published. Immediately.' Johnson laughed heartily and it was apparent that he had been in good spirits all along. In truth, he was nothing more than tired from having stayed up late to read Gobey's pamphlet. Johnson shook Gobey's hand to seal the deal.

Weak on his legs, Gobey almost collapsed on hearing the news. Joy engulfed him. 'Do you mean it, sir? Is it true? You shall publish my pamphlet, my work? Are you sure I'm not half-right and therefore half-wrong?'

'Tom Gobey, you are most right with this one, and I shall have it printed and sold in your good name.'

The months that followed saw Gobey published many times from Johnson's house. He was a frequent contributor to the *Analytical Review* and brought out many pamphlets that sold abundantly in the contentious political climate. He continued to be nurtured by Johnson and their friendship grew into a deep and mutual respect. Gobey earned modestly and, for the first time in his life, he was able to save a small amount of money. He never lost sight of his mudlark origins and deeply regretted that his mother had died without experiencing the benefits of her son's success. He wished he could have seen her in her first pair of shoes – laughing and not knowing how to walk in a way that wasn't flat-footed.

Now working as a pamphleteer, Gobey gave up his post as a printer, only helping Johnson when the publishing house was particularly busy. In Fetter Lane he hired premises with Johnny Steadman and they started their own pamphlet house, a small concern that mostly produced handbills and short publications, used for agitation purposes and handed out on the street.

It was on the street, distributing handbills, that Gobey had first met Eileen Dineen. He seemed to remember they had in some way collided, knocked into each other. He had stopped to apologize and was immediately struck by her presence. There was something familiar and comforting about her, as if they had met in some past existence. She had wit, charm, beauty and a natural warmth that made conversing smooth and effortless. He found she was Irish and had a lilting tone to her voice – a voice that just fell short of song in her longer sentences. She was also a radical with a particular interest in the struggle for women's rights. It turned out they moved in the same republican circles, but had never met until this day.

Now, standing at the window of his Newgate rooms, Gobey treasured the memories of getting to know Eileen. Their first meeting was every bit as momentous as the French Revolution – for he was blasted with enthusiasm, blinded with love for that sweet Irish girl. He came to see there were revolutions of history, where the balance of power was overturned, and revolutions of the heart, where the Bastille of emotions was stormed, altering things forever. And altered he was, from the first day they had met – things would never be the same. Something had stirred inside of him, something exquisitely powerful and impossible to manage. His feelings for Eileen would not leave him – not in a state dungeon or prison hulk, not on the fathomless ocean or in the penal colony.

Gobey gazed into the courtyard of Newgate prison. He was tearful and his chest felt weighted, as if someone had replaced his heart with a stone. He had felt this oppression while mourning his parents – the crushing sense of sorrow, a hollow feeling in his gut. It seemed he was in mourning again, grieving for his sweetheart, yearning for her resurrection.

Gobey's mind tripped back to better days, when his life was giddy with love, his heart overspilling with joy. He recalled a day in London, campaigning on the streets. It was winter and the windows were white with frost. The sky was full of coal smoke that cascaded down towards the river. He stood with Eileen on a street corner, distributing handbills and calling out slogans. 'Liberty! Equality! Fraternity! Follow the French, unshackle the poor!'

The day was unremarkable in itself – they had distributed many handbills, sold some pamphlets and debated the iniquities of privilege with some disagreeable aristocrats. Leaving the streets, they adjourned to a tavern and found a bench in the corner. There was a peaceful clientele inside, seated at the tables and speaking in low tones. The fire was crackling its way through a log, smoking and spitting sparks onto the hearth. They shared a pie and a pot of ale and were full of merriment, teasing each other about the day's events – who had said what to whom – and who had argued the most vehemently with the aristocrats. They mimicked the voices and gestures of people they had met on the street, shrieking with laughter and shedding tears in the process.

Looking back, Gobey recalled how they were utterly absorbed in each other. The tavern might have been empty for the notice they gave to the people around them. They were insular as a couple, an island afloat on the dreamscape of the city. And it felt to him then, as it did now, that they were in some way conjoined as a single organism. They laughed and cried at the same things and were stirred by injustice and stilled by the beauty of art and nature – like Romantic poets, they never tired of exploring the inward life of the imagination and emotions. And when they argued, and sometimes they did, raising their voices and remonstrating with their hands, it was always soon forgotten, as neither had a tendency for grudges or sulking.

They left the tavern and entered the crisp London air. The frost had accumulated on the shop fronts and ledges of the houses. The light was failing and a blue glint tinged the atmosphere. A frieze of stars was becoming visible above the river, a walkway to the sky. Lanterns were being lit in the windows, red and yellow auras colouring the street and glowing in the faces of the passing people. Wrapped in their long coats they walked in a huddle, Gobey taller, with his arm on her shoulder, and Eileen nuzzled into his side. In the white ministry of frost, London was consecrated, blessed and purified of a million inequalities, a miasma of squalor – it seemed that nature had levelled the playing field where man had so miserably failed.

They arrived at Gobey's rooms in Bloomsbury, gasping from the cold and rubbing their hands for warmth. They raced up the stairs and Gobey reached the top first, but Eileen tugged his coat and squeezed by in front of him. Then he caught her on the landing and kissed her against the wall.

They bundled inside, fleeing the weather. Gobey knelt to the fireplace and used a flint, tin pot and some tinder to start the fire. Behind him, Eileen was lighting the lanterns around the room, the shadows creeping up the walls. Gobey built the fire with thin layers of wood, until the flames were ready to receive coal. When the fire was blazing, he turned to find her naked, standing before him. She was shivering and laughing and hugging herself to keep warm.

He embraced her and massaged the goose pimples on her arms. He steered her towards the fire, massaging and caressing, until her skin was smooth under his hands. He undressed and they slipped beneath a blanket on a large sofa that faced the fire. She shrieked when he joined her, the coolness of his limbs making her shiver. In the act of love, they drove winter from their hearts and the cold bite of the frost could not set its teeth upon them.

Later, entwined in the firelight, she stroked his hair and sang a lilting ballad. In that tender moment, he felt like a boy again, in utter surrender to forces beyond his control. Never had he felt more secure, never had he felt more liberated. There was not a thing in the world he would have changed about her – not a lock of hair, not a word of speech. And it was this moment he would recall, again and again, in the prison camp, when his spirits were crushed and desolate.

CHAPTER 5

In these early days working for Johnson, Gobey was at his happiest. He had mastered the art of the pen, had transcended his roots as a mudlark and was hopelessly in love with Eileen Dineen. There seemed little in his life that could go wrong, and the future had much promise. In the wake of the French Revolution, in the Age of Reason, he truly believed the old regimes of Church, Government and monarchy were about to be replaced by a just republic. Gobey envisaged the day when the workers would be represented in Parliament, the poor would have an equal share in the nation's wealth and religious tolerance would be guaranteed.

Now pacing his Newgate rooms, he looked back on events with wiser eyes. And had he not been so blinded by youthful idealism, he might have read the signs and taken heed to avoid his downfall. But in truth, it was difficult to read history while history was in the making, and it was only with the passage of time that he came to fathom his own dire narrative.

Gobey recalled how the tide began to change against his radical circle. The first sign came in 1790, when Edmund Burke had published a pamphlet, *Reflections on the Revolution in France*. Burke condemned the French revolutionaries as anarchists, hell-bent on destroying the Church and constitution. Gobey had visited Johnson's office and found the publisher waving a copy of Burke's work in air. 'Have you read this?' he said, throwing the pamphlet down. 'It's an outrage, an outrage.'

Gobey had read the piece, but thought it nothing more than the conservative ranting of an old man. 'I've read it, Joseph. It seems most odd that Burke should support the American Revolution and condemn the French for the same.'

'Odd? It's more than odd, it's dangerous. I'm sure if Burke had his way, he'd have us all strung up – dissenters, atheists, republicans and all.'

'Maybe you should put out a pamphlet against it, promoting the Revolution.'

'I am doing just that, Tom Gobey I'm publishing one by Mary Wollstonecraft – *A Vindication of the Rights of Men.* It questions hereditary property and honours, the privileges enjoyed by the rich over the poor. And Tom Paine is to follow up with another pamphlet, *The Rights of Man.* This should keep Burke quiet for a while, silence the old fool.'

And Gobey, thinking no more of the matter, had replied, 'I'm sure it will, Joseph. I'm sure it will.'

But not even Johnson, with his careful publisher's instinct could have predicted what was coming next. A full-scale pamphlet war broke out between the loyalists and the reformers. The loyalists continued to condemn the French Revolution and to support the Church, Government and monarchy, while the reformers persisted in challenging them. And Gobey, like a pawn in the game of politics, was drawn deeper into radical life, forever penning and constructing new arguments against the traditionalists.

The hostilities continued, until in 1792, Gobey received a message to visit Johnson's house. When he entered the publisher's study, he found Johnson in pensive mood. He was seated at his desk, surrounded by piles of pamphlets, handbills and assorted reading matter. 'Take a seat, Tom Gobey'

Gobey sat facing Johnson across the desk. Johnson was looking pale and gaunt, folds of loose skin hooded his eyes. His breath was laboured and he exhaled noisily before speaking. 'Oh, Gobey, my fellow. We are in trouble. The friends of freedom are in trouble.'

'How so, Joseph?'

'Events in France have overtaken us. The revolutionaries are massacring the royalist prisoners, persecuting the clergy. It's exacerbating ill-will against us at home. Now the Government have joined the affray. They live in fear we shall rise up and topple the system. They want to drive us down, to silence us in any way they can.'

'Are things truly so bad?'

'They are, Gobey, they are. Between the King and Pitt, they'll have us hauled through the courts and imprisoned.'

Impassioned by his new life as a pamphleteer, Gobey did not share Johnson's fears. He thought the publisher was overworked and perhaps overreacting to the situation. There was something slightly manic in his countenance. 'Well, Joseph, I'm sure we'll survive whatever is thrown at us.'

'They've introduced a Seditious Writings Act to silence us. And there are spies, Government spies tracking us and watching our every move. They're studying our literature, trying to catch us for any small thing that might fall foul of the law. We are being watched, I tell you.'

Gobey was truly worried about Johnson's state of mind. He suspected he was paranoid and giving way to unnecessary anxiety. Gobey was not blind to the fact there was a growing hostility towards the French Revolution, but he didn't share the publisher's fear, or anticipate the devastation that was about to unfold. And yet, there were so many signs, so many that he might have heeded to moderate his radical activities.

On a mild September night, Gobey had dined at Johnson's home. They had finished dinner and were seated at a long table, drinking port and brandy. The room was dimly lit with lanterns, a soft light bathing the faces of the company. Thelwall, Priestley and Godwin were present, deep in discussion on the politics of the day. There was a congenial atmosphere and a sense of camaraderie between the men. They were discussing the problem of property and how it might be distributed to achieve a more equal society.

Godwin ran a hand over his thinning hair, a scalp that was beginning to shine. His nose was slightly bulbous and his face was flushed from consuming fine port. With his elbows on the table he said, 'Well, I think whatever comes into my possession without violence to man or society – whether it be house, carriage or watch, or some other item – might fairly be called my own.'

Thelwall raised his eyebrows, his eyes slightly slanted at the corners. His hair was dark and sculpted around his ears. He fingered his neck scarf as he spoke, 'Yes, yes, William,' he smiled at Godwin. 'Do keep your house, carriage and watch – by all means do. But I'm with Tom Paine on this one. I follow the French National Assembly that sanctions the ownership of property, unless it is required for the greater public need. Then the state can appropriate and redistribute the property as it deems fit.'

Priestly shook his head, laughing, his short fringe bouncing on his forehead. His eyes sparkled and his lips were moist from the port. 'Gentlemen, gentlemen,' he said, gazing around the table. 'Since when has there ever been an obligation to throw our goods into common ownership? Never I say, never. What this country needs is equal rights, not equal property.'

Gobey sat in silence, harbouring his own radical beliefs. He was the youngest in the room and felt overawed by the distinguished company. Around the table were some of the finest freethinkers in the world, famous and infamous, men who often made the newspapers. Listening intently, his eyes followed the voice of the speaker, from one to the other, up and down and across the table, following the debate wherever it travelled. He caught Johnson's eye and found the publisher smiling at him.

Ever the egalitarian, Johnson raised his voice to gain the men's attention. 'Gentleman, we have an up-and-coming pamphleteer in our midst. We have discussed, deliberated and pontificated all night, but have not yet thought to ask his opinion. Let us consult the voice of the nation's youth.'

The men fell silent and all eyes turned to Gobey.

Johnson continued, 'Young Tom, what say you on the matter of property?'

Gobey felt the room shrink, the walls closing in. His face felt like a portrait, stared at in a gallery. He swallowed and found his throat dry and itchy. He reached for his glass to moisten his vocal cords and found that his hand was shaking, visibly moving against his will. One small sip of brandy seemed to take aeons to ingest. When he placed the glass down, the sound rang in his ears. 'Gentlemen,' he said, his voice alien and trembling, strange even to himself. 'I think we should abolish all property rights. All property should be brought into common ownership. Every working man and every working woman should have a share in the common property of society.'

Godwin, who had begun the discussion, was most intrigued. 'A bold proposition, young Gobey, 'A bold proposition, young Gobey, a bold proposition. But how are we to encourage the aristocrats and landed classes to relinquish their wealth and goods?'

'With the greatest respect, sir. We don't encourage them.'

Godwin wiped his shiny forehead with his hand. His nose was glowing red in the lantern light. 'We don't? Then what should we do?'

'We should take it, appropriate all the nation's wealth for all the nation's people.'

'But how will we take it?'

'By revolution, sir. The same as the French – by revolution.'

The room fell silent. A clock could be heard ticking in the hall, the echoey shifts of the pendulum. It was widely known that Godwin was in favour of transforming society by use of the pen and not the sword. The political philosopher scratched his head and appeared to be dumbfounded. The men were thrown deep into thought, and when it seemed that no one was fit for speech, Johnson roared with laughter. 'Ha ha!' he said, clapping his hands. 'Gentlemen, we must concede defeat on the matter of property and give way to young Tom Gobey, who is growing more radical by the day.' Johnson looked to Gobey and raised his glass, 'Gentleman, let us make a toast to our French allies across the Channel. Long live the Revolution!'

The men raised their glasses above their heads and bellowed in unison, 'Long live the Revolution!'

On that celebratory night, Gobey might have sensed that his politics were becoming too radical for the times. But he did not – in fact, the occasion spurred him on, taking heart from the thought that he had constructed a theory on property that was more extreme than that of his distinguished friends. It made him more determined to define his own arguments and develop a theory of government to benefit the urban poor. And thus, he began work on his most radical pamphlet yet – a piece that challenged the authority of the clergy, monarchy and government.

While Gobey was labouring at his desk, the world was unexpectedly changing around him. The Government was infiltrating radical circles, intercepting their post and employing spies to gain evidence against them. Loyalist associations were set up in opposition to reforming groups and societies. Church-and-King mobs were sent to break up meetings and exact violence against those who challenged the status quo. Even when the situation was pointed out, Gobey was so full of zeal that he failed to comprehend the gravity of events.

John Thelwall had tried to steer Gobey towards a more cautious path. He warned him to keep his radicalism out of print and to only voice his ideas behind closed doors, in the company of like-minded people. Thelwall had invited Gobey to a meeting of the London Corresponding Society, a radical group he had helped form. On the night in question, they made their way down to Chalk Farm for the meeting. They were drinking in a tavern and in fine spirits, discussing their vision of a new republic where the balance of power would remain with the masses.

In the rooms above the tavern, they arrived late, entering with the meeting underway. The room was smoky and the ceiling stained yellow from the smoke. There were lanterns hung on the walls and naked candles alight on the windowsills. A fellow called Thomas Hardy stood to address the audience. He was a shoemaker, who spoke with much eloquence against privilege and hereditary wealth. He went on to attack the high taxes, unjust laws and restrictions on liberty. When he finished, the crowd roared and applauded, stomping their feet and raising their fists in the air.

Standing at the back, Gobey was overjoyed in the moment. Never had he seen so many mobilized workers gathered for the purpose of protest. Here were men like himself, emanating from the poorer classes and determined to liberate their brethren from squalor and poverty. Among these working men, Gobey felt a sense of belonging and camaraderie. All things seemed possible in their company – the disbandment of the monarchy, the dissolution of Parliament, the disempowerment of the Church.

While the men were busy in debate, Thelwall nudged Gobey with his elbow. 'There,' he said. 'Over there, can you see him?'

Gobey gazed around the room and could see a great many people. 'Who?' he said. 'Who are you talking about?'

'Do you see the fellow in the corner?'

'What fellow?'

'The one with the notebook, the one writing as we speak.'

Gobey focused on the man in question, a rotund specimen in a dark suit. Head down, he was writing in a small notebook that rested on the flat of his hand. 'What of him?' said Gobey. 'Who is he?'

Thelwall spoke from the corner of his mouth. He kept his eyes on the man as he addressed Gobey. 'He's a rat, that's who.'

'A rat?'

'A slimy, filthy rat.'

'How so?'

'He's a Government spy. Here to keep an eye on us, to report back on our activities.'

Gobey narrowed his eyes, as if the man might become clearer, more fathomable in his intentions. He didn't look any different from any other man in the room – except he was busy writing in his notebook. That didn't seem unusual in a meeting of this kind, where an agenda was followed. For the purposes of his own pamphlet work, he might have taken a few notes himself. Gobey considered that the man might be a journalist, working for one of the many city newspapers or journals.

While he was pondering these things, Thelwall nudged him again, 'There, citizen Gobey. Over there, spot ye another rat, another slimy informer.'

Gobey's eyes fell on a tall man leaning against the wall. He had his arms folded and although he appeared to be relaxed, there was something in his demeanour that said he was uncomfortable in that environment. He was furtively looking around, nervously processing the events of the evening. But before Gobey had time to further reflect on the man's purpose, Thomas Hardy stood once again to address the meeting. 'Gentlemen, the people of Great Britain are not effectively represented in Parliament. And as a consequence of this partial, unequal and inadequate representation, we have been subjected to high taxes and harsh laws. We, the industrious people of Great Britain are thus forced to bear the brunt for the excesses of the rich.'

Inspired by the speaker, Gobey was distracted from what Thelwall had said about the spies. His mind was now cogitating his own political theories and he was desperate to begin work on his forthcoming pamphlet. He shook Thelwall's hand. 'Citizen,' he said, 'I must depart. I'm struck with ideas and must return home to transpose them to paper.'

'So soon? The meeting has some way to go.'

'I must, I must, lest I should lose my thread in the process. I thank you heartily for bringing me here. You have started something glorious – the London Corresponding Society is a noble thing, a noble thing. Oh, to have the workers mobilized and ready for a fight, a noble thing. And now change is in the air, truly in the air. Make way for the Revolution.'

Gobey turned and began to leave. As he crossed the floor, he heard Thelwall call to him: 'Citizen Gobey. Beware of the spies, I say. Beware.'

He briefly turned to acknowledge Thelwall's warning, but by the time he had left the premises, he had forgotten every word his friend had said. There was no room in his mind for anything other than the production of a pamphlet to overturn the system, to topple the powers that be. Looking back, he saw he was giddy in the moment, carried away with the impetus of change that had swept across the Channel.

Desperate to begin writing, he looked for a carriage to take him to Bloomsbury. He made his way through Chalk Farm, past the braziers of the street vendors. It was winter and windless, not a flutter of breeze in the atmosphere. The mist stood in isolated pockets, only visible in the beams of light from the shops and houses. It was cold on the street, but his heart was ablaze with the fire of revolution.

He took the road to Camden Town and was about to enter a carriage when someone called from behind. 'Tom Gobey! My word, is it you?'

He turned to find his friend, Samuel Coleridge – a poet who was a year younger than Gobey, a good-natured fellow with an enthusiastic disposition. Coleridge had been studying at Cambridge, but had decamped to enjoy the pleasures of the city. Their paths had crossed through radical circles and they had got on famously, sharing the same lust for radical politics. Gobey was most pleased to see him, 'Good Sam, how is thee?'

Coleridge's hair was wild and unkempt, his eyes were large and glossy. 'Most well, Gobey. Most well, methinks.'

'Escaped again from Cambridge, I see.'

'Knowledge alone cannot feed the soul. One must have a good fill of the senses, I say.'

Gobey patted his shoulder and laughed. 'You are not wrong, Sam. Not wrong at all.'

Coleridge skipped a little and was most animated with his gestures. 'Say, where are you going in such a hurry?'

'I'm off to work on a pamphlet – it has all me heart and attention at the moment.'

'Does it make a turnip out of King George and a sausage out of Prime Minister Pitt?'

'It does, Sam. Most definitely, it does.'

They laughed and shook hands. 'Say,' Coleridge beckoned with his head towards a tavern that was close by. 'We must have a sup and some small converse.'

'I really should be getting back to the job at hand.'

But Coleridge, always most persuasive in matters relating to pleasure, would not let Gobey leave. 'Well,' he said, with a glint of mischief in his eyes. 'Most pamphlets could benefit from a little lubrication, it frees the mind from formal thought. Come, do come, just for one and no more. I can't stay long myself, for I have a meeting with a certain lady of the night.'

Gobey laughed and succumbed to the inevitable. They entered a tavern on the corner and cut their way through the smoke. They found a table in front of the fire and sat within its illumination. They ordered pots of ale and were in high spirits, discussing the French Revolution. Coleridge had befriended the religious dissenters at Cambridge and claimed to have been almost expelled for singeing the words 'Liberty' and 'Equality' into the college lawn.

The one drink that Coleridge had promised turned into many more. They spent the evening discussing politics and promoting ideas to transform society. Gobey had spoken about the theories of his proposed pamphlet and Coleridge had sucked the air through his teeth and said, 'Be careful, you could land yourself in trouble with such proposals.'

Coleridge went on to explain that a dissenting meeting in Cambridge had been attacked, and that an effigy of Tom Paine had been burnt on Market Hill. He had been dosing on opium to calm a rheumatic fever and it gave his eyes a strange luminosity. It made him look like a man half-mad, or one prone to prophecies. Before they went their separate ways, Coleridge had drawn close and spoken with a hiss in his voice. 'Watch yourself, Tom Gobey. These are dangerous times, dangerous times.'

But Gobey was incapable of watching himself, of calming his passion. In the same evening he had been warned twice – first by Thelwall and then Coleridge – but to no avail. For he was so embroiled in the quest for freedom that all signs and warnings failed to impact on his mind. For Gobey was not acting with his mind, but feeling with his heart, a heartfelt certainty of the morality of revolution.

He left the tavern with Coleridge's words looping in his head. *These are dangerous times, dangerous times*. He stood groggily on the street. The ale had him off balance, stumbling to regain his footing. The cold night air sobered him a little. He crossed the road and hired a carriage to take him home.

The coachman geed the horses and they set off through Camden Town. The streets were dark and misty, the tavern lanterns shimmered in a haze. From the window, he languorously watched the revellers, drunk and animated, carnivalesque in the theatre of the night. There was much to gain his attention: the doxies, thin as slinky cats, sliding against the walls; the hawkers layered with rags and calling out in yodelling echoes.

London travelled outside the window, a wonderland of mist and disembodied voices. He passed the coiling alleys and cobbled streets, the nooks and shadowy courtyards. The river was like a sleeping serpent, bedded down for the night.

From the left window of the carriage, there was a house fire in the distance. The building was engulfed and the flames were spewing from the windows and rising through the roof. He watched the destruction knowing there was nothing he could do to reverse the process. He hoped there was no one hurt – men, women, children, dogs, cats or rats – that they would all remain untouched by the blaze. The inferno, in its terrible beauty, made an aurora borealis of the night sky.

Gobey arrived at his rooms feeling almost sober. He climbed the stairs, two at a time, eager to begin his work. His mind felt lucid, as if he had processed the contents of a thousand pamphlets into one distilled hypothesis. Seated at his desk in the candlelight, he began to write.

He worked all night, the scratching sound of his quill filling the silence of the room. Like one in a frenzy, he hardly paused for reflection or rest. He filled page after page, underlining the headings and making notes in the margins. The desk was scattered with the notes and scraps of writing he had made over the previous weeks. He worked with urgency, frantic to finish the work, lest his ideas should depart with the arrival of a new day.

As the first glint of dawn struck the window, he put his quill down. He had drafted the full pamphlet and felt depleted. His temples throbbed from the drinking bout with Coleridge, and it was only now he had stopped working that he fully felt the depth of his fatigue. He was hanging tired, desperate for rest.

That morning, as the first shafts of light crossed the river, he fell face down on his bed. While London was waking, Gobey slept, removed from time and preoccupation a deep slumber without dreams. In that night's work his fate had been cast, his destiny sealed like a corpse in a tomb.

In the days that followed, he crafted and redrafted his pamphlet. Gobey was his own worst critic, frequently scrapping whole sections to start them again. He compared his work to Paine, Godwin, Priestly and Wollstonecraft, and only when he felt the pamphlet was of equal standing did he lay down his quill and call it finished. He had it rushed off to Johnson for approval, in the hope it might be published to popular acclaim.

Three weeks passed and Gobey heard no word from Johnson. This was unusual, for the publisher normally responded in the following week. Then one day, quite unexpectedly, Johnson visited the pamphlet house in Fetter Lane. He was carrying Gobey's manuscript in the fold of his armpit. Gobey was working alone on this day and was most pleased to see him.

'Do come in, Joseph, it's a pleasure to see you. Will you take some refreshment, a drink of some kind?'

'No, no, Gobey. I'll not stay long. I've business elsewhere and must rush.'

It was the first time Johnson had visited the pamphlet house and it was good to receive him. Gobey led him into his study, a room overstocked with pamphlets and reading matter, leaning in towers against the walls and piled high in every corner. Although he was smiling, Johnson looked a little tense, a hint of apprehension in his eyes. 'So,' he said, gazing around the room. 'This is where great revolutions are made, is it?'

'It is. It is, indeed.'

Gobey offered Johnson a chair, but the publisher refused, preferring to stand and finish the business he had come for. Their eyes met and they stood in silence for a moment, both waiting for the other to speak. Then Johnson moved to a table by the window and placed the manuscript down. 'Look,' he said, turning to face Gobey. 'I won't prolong things I'm truly sorry to say that I can't publish your pamphlet.'

Gobey was a little surprised, for it had been a long time since Johnson had rejected any of his works. He was hurt at the news, but tried to make light of it. 'Is it half-right and therefore half-wrong?'

'No, no, no. It's beautifully written, a carefully constructed argument, a most valid piece of work.'

'Then where is the problem?'

'It's too radical, it goes too far. I have the upmost sympathy for your arguments and the greatest respect for all your theories. But if I publish this, it will find me in trouble, land me in court. The title in itself is likely to cause offence.' Johnson leaned over the desk to read from the manuscript, '*Monarchy, Clergy and Government: The True Designs of an Unholy Trinity*.'

'Every word is true, Joseph. The royal household, the Church and Parliament, all conspire to keep the working man down. They oppress and impoverish the people of England, while they live in privilege and luxury.'

'I'm not questioning the ethics or veracity of the piece, only that now is not the time to publish it. It will incite trouble and bring damage to my reputation and publishing house. Can you not tone it down, dilute your accusations, hint at where the inequalities lie, instead of blatantly pointing the finger?'

Gobey shook his head. 'I can't. I can't change what I feel to be true.'

'Then I can't publish the thing.'

Heavy of heart and resigned to the situation, Gobey said, 'Joseph, you've been a mentor and an inspiration to me. I cannot thank you enough for your support and kindness. I will always be indebted to you, always. But please try to understand that I can't alter this work. If I did, I would be a Judas to my own people, to all the mudlarks and beggarly classes that dwell on these streets.'

Johnson spoke with his arms outstretched, his eyes full of benevolence. 'Gobey, my boy, let us not quarrel over this. Let's not see the matter come between us.'

'I never would, Joseph. I never would.'

The men hugged and parted, smiling warmly and knowing that the goodwill between them remained intact. Gobey led Johnson to the door and the publisher turned one last time, 'Temper your pamphlet, remove the radicalism and I will gladly look at it again.'

Remaining true to his heart, Gobey did not temper his pamphlet. Instead, he found another publisher, J.S. Jordan, who had already published Tom Paine's *Rights of Man*. Gobey's pamphlet was printed and widely distributed. In the weeks that followed, he began to be watched by spies and harassed by Church-and-King thugs. A short while later, he was arrested at the pamphlet house on Fetter Lane. Gobey was tried and convicted under the Seditious Writings Act of 1792. The indictment against him was written on a six foot parchment roll:

> The said Attorney General of our said Lord the King giveth the Court to understand that Tom Gobey, a London pamphleteer, being a seditious, ill-disposed and anarchic person, did wickedly and maliciously attack the King, the Church and the Government for purposes of unrest.

Despite being defended by the renowned lawyer, Thomas Erskine, Gobey was found guilty. Erskine had done his best, in that he got the charges reduced from treason to sedition (thereby saving Gobey's life), but the pamphlet had proved too radical to defend. Godwin and Johnson had both spoken in court on Gobey's behalf, but it was no use, the young pamphleteer was sentenced to seven years. An article in the *Morning Chronicle* told how Johnson had wept bitterly when the young man was led away.

They were all down the river now – those days of unheeded warnings, of revolutionary zeal, of attending meetings, of frenetic writing and utopian dreams. And it would have all been worth it, he thought. Every year of the seven would have been worth it – if only things had changed in the process. But now back in London, he could see that nothing had changed – the rich were still rich, the poor were still poor, and all the old hierarchies were very much intact.

From his window in Newgate, Gobey gazed down into the courtyard of the prison. Some convicts were leaning against the wall, their breath billowing in the cold air. He supposed them to be victims of poverty rather than perpetrators of any crime. Of all the causes he had fought for, there was only one left that was driving him on. Eileen Dineen, the crux of his universe – he would trawl the city to find her.

CHAPTER 6

Several days passed, with Gobey struggling to adjust to city life. The years of imprisonment had calmed his spirit, made him sensitive to bustle and noise. On the streets, he found himself listening for birdsong, any small sound of nature to pacify him. Each day he returned to the bone-setter for news of Eileen, but left with no word. He took to wandering the city at night, as if an essence of her might be found in the darkness.

On one such night, he found himself lost in the city, randomly roving in search of his love. He stood in the road and saw a marauding press gang approaching from afar. Armed with clubs, hooks and cudgels, they came clattering from the docks, striking posts and pillars as they passed. They were clearing out the taverns in search of men to take the King's shilling, to fight the war. The street emptied before them, a scampering on every corner and men climbing walls, fleeing on horseback to dodge the gang of ruffians.

Gobey slipped into an alley and leaned against the wall. The ground behind him vibrated from the passing road carts. The city smoke seemed to filter in from all directions. He steered a cautious path over the rubble and splintered planks, the wet leaves smeared over the ground. The eyes of the rats glistened along the pathway as they scurried along.

He continued along the backstreets with the wind rustling behind him. The moon passed from behind a cloud and life stirred in the shadows – sooty faces peering from courtyards women on steps with screaming babies. Along the street a cockfight gathered a crowd of wagering men. They spat and jostled, studying the bloodied birds tearing each other's eyes in a flurry of feathers. Some grubby boys stood around upturned boxes, rattling dice, slapping cards and shouting at each other.

Gobey made his way down to Newgate. The ghostly cries of the prisoners pinged along the brickwork towards Moor Fields. The inmates were hollering at the moon, its blue face staring down at them. The rats danced beneath the moon's illumination, scattering through the puddles. There were prowling shapes everywhere – a thin cat slunk under a barrow, a white goat trotted through an alley like a will-o'-the-wisp. There were beetles seeping out of the woodwork, birds chattering as if the sun was up. The fields were alive with the marbled eyes of frogs, and the sheep circled in a halo of blue light.

This night was not for sleeping. Gobey purchased some provisions and climbed the stairs to his rooms. He pissed in an old chipped pot, the urine thick orange and sluggish in the passing. He ate a slice of oily mackerel from a newspaper and swigged at a bottle of rum. The liquid inched into his gut with creaking protests, a knot twisted as if his intestines were wound round a stick.

He lit the lanterns and shuffled around for more candles to drive out the dark. A shaft of moonlight struck the wall behind him. He sat at the table by the window, and a pearly beam struck his face. He sat staring at the moon until a dog howled in the distance. From deep in the prison, a convict replied to that howling. *Owl-owl-owl-owwwwwwwl* – then dog and man bayed together, a joint communication of some past sorrow. He was struck by the truth of it, the sincerity of loss.

He stood at the table with his new boots murdering his feet, chafing at the heel. He was hopelessly weary and aching in the legs. He took off his boots and lay on the bed, but could not settle.

He rose and lit a candle at the window. There was a man against the wall outside – stone cold in his resolve, solid as brickwork. Gobey's legs began to tremble, his heart paced. He studied that stunted form, those thick-arched shoulders and short bulky legs. Then Mr Sticks stepped sideways into the moonlight and looked up at him.

Gobey jerked back from the window and slid on his boots. His hands were shaking, his breathing laboured. He clasped a wrist to calm himself, but the tremors ran a circuit of his bones. He handled the razor and tucked it in his belt. He took a swill of rum and swallowed with a choking cough that wouldn't cease.

In the hallway, he stood on the banister, slid back the panel and climbed into the loft. He traversed a beam with the moonlight torching his steps in a wavering line. He eased open the window and shifted onto the slippery roof. The night air was thick with coal smoke, the carbonized stench carried in the wind. He crawled over the dewy slates and peered down to find that Mr Sticks had vanished.

Gobey stared at the milky-faced moon as something passed over the surface – maybe a bird, or maybe he blinked. From close by, he could hear a low vibrating sound. From a chimneystack, a grey cat opened its eyes. They looked at each other. The cat continued to purr from its sleepy coil.

Gobey slid down the slates to make a rear exit. The howling voice from the prison started up again, *Owl-owl-owl-owwwwwwwl.* He clambered along the ledge of an adjacent house. Stepping onto a windowsill, he hung at arm's length and dropped into an alley. He scattered the rats along a leafy gully and over the sides of the walls. The shadows played tricks with his eyes, forming into waiting men and metamorphosing into mist as he reached them. He started to run, run with the knowledge that a moving target was the hardest to hit.

He crossed a field and stood against a tree to catch his breath. The moonlight ran along the branches, glowing against the bark. His back was wet and sticky, his shirt clinging like a steaming lover beneath his jacket. He crossed the fields with the owls screeching all around, but he couldn't gauge their whereabouts.

He walked for an hour with the fear inside him. He kept looking over his shoulder for a sudden attack. The last vestige of autumn met winter on the street, and as if to mark the occasion, the mist gave way to frost – it stitched along the blades of grass, knitted across the surface stones and hardened the mud. The windows of the houses had started to ice over. The puddles crunched into brittle crystals as he crossed them.

He stopped at an old boarding house with no light inside. He banged on the door, called up at the windows, but no one stirred from within. A pack of dogs barked along the road, the frost clung to him like barbed teasels. He continued down the street and found an old shed behind one of the houses, crooked and barely standing. He forced open the door and a voice flew out at him – 'No room at the inn!'

Walk he must, onwards on that desolate road. He left the world unaltered behind him – the white-needled grass, the stiff-frozen leaves, a mangy dog pissing up a door. He came to an upturned cart with one of the wheels spinning. He looked up and down the street. A newspaper rolled over and fluttered away like an injured bird. A low ebb of voices rose as he approached a corner house. A man stood outside, beneath the yellow shafts of a lantern. He had long, straggly hair, torn and brittle, a worn military overcoat with loose epaulettes. The man addressed him in a voice close to song. 'Poppy juice, poppy juice, best opium in town, grog to wash it down. Warm inside, chummy, warm inside. Poppy juice for you, warm you right through, chummy. Warm you right through.'

The man had a black eyepatch with a red dot. He gathered Gobey off the street, patting his shoulder. 'Poppy juice, poppy juice, best opium in town. Kiss the stars before the dawn comes down. Drink the milk of paradise, set the weary night free – sip, sup and supper on the juice of liberty. Look to the heavens and the good Lord looks down. Poppy juice, poppy juice, best opium in town.'

They entered a large room with a red simmering fire in the grate. There were figures crouched against the walls, sleeping on mats on the floor and standing in small groups. The air was heavily scented, sweet and sickly with intoxicating vapour that rose towards the ceiling in coils. Hoarse laughter and garbled strands of conversation drifted through the smoke.

Seated on the mat, Gobey raised his knees, hooking his arms around them. The man squatted beside him. 'What's it to be, chummy? How do you like your paradise? In the dip of a spoon, in the well of a pipe, or in the sweet tides of a sugary wine?'

'A drop of wine.'

'A drop it is.' The man left and returned with a glass held in both hands. Gobey paid him, and watched him slip through the smoke and out towards the street. He drank and gazed around the room – two women sat with their backs against the wall, holding hands and consoling each other. He could just grasp fragments, the scratch of their conversation. Their noses were chewed with syphilitic sores. He stared at them for some time without inhibition, stared until he found himself laughing. One of the women looked up and he put his hands to his face. Still he laughed, with his shoulders rocking and his laughter echoing in his head.

People were sucking on pipes and blowing the smoke into blue circles – it swirled and hovered like pond mist above the floor. Three old women sat drinking over a barrel, telling tales around a candle. On its perch, a green parrot watched the comings and goings of this sleepy gathering.

The man with the eye patch called into the darkness. 'Poppy juice, poppy juice, best opium in town.' There was something comforting about his presence. He stood like a watchman over the night, a guardian for lost souls.

Gobey turned to the wall and tried to sleep, to melt into the floor. He felt a creamy satisfaction, a euphoric sense of lightness. Under the influence of opium, he thought could see Eileen's eyes – the different shades of green, the detail of her dark eyelashes. Now he could scent her hair, feel the milky softness of her hands.

All sense of time fell away. He didn't know if he was asleep, dreaming or imagining these things. Over his shoulder, he could sense people lying down and getting up, transient ghosts dissolving through walls. The room was filled with a low burr of voices. He thought he could hear the old women at the candle whistling through their vaginas – strange harps from barren lands.

He rolled over and smelt the waft of someone's breath. A man was resting on the floor next to him. It took a moment for the realization to dawn – the trunk neck, the sheen of greasy skin, the bloodshot eyes. Gobey snatched the razor from his belt and brought it down. The flesh sliced on Mr Stick's face, and the blood sprayed up Gobey's arm. Gobey leapt to his feet and bundled his way to the door, shoving through a group of sailors.

Outside, the cold air hit him, the ground crunched with frost. Gobey ran in a wild scampering fashion, slipping and flailing with his arms. He dropped the razor and turned to retrieve it, but Mr Sticks was running at him, a large flap of skin lifting from his cheek.

The man with the eyepatch stepped aside to let them pass. He leant against the wall and called into the cold night air. 'Poppy juice, poppy juice, best opium in town.'

Gobey passed a wall that was too high for vaulting. He looked around for a weapon – a pail, a plank, a bottle – anything to grip and swing. He ran down a passage with the frost glistening on the ground. He followed the path to a dead-end fence, where he dislodged a panel and slipped through to the other side.

He covered stones, cobbles, brick rubble and crisp hardened fields. He worked through a labyrinth of winding alleys, crossing a courtyard, a cemetery and an old deserted waste ground. Walking now, he turned and looked behind for the squat, pursuing figure. Nothing stirred in the dark. He passed a cow, its softly reproving eyes following his progress.

The smell of the Thames drifted towards him. The river ran copper in the first shafts of sunrise. He came down a cobbled alley onto the slippery stones and squatted to rest. He stood and watched the spectacle of dawn – the blue sky unfurling for miles, the fleeing geese, following the line of the river.

The light crept over the houses. The first fires smoked from the chimneys, and a cat passed, like the ghost of a cat from the shadows. He leaned on a rail with his back to the river, facing a steep hill. Then, rising up, the head of Mr Sticks gradually came into view – a hand held his face together, his free arm worked like the pump of a well. As he rose, the sky reflected in his eyes, cold and dead as a bygone winter.

Gobey cut down to the river and trudged along the sludgy shore. He followed the arc of the bank into the call of seabirds, into the oncoming breeze and boggy aroma. He walked with the sun rising, the fish flashing silver above the surface. A heron, in a slow cumbersome sweep, crossed the water. The tide was coming in, seeping across the mud towards him. Mr Sticks followed in the distance, holding his face and grunting into his hand.

Gobey pushed on, the water covering his ankles, the tide gushing noisily from upstream. Out on the river, the current was turning with great momentum, whirlpools circled on the surface. He threw himself against the tide with the river passing around him. The water streamed through his legs and rose to his waist, the mud sucked at his feet. Clinging to a tree root, he managed to pull himself above the bank and flop onto the grass to escape the river.

Flat on his back, he tried to restore his breath; dragging the air through his mouth. He clambered to his feet, dazed and unsteady. For some minutes he laughed hysterically, counting his blessings and celebrating the solid earth beneath him. The water advanced over the bank and swallowed a fence in the distance – only the tips of the posts were showing. He watched the tide run its course, drifting over the land – no river was more dark, no river more forsaken.

CHAPTER 7

Cold in the marrow of his bones, Gobey walked by the river. He stomped and hugged himself to build some heat. He was almost entirely soaked. The water oozed in his boots The marshes shimmered and held a silvery image of the sky – desolate, waterlogged, endlessly grey. The wind tore the reeds and battered the earth in angry spasms. The gulls hung above him like wax exhibits, stationary clumps of flight.

Gobey lurched across the marshes in grim determination. He roared into the squall. 'Eileeeeeen!' As if the wind were a messenger for lonely hearts.

He travelled towards the silence, only bird calls and wind-howl around him. The blue shadow of a cloud passed over the sky. The light was taking on an ashen hue the complexion of a corpse. He could not say for the life of him what had happened to his life. Seven years in the wilderness and what was there to come back for – a game of chance?

He faced a house in the distance, a bog abode of grey stone . Remote and inhospitable, it sunk into the landscape. A house embedded in soil, built on silt and sludge from the river. Shaped by the rain, carved by the wind's sleek fingers. Battered from every direction, it knew not which way to fall. He walked head down, boots squelching into the growing silence. He walked until he could see the reflection of the windows – the sky in the panes.

He pushed against the door and stepped inside. A mildewy musk inhabited the room, mould stained the walls and straggly plants grew through the boards. There were a couple of old saddles against the wall, reins and horse paraphernalia scattered around. He closed the door on the wind – it had driven the life out of him, howling and moaning across the marshes. In the corner, he settled down among the straw and old newspapers. He curled in a ball with the bugs in his hair and the gulls sniggering over the roof – sniggering like gambling men, concealing their loss with laughter. He slept in a deep unconscious fall from the world around him.

He didn't hear the door shunt open. Nor did he feel the wind brush the straw beneath him. The boggy odour of the marches drifted inside. A figure tapped across the boards, removed his tricorn hat and placed it on the sleeping man's head. He drew the cork from a bottle with his teeth and spat it out. Taking a nip, he sloshed the liquid and swallowed. He drove out a strangulated fart and it was this that drove Gobey from his slumber. He stirred on the ground, stretching his limbs. 'Well, well, our Johnny. Good day to thee, matey. Good day.'

Steadman grinned and shifted on his wooden leg. His plaited beard swung like a pendulum. 'You couldn't stay away.'

Gobey rubbed his eyes, removed the hat and handed it up to him. 'I didn't have the choice. There's a fellow out there at war with me. Wants to do me in, good and proper. From dock to den to river he has me followed.'

'He ain't out there now, is he?'

'Methinks not.'

'You sure?'

'I'm not sure of anything.'

'I'm not liking the sound of this.'

'Nor am I, matey. Nor am I.'

Steadman helped him up, and they took the creaky stairs. The rooms at the top were comfortably furnished with rugs, armchairs and a long rough-surfaced table. The flocked wallpaper was hanging in strips, and there was a red upholstered sofa smudged with coal and food stains – one of the legs was snapped and propped on books. Piles of pamphlets were leaning against the walls, mountains of silent revolution.

They lit a fire and filled two mugs from a barrel. Steadman toasted some bread on a prong and sliced a block of cheese on the table. 'Who's this fellow, then?' He spat into the hissing fire. 'This fellow after your guts?'

Gobey undressed and hung his clothes on a chair to dry. He sat draped in a blanket on the ground. He took a large mouthful of ale and savoured its passage. 'I don't know the fellow. I've been raking it over, but I can't place him. A little miscreant, short and stocky – a face like a snarling dog.'

'He got a name?'

'Mr Sticks. Mr Sticks, I believe. You heard of him?'

'Can't say I have.'

They sat drinking and staring at the crackling fire. Steadman farted a slow squeezed affair forced out with a whistle. He gazed innocently around the room, up at the ceiling and down at the floor.

'You're a childish man, Master Steadman. An infant with a beard.'

'Take no notice of the mice in here.'

They chinked mugs and drank in large mouthfuls. Steadman held a lasting grin, eyes moist and full of merriment. He fingered his beard like a flute, a mock playing. There was nothing he liked more than drinking – drinking and farting and the resulting laughter. 'This Mr Sticks, what did he do?'

'It's not what he did, it's what he wanted to do.'

'What's that, then?'

'He tried to have me with a musket.'

'Yeah?'

'Yeah.'

'Is that the cause of the scratches on your face?'

'I guess so.'

'You were lucky.'

'A queer old fate going on.'

'How do you mean?'

'It sprayed all around me and caught some poor old barber. It had his brain out of his head. Horrible, horrible to see him like that.'

'Stomping bells of hell.'

'Me ears are still ringing.'

They stared dreamily into the fire. The flames entwined a blackened log that sent a succession of red sparks crackling up the chimney. Outside the wind howled like a crying woman, pausing to find voice and erupting in a growl. 'I slashed him with a razor. I had to

– I had to try and stop him. He's hell-bent on slaughtering me I'm sure of it. I tell you, this fellow's not normal. Even with his face in tatters he chased me across town, down the river and over the mud. It was only the tide that saved me.'

'What a savage.'

'I tell you, Johnny. There's something about him, something dead inside. You wouldn't want to meet him. You wouldn't.'

'I've no plans to, son.'

Gobey drank and stared into the mug and drank again. He wrapped the blanket tight over his shoulders. He could smell the river on his skin. The memory of the rising tide kept coming into his mind and he shuddered to drive it off. He went to speak and stopped, then started again. 'Could a man swim upstream?'

'Not on this stretch, the current's too strong.'

'You sure?'

'He'd have to be an eel, a slippery bastard.'

Steadman crossed the room and filled the mugs at the barrel. His pole leg tapped as he walked. Gobey shivered by the fire with his chin tucked over the blanket. 'I hope he's drowned. I never want to see him again. Ever – not even dead.'

'You won't have to, son. Take a drink now and forget the whole business. Old Tamesis will have swept him away.'

'Say,' said Gobey, warming his hands at the fire. 'Tell me do about the old friends of freedom. You say they've all disbanded.'

'Yeah, mostly. Do you remember John Thelwall?'

'Of course, of course. I attended one of his meetings at the London Corresponding Society.'

'He was up for high treason, you know. Dogged by spies who had him charged and sent to the Tower. Thankfully, he was acquitted – they couldn't prove the charges.

'Glad to hear it, he was a good fellow, citizen Thelwall. A right good fellow. Where is he now?'

'In retreat, when I last heard. Retired from the dangers of political life.' Steadman picked some crumbs from his beard and continued. 'And you've probably heard about Tom Paine. They were out to get him, good and proper. He fled to France and was elected to the

Republican Convention, the National Assembly.'

'I heard that. A good fellow for stirring it up, our Tom. No flowery language, a direct route to the working man's heart.'

'And Priestly had his house and laboratory burnt to the ground by a Church-and-King mob. He's had enough and sailed for America. He'll not return – no, nay, not at all.'

'Who could blame him?' said Gobey shrugging his shoulders. 'What about Godwin, what happened to him?'

'Virtually a recluse, now. Greatly besmirched by the loyalist press, greatly abused.'

'And what of our good boss and mentor, Joseph Johnson?'

'Greatly reduced as a man. He's shortly to go on trial, and they say he's certainly for the jailhouse. He published a radical pamphlet by Wakefield and is about to pay the price. He's keeping a low profile, scaling down his publishing interests.'

Gobey gasped, a shiver running the length of his spine. It was awful to imagine that Johnson had been so careful to keep the youthful Gobey out of trouble, but had now succumbed to the same fate himself. He shuddered to think how the dignified publisher would take to the humiliation of prison life. 'I must pay him a visit, before the law gets its wicked hands on him.'

'Do,' Steadman sniffed and nodded. 'Do. He would be overjoyed to see you, I'm sure.'

They sat without speaking as an ember frazzled in the grate and burnt out. Something in the fire was still hissing and they stared at it for a moment. One drank, then the other. You could hear the liquid slipping down their throats.

Gobey tossed a piece of coal onto the fire, the black smoke billowed around it. The wind howled through the chimney and shook the flames in the grate. His face was hot, the back of his neck was cold. He left the chair and picked up a copy of *The Rights of Man*, but couldn't concentrate and sat down. He looked over at Steadman. 'You knew, didn't you? Back there in the pillory, you knew about Eileen.'

'Knew what?'

'Knew she had a fellow.'

Steadman paused for a few seconds. He took a breath and expelled it. He raised his hands to the hopeless situation. 'Yeah, I did, son. I had the knowledge.'

'Why didn't you tell me?'

'How could I? There's you just off the boat, how could I stand there and say that? I couldn't do it, Gobey. I just couldn't. I'm sorry, I'm a weak man, I should have –'

'Hey-ho Johnny, you're a good man. I would have done the same.'

'But I should have –'

'It's all right, don't flog yourself, matey. Just tell me this – what's he like? This fellow with my girl. What sort of a man is he?'

'I ain't seen him, but I've heard he has wealth, lots of it.'

'The bone-setter said he knocks her about.'

'Yeah.' Steadman's wooden leg tapped on the floor – it seemed to work of its own volition, skittering over the boards in a circle 'It's not good, son. Not good.'

Gobey went to the fire and stood facing the flames. He spat and the hiss came back at him. He turned to Steadman. 'I can't stop thinking about it. It's not right, not right.'

'It's not, not right at all. But what can you do? If she chooses him, how can you change it?'

'I don't know, I don't know what I can do.'

'Nowt.'

'Do you know where she lives?'

'No, son, I don't. Honestly I don't.'

'I'll go back to the city and find her. That's all I can do.'

'Maybe you should just leave things alone.'

'I can't.'

'Maybe you should.'

'I just can't. I ache for her. I get this feeling in me chest like jagged glass, like I'm bleeding from the inside. The wound runs too deep and I can't reach it. She's in me bones and I can't get her out. That's the way it is. On the Bay, it was the same. On the other side of the world and nothing had changed. She lives in me dreams, sleeps with me thoughts. I can't foresee a time when I won't think of her.'

'You best try.'

'All the trying in the world won't change it – not this, not her. You hear stories, don't you? About people who love for life, spend their days yearning for the one person. The one person they can't have. It's like their soul has been ripped out and they're waiting for it to return. That's me, ripped up and waiting. Me insides are raw.'

'You might have to work at it.'

'Every day for seven years I've worked at it. I've told meself a million times she might not be there when I return. A part of me doesn't expect her to be. Christ knows, it's too much to ask of anyone, but it don't stop me wishing, and men have been wishing since the first suck of breath. Long before you, me, and that old stinking river – men have been wishing.'

'Wish away, my son.'

Gobey nodded. He drank and swallowed as if something was caught in his throat. When the firelight left his eyes they were black, a filmy sheen covering them. Beneath the blanket, he was hanging like a man on a rope. 'Have you ever loved?' he said. 'Have you had the yearning so bad, that all you got is centred on it?'

'Yeah.'

'Tell me.'

'I've had it.'

'Speak to me.'

'Had it and got it now.'

'Tell me good things.'

'It was love at first sighting. Couldn't put it any other way. When I looked into those big brown eyes, I knew things would never be the same. We go back a long ways, a long old ways. The power of the thing is greater than me. Wherever I am, whatever I do. I don't suppose it will ever leave me. I'll always –'

The boards creaked by the window – a movement in the shadows, something made a slow crawl across the room. Gobey leapt up and threw his back against the wall and Steadman reached to console him. 'It's all right, son. It's all right. It's only Plato. You remember the old dog, he wouldn't hurt a fly.'

'Jesus-flogging-Christ! I thought it was Mr Sticks crawling from the river.'

'It's only Plato.'

The dog shuffled in front of the fire. A more tatty specimen was hard to find; its coat was covered in mud – dry and flaky it sprayed dust as it flopped down. It was not so much a dog, as all manner of dogs – collie, terrier, dingo, wolf. He did remember Plato. The poor old thing had seemed old before he went away, but now it was ancient – its snout had gone grey and it had few whiskers.

'I didn't know he was here.'

'Seldom leaves the spot.' Steadman pointed to the bed in the corner. The wall was grimed where the creature had been leaning. The dog had a strange blended smell of freshly baked bread and sweet biscuit, except for its breath – pure maggots, a vile meaty gas lived in its mouth. 'He's getting on a bit, my Plato. Sleeps most of the time. Hardly get a peep out of him these days, but he's still the best dog in Christendom.'

'And I thought it was you farting.'

'Nay – never'

'Remind me why you call him Plato.'

'He's wise beyond his species, he communicates with his eyes. Look at him. Don't tell me that dog hasn't got an intelligent mind. Look – what a beast, what a thinker. There's more humanity in that creature than half of Parliament, all the monarchy.'

Gobey stared at the dog and it blinked. He had to admit a sense of wisdom, a quiet knowledge lurking behind its eyes. Plato looked at the cheese, then up at him – three times it repeated the motion, until he fed it, and it gently licked his hand to savour the flavour. Its fur was singeing at the fire, but it wouldn't move. And whenever its name was mentioned, the dog looked up to see who was talking about it.

Steadman pointed affectionately at the dog. 'There's me love, me heart, me soul. That's where all me yearning rests. From the moment I saw those brown eyes looking up at me – that old tail wagging and them bulging paws. There'll never be another for me like Plato.'

'The one for you.'

'Hook, line, and sinker.'

The night drifted in at the window and they drank at the fireside recalling the old days. They laughed until they wept, and wept themselves back to laughter. Good days, bad days, days in a life of republican struggle. Blasted in the drunken hour, they feared not the things to come, but things were coming – blind, insensate, unimaginable things hurtling towards them. And there was nothing in the ale, or the hollow of their hearts to fend them off. Parched from laughter, they bedded on the floor by the fire – Tom Gobey, Johnny Steadman and Plato the philosophical dog. When the candles fizzled out, the night ran amok around them. The darkness entered their sleep, their dreams ran down the river, travelling the way rivers do – from one place to the next, from base to destination in search of the life to come.

CHAPTER 8

No ordinary morning, that much he knew. Before his eyes had opened, he sensed the change – the hoary bite of the air, the strange lack of sound. Not a bird in song, no noise from the river. Without looking to the window, he knew it had snowed in the night. He could feel its silence, a deadening insulation wrapping the house. Gobey got up and enlivened the embers in the grate with a poker. He tipped coal on the fire and blew to entice the flames. Steadman slept with his arm looped around the dog – old lovers, sharing the breath between them.

Gobey went to the window. The powdery flakes sucked at the glass. His eyes followed the snowdrifts over the landscape – the bare white trees were coated, the ground had a smooth carpet. From the roof, a small avalanche of snow fell outside the window – it made a heavy crash on the ground.

He stood at the fire, a chill running through him. He clapped his hands and stomped his feet. From the floor beneath the blankets, Steadman moaned up at him, 'Bang a drum while you're at it.'

'I can't get warm, Johnny. It's gone and snowed in the night. The cold has frozen me bones.'

Steadman farted by way of reply. The dog left the comfort of the blankets in a stumble, an arthritic stiffness to its hind legs. It hobbled woodenly over to the door and began scratching. 'Can you let the old dog out, my son?'

Gobey went downstairs with Plato shuffling before him. He dragged the front door open, the ground snow falling onto his feet. They went outside and the dog ran over the marshes. It moved faster and with more vigour than it had shown before, rolling over wildly. There was nothing more beautiful to his present mind than the snow.

The snow, and a mad dog all for anarchy on this desolate morning.

Back in the house, he built the fire. They ate a lumpy broth with toasted cheese and pickles. For every bite Steadman had, Plato also enjoyed a morsel. The old dog never left his side – it sat staring at its master, grateful for all gifts received. The snow drifted by the window. They talked for some time by the firelight, mustering hope for the days ahead. 'So,' said Steadman, chomping vigorously. 'Are you going to help with the pamphlets, then? It'll keep you out of trouble.'

'Get me in trouble, you mean.'

Steadman laughed. 'I'm knocking up some handbills, mocking the King and all. How about you write something about the war, something about the hardship, the higher taxes? The *war* on the *poor* and such?'

'Me heart's not in it.'

'How about something on the French Revolution?'

'It's a hard thing to support now. What with all the bloodshed and the French becoming dictators.'

'True enough, true enough.'

'There's only the spirit of the Revolution to admire now. And that will always stay with me. It's only the spirit that needs to live on.'

'Aye, the causes that shaped the storm.'

'You still got the pamphlet house?'

'Same place on Fetter Lane.'

'The good old days.'

'We had some laughs down there.'

'We did.'

Gobey smiled – those days were sweet to him. He recalled the mood of camaraderie among that small band of radicals who had worked together. They were days filled with Eileen – her glowing presence, her constant laughter. Days when she was never far from his side, seldom from his mind. One incident struck him with some force and stood out from the rest. It was mid-summer, and the heat so great that all the windows of the pamphlet house were open. The breeze was shifting the curtains, lifting the papers on his desk. He was suddenly aware that the sky had grown black. A storm had blown in from the river, spooning darkness inside and forcing him to work by candlelight.

Alone and restless, anticipating the downpour, he waited for the rain. The first sign came in weighty droplets. Soon it was crashing in sheets, the aroma of the soil rising, the scent of pollen in the room. The thunder cracked and shook the windows, branched lightning struck the sky.

At the window, he saw Eileen rushing through the rain. She pattered through the hall to stand in the doorway. Drenched from head to toe without coat or shawl, her dress clung to her. The fragrance of summer was all about her. She laughed with a wild exhilaration. In the moist heat they kissed, and he felt the explosion of that kiss, as if it had been the first and last in a world blown asunder. That fleeting moment had fuelled him for years, through night terrors and days of hard labour – it had crossed fathomless oceans and dense cities to reach him.

He was running away with these thoughts, but Steadman's voice jolted him back to the fire. 'So how about it, then? Fancy a little sedition, my son? A few pamphlets? It will take your mind off things.'

Watery at the eyes and swallowing uncomfortably, Gobey shook his head. 'I'm done with all that, its over for me. But let me have the key to the pamphlet house. I'll call in for old lang syne.'

'Why don't you stay here and rest a little?'

'I'm going back to the bone-setter to wait for Eileen.'

Steadman searched his pocket and handed him the key. 'She won't be there today, son. Not in this weather.'

'I'm going anyway. Every day, until she turns up.'

'Son,' Steadman looked earnestly up from his plate. 'You might have to let her go. You just might have to. You'll not be the first to get out of prison to find circumstances changed. It happens, it's a bastard thing, I know, but it happens. I hate to say it, son, I really do, but you need to think about extricating yourself from Eileen. She's got someone else now. You might have to accept that. He may be a bastard, but if she loves him, there's nothing you can do about it. Go easy on yourself, you've been through enough.'

Gobey stood up and brushed the crumbs from his trousers. 'Fare thee well, my agitator friend.' He smiled and made for the door.

'Wait,' Steadman called him back. He tapped across to the wardrobe and removed a long overcoat of stitched fur. He swung it around Gobey's shoulders. 'Look after yourself, you hear me? Don't go doing anything foolish.'

'Fill me mug, I'll be back to drink it.'

'I'll fill it.'

'Good man.'

'You take care, now.'

'And yourself.'

He watched from the window as Gobey trudged in the snow. The wind buffeted him, but he pushed on with his head down. Steadman followed his journey across the marshes and out towards the river – shrinking now, only distinguishable from a fence pole because he was moving, edging across the landscape. There was a fellow who would not give up, not until he had the life knocked out of him, the last breath squeezed. Try as he may, he couldn't help seeing Gobey walking into trouble.

CHAPTER 9

Take the crow's view overhead, gliding through the sky with a lone figure on the marshland. Tom Gobey with his odd fur coat, sinking to his knees and moving against the wind. Snow or no snow, he was heading back to the city, to the bone-setter's to find Eileen. Squall, blizzard, hurricane – nothing would stop him. He would have kicked an autumn leaf around the world to find her. His legs were weary, aching from deep within the muscles.

So close to the river, but there was no sound, no intimation of water beyond the stark trees. Reaching the bank, he found the Thames frozen, the great river stilled. The silence was shocking. The still spirit of ice had him mesmerized. The river pooled towards the city like the icy breath of a snow God – majestic, immaculate, untraversed. The ducks were padding around, sliding and quacking, not knowing what to do with themselves.

To test the strength of the ice he tossed a log out – it skated along with a strange, resonating twang. Near the bank, he rooted for stones and pelted them against the surface. They pinged across the ice, like the warped chirruping of seabirds. There was no way of knowing what the tide was doing below, swirling around or standing still? And what of the fish and eels, were they dead and crystallized or sleeping until the thaw?

He stepped onto the river, the ice was solid and impenetrable. He couldn't see beyond a few inches of the misty surface He gazed at the driftwood, frozen rope, boats fixed rigid and brittle newspapers strewn around. He pushed off, each step made tentatively. He pranced like a puppet. At times the ice shuddered, the eerie sound making him think something beneath was trying to escape. And for reasons blind to him, he thought that something was a whale – a great blue monster beneath the ice.

The snow fell in large flakes a swirl that blinded him. His progress was slow and methodical, slipping when he tried to speed up. Three times his bottom hit the ice and three times he clambered to his feet cursing. His slippery new boots were not helping matters, the leather soles gliding across the ice. He took short bird steps with great impatience. Onwards, with a long day's skating ahead of him.

The snow settled on his hair and shoulders and he shook it off like a wild dog. The fields ran white, without a blade of green or a glimpse of mud. Chaste and unaltered, the snow was building on the hills and thickening the trees and holding the fences to ransom. A dead insulation blocked his ears – no birdsong or flutter of wings, no callings of nature. The sheep in the distance stood like white boulders rolled together. He had the sense that the world was slowing, curling into a snowy foetus.

On he slid, down a dip in the river and past a punt stuck in the ice. There was a dead cat curled in the boat – a frozen ball of fur. He followed the steam of his breath and passed through it. The snow settled on the ice and he turned to view his own footprints, a long crooked line of tracks. He had walked like a duck, with little space between each step. His calves were aching from the effort of his strange waddling.

He passed the morning in this slow laborious way, skating and regaining his balance. The ice echoed with an eerie ring that ran all around him. He inched down the centre of the river and kept wandering about the fragility of the ice.

Approaching the city, he saw there were others on the river – scavengers searching for debris, fishermen untangling nets, kids skating and sliding on sledges. There was a frost fair up ahead, carts and carriages had been driven onto the ice. Stalls, tents and booths had been erected. There were children having donkey rides, men turning chestnuts in hot coals. At Blackfriars Bridge, a woman in a fur hat was selling books from a long table. Up from the bookstall a sheep was being spit-roasted and sold as Lapland mutton. Further along, a merry-go-round spun with the kids hopping on without paying. An old man was chasing them, shaking his fist and looking irate.

A boat was angled in the ice, a band of musicians sat on the mast – blowing horns, sawing fiddles and thumping heavy drums between their legs. Above the music, a discordant whinnying could be heard. From the bank, a street pugilist with a crushed nose was trying to lead a horse onto the ice. He was tall and broad, his long overcoat trailing the snow. He swung a looping punch into the horse's neck. The colt buckled and made an awful cry through its teeth. The man tugged on the horse's muzzle to restrain it.

All of Gobey's instincts were saying, don't get involved, but he somehow gravitated towards the commotion. He crossed the ice to the bank and stood behind the stooping pugilist. When the man raised his fist, he tapped his shoulder. 'Steady there, you don't have to strike the poor thing. Be gentle, it will come down with a little persuasion.'

The man whipped around in rage. 'Who are you?'

'No one special.'

'You better mind your own affairs, I'm not in the mood.'

'Look,' Gobey pointed at the horse, slowly reaching out and patting its neck. He gently walked it onto the ice. 'That's no way to a horse's soul. You've got to speak to them, caress their nature.'

'Up the road!'

The man snatched the rope and made off to a cider stall on the ice. He stood drinking and snarling at the horse, taunting the animal until it turned away from him. The colt's eyes were black, its posture awkward; its hooves scraped over the ice, a repressed dancing in its powerful legs.

A drunk staggered onto the river with a horn in his hand. The snow was too bright for him. He stood squinting and blinking, with slits for eyes. Gobey approached him, 'Halloa. You're looking well, matey, looking well on this cold day.'

'I am?'

'Fine and healthy.'

'Well, thank you,' the drunk staggered and caught his balance. 'Thank you kindly, sir.'

'Want to earn yourself a nice penny? A nice clean bit of coinage? The easiest money you'll ever earn. No hard labour, no backs broken.

A cool penny for your pocket without fighting the war.'

The man had a grubby face and smelt of fried bacon. His eyes had red-crushed veins that looked beyond repair. 'A penny?' he said, spraying spit. 'I'll run a mile on me rump for a penny. Faith I'll fight the French and stalk the King. I'll sell me wife and her mother for less.'

'You want it?'

'Faith yes.'

Gobey slapped the coin in his hand and bent to whisper. The drunk nodded in a rigid, deliberate way. At no time was his head still, or his eyes fully open. He made a slow, zigzagging totter to the man with the horse and stood behind him. He raised his thumb and blew the horn with all his might. The pugilist crouched and shuddered as if struck about the head. The colt reared, wriggled free and skated on its hooves. People scattered as it came flying under Blackfriars Bridge, back-heeling the ice into flying fragments. It came charging with eyes large and wild – out into the great white yonder of falling snow.

Gobey left the river and slipped into the crowds. The road was slushy and the carriages were skating, veering around corners with the wheels locked. The ground snow was deep and difficult to traverse, crunching and squeaking underfoot. On Blackfriars Lane, people were tumbling in the snow and sliding on patches where the ice was thick and slippery.

Before visiting the bone-setter, he thought he'd call on his old employer, Joseph Johnson , since his bookshop was only a few streets away. He trundled past St Paul's Cathedral, the edifice vast and magnificent, reassuring in its solid structure, dependable in a city bound for change. The dome was covered in snow and fuzzy in the winter light.

At St Paul's Churchyard, Gobey entered Johnson's bookshop. The familiar smell of paper transported him in time, as if he'd never been away. The mind holds scent like memories, he thought. And all for a moment, he could have been living his youth again – the young pamphleteer, his heart ablaze with radicalism.

An elderly man was seated in an alcove between the bookshelves. There was a lantern on a small table beside him. He was hunched over and reading a book on his lap. As Gobey approached, he saw it was

Johnson, somewhat aged and looking gaunt and haunted. The skin on his hands was as thin as rice paper, barely a membrane covering his veins. He looked as old as a biblical prophet, yet Gobey calculated he was no older than sixty-one or two.

Johnson looked up and didn't recognize Gobey. He thought he was a customer looking for books. The publisher called for his assistant, 'Patrick, be a good fellow and see to this gentleman, will you?'

But once he had met Gobey's eyes, some recognition stirred in his mind. He stared intently, trying to place the fellow before him. Then Gobey said, 'Good Joseph, it's only me, Tom Gobey.'

It took a moment for Johnson to fully comprehend those words. Then he gasped and sprung from his chair, 'Gobey, my boy! You are back! Back with us, back once again.'

'Yes, yes, I am back.'

Johnson's eyes were teary, his breath laboured and his voice hoarse. He hugged Gobey in such a violent way, it seemed he might crack his own frail ribs in the process. The assistant he had called arrived, and stood dutifully, waiting for an opportunity to intervene. Johnson released Gobey and turned to speak. 'It's all right Patrick. This is no customer. This is an old, old friend of mine, Tom Gobey. A fine pamphleteer, a fine exponent of the pen.'

Johnson led Gobey to a room at the back of the shop. It smelt of antiquated books, the weighty aroma of knowledge. They sat at a table and, from a decanter, Johnson poured two large glasses of brandy. Each observed the other, both inwardly noting the changes of time, the alteration of their appearance. The publisher thought Gobey had not only lost weight, but his youth and innocence. Something of his boyish enthusiasm was long behind him. Being leaner now, he seemed taller and had grown handsome – an ascetic luminosity had overtaken his face. More noteworthy than this, Johnson would have said there was a longing in his dark eyes, a yearning for some unfulfilled dream.

Gobey put his palm on the back of Johnson's hand on the table. A comforting gesture that spoke of old friendship, of the warmth of his heart. He removed his hand as he spoke. 'I hear you're up in court, Joseph. Facing a sentence.'

Johnson's eyes saddened, his face looking haggard in the

candlelight. 'They've been after me for years, and now have me up for publishing Wakefield's pamphlet.'

'Is Erskine defending you?'

'Yes, he's the best fellow for the job. He got Thelwall, Hardy and Horne Tooke acquitted of treason. But alas, I fear, not for me. He assures me a sentence is due.'

'I'm most sorry, most sorry.'

'Good Tom Gobey, you have no need to feel sorry for me. You have suffered the harshest punishment of all. You have been banished for seven long years in the wilderness, I will only spend some months in the King's custody.'

Gobey knew that Johnson was wealthy enough to have a comfortable time in prison. He would probably hire quarters within the jail and continue the social gatherings he was accustomed to. He thought the publisher's despondency was not caused by the fear of imprisonment, but by the humiliation of being hauled through the court – the newspapers would follow the case and his downfall would be played out in the public domain. There was something in his demeanour that said his days of radical publishing were over, beaten down by the law. It seemed that Johnson's disappointment had aged him.

And yet, when Gobey offered sympathy, Johnson rallied himself in the old way. He laughed and made light of the matter, and there was much in his eyes that spoke of a joyous heart. The two friends revelled in the knowledge they had not been broken by the law. Whatever way their lives had unfolded their spirits remained intact.

They talked about the old days, recalling better times when the French Revolution had captured their imaginations. They remembered past dinners at Johnson's house, where there was more than boiled cod and rice pudding on the menu – for there was always a healthy diet of dissent, anarchy and vibrant intellectualism. How these evenings were spent in debate, discussion and much laughter.

For a lost hour, it seemed the last seven years had not happened. They picked up the threads of their friendship, as if Gobey had not been away. But as Johnson walked him back through the shop, he had a strange feeling he would never see the publisher again. There was something inexplicable in the air, a curious finality to the moment. And although they had agreed to meet for dinner and Gobey had promised to visit him in jail (should he be convicted), it seemed that destiny would prove otherwise.

Outside the bookshop, Johnson hugged him and returned to his premises. It was like being held by his father, cradled and protected by the wisdom of an older man. He felt the emptiness of parting from the publisher but something warm and intangible was left behind. It was a joy to see him, a blessed experience. Gobey carried a radiance into the winter's day, a beacon against the icy wind and the falling snow.

En route to the bone-setter's, Gobey took a seat in a smoky tavern. He bought a mug of ale and a hot pie that was steaming. He stared at the fire, its flames twisting in the hearth. The chimney must have been blocked, for the smoke crept insidiously across the room, over his boots and up into his face. He sat until he was half-choked, until he could stand it no more and had to flee.

On the street a group had gathered to watch two men performing. They had long beards tied together, and were whirling like entranced dervishes round and round. Wrapped in the old fur coat, he crunched through the snow towards some doxies who called out, 'Hey you, bear skin. Need somewhere to stick your pole?'

He turned away from their catcalls and continued along the road. Beside the butcher's shop a group of lads watched his progress. As he approached, they pelted him with snowballs, laughing with the cold air expelling from their mouths. He joined in the fun, scraping up the snow and flinging it back in armfuls. He danced a jig to torment them. With their greater numbers they drove him into submission, cowering and ducking from the onslaught.

Down the street, a carriage came speeding into view, the horses gasping, their hooves thudding loudly. The coachman cracked the whip and made a geeing cry that echoed around the buildings. Gobey skipped across the road, leapt onto a ledge at the back of the vehicle and was hauled away from those wild, chasing lads. He poked his tongue at them, and they roared with merriment.

From the back of the carriage, he watched the world roll by in a swoon. Life in the city with the snow drifting: the vendors calling through the cool air; the smoky taverns bustling with wealthy merchants; the effeminate aristocrats staggering from bawdy houses to sleek black carriages along the road.

There were voices raised from inside the carriage, some bickering at hand. A short bout of squabbling was followed by a long reign of tense silence. Then they started up again, these razor-tongued adversaries, slicing at each other. He edged along the side to glance through the window. A cascading dress puffed from a woman's lap, her hair was piled high – this English Marie Antoinette, sparkling with sequins and clustered jewellery.

He swung back from the window astonished at what he had seen – a face almost powdered to extinction, but not the eyes. Not the eyes. Sure as the sun came up each morning, those were the eyes of his sweetheart – in another life, with another man. The coach bumped, and Gobey toppled in the snow, landing heavily on his spine. He tried to scramble to his feet, but his legs collapsed from under him. He screamed from the ground, 'Eileen! Eileeeeen!'

The coach disappeared and again he tried to stand, but his legs had no substance. He crawled from the road, away from the passing carriages. The fur coat had ridden up his back, high on his shoulders. He stared at the sky, a glut of wavering snowflakes falling. He called to a woman pushing a barrow, 'Lady, can you lend me a hand? Give me a lift up the road to Fetter Lane?'

'No, lovely, I can't. I've got work to do. I ain't got all day to be messing around with the likes of you.'

'Please help me,' he lisped through the cold air. 'Please'

She took a moment to assess the situation. Then she gripped him beneath the armpits and lifted him with a grunt. A young lass who looked old – no teeth, thinning hair, a lined face. Her breath smelt of stewed cabbage. He levered himself onto the barrow and dragged his legs across. If only his teeth would stop chattering, dancing in his head. He began to retch, but couldn't vomit.

They rolled into Fetter Lane and stopped at the old pamphlet house, but he couldn't find the key. 'Bang the door open,' he said. 'Run it with the barrow. Give it a good knock, girl.'

'I ain't doing that.' Her hands left the cart and she shook her head and stomped up and down. 'I ain't breaking in there. Not for you or the King.'

'It's me comrade's place, Johnny Steadman. If you're from round here, you might know him – little gent with a peg leg.'

'I don't.'

'It doesn't matter. I'm not robbing anyone, I just need to get out of the cold. Please now, give the door a good shunt will you?'

'Ya need a doctor.'

'I'm all right.'

'But ya can't walk.'

'I'm fine.'

She shook her head and lifted the handles. Backing onto the street she made a headlong rush at the door. It burst open and the momentum propelled them inside. The barrow struck the wall and he rolled onto the floor. 'Jesus hell! Are ya dead?'

'I'm all right,' he groaned. 'You can go now.' She dragged him by his fur coat, across the boards and into a dusty room. There was a tatty table and chairs, hoards of books and pamphlets stacked against the walls. There was nowhere for him to rest, so she left him on the floor.

He groaned up at her. 'Thank you. Close the door on your way out.'

'I can get a doctor.'

'No need.'

'I'll bring him back and all. It's no trouble, no trouble at all.'

'I just need to rest.'

'Someone should study those legs of yours.'

'I'll be up and running after a rest.' The woman went to speak, but he interrupted, 'Fare thee well.'

'And luck to ya, mate. Luck to ya, all the way.'

'And luck to you.'

Before leaving, she wedged the front door with a folded newspaper to keep it shut. The barrow creaked onto the street and rolled through the ground snow. His legs wouldn't stir, the cold ran through him. He tried to whistle to stop his teeth chattering, but his lips only quivered. Every breath stabbed his ribs. A spasm had hold of his back, it cramped and made a fluttering sensation. He listened to the rocking carriages on the street, men calling to each other. There was a sudden burst of laughter and a drunken doxy weeping for her tomorrows.

All he could think of was Eileen – gone to the aristocracy, wearing the garb of French royalty. He had barely recognized her in the drapery of excess. Such clothes, such jewellery – the stacked hair, the powdered face. In the wild excursions of his mind, he could not arrive at a suitable account for her transformation. What had happened to her life to drive her this way? What new world had been conjured in his absence?

The snow drifted in his peripheral vision at the window. The wind picked up and began to growl. The cold was getting to him in a way that couldn't be ignored. He looked around for something to use as a cover, but there were only pamphlets that he toppled from against the wall. He slept among them on the floor, the shivers jiggling every bone.

He woke to pain, deep in the base of his spine. He was too weary to drive his thoughts in any particular direction. His mind went out to the fluttering of snowflakes, the restless moaning of the wind. Way down the river a blizzard was blowing in from the north. Way down the river and running against the gale, heedless of the wind and the driving snow went the freed horse – running, as if it might leave the earth and sprout wings to flee the city.

CHAPTER 10

Behold London, covered in snow, silent at dawn with the flakes falling in profusion – the white-puddingy fields, the trees with hanging icicles. The wind crossed the river into the dark alleys, where it howled like a soul gone mad for a lifetime of purgatory. At the grand house, the servants had stirred, their sleepy limbs going through the perfunctory motions of their duty – lighting fires, emptying chamber pots, boiling eggs in pans at the range.

It was a large house, exquisitely furnished and finely kept according to the aesthetic tastes of its owner, Master Saffronetti. Retired from the opera, and now operating as a moneylender, he had a great sense of grandeur, of growing self-importance. Rightly or wrongly he believed himself to own half of London, since half of London to his estimation was in some way indebted to him. Among all his possessions – land, houses, paintings, jewellery – none was more precious than the splendid object that was Eileen Dineen. Bound to him by a contract of debt, she had fallen into his keeping with no means of release.

Eileen rose sleepily from the bed and into her daily sorrow. For seven years she had woken and thought of him – her Tom, her sweetheart – with the same wrench in her stomach. Last night she had dreamt of him, a vivid dream that spilled into the morning and left an aftertaste, a sharp pain in her chest. And now she would have to carry it around all day – the disquieting knowledge of his absence, with only patchwork dreams to keep him alive.

She recalled a time of hot summers, when they loved among the fields by the river. Tom Gobey in the daisies, the sweet scent of honeysuckle faint in the breeze. In those years following the French

Revolution, they truly believed the liberties won by the French lower classes would sweep across the Channel and emancipate the masses. How they had worked in the pamphlet house, dedicated to rights of the poor. Intoxicated in their quest for equality, they could not have foreseen how the tide would turn against them.

They had arrived one morning at the pamphlet house to find the windows broken. Not one, but all of them, a mass of glass on the ground. That night they left the premises and were jostled by a Church-and-King mob, cursed as atheists and republican rebels. From henceforward, they arrived each day to find a spy standing outside with a notebook.

Weeks passed with them being watched, followed and abused. They had reason to suspect that their post was being tampered with, as some letters didn't arrive and others looked to be stained by finger marks. The premises were frequently burgled and piles of pamphlets stolen. Then, one morning with the rain slanting through the broken window, the front door crashed off its hinges. A magistrate and two soldiers marched hollering into the room.

And still now, as if it were yesterday, Eileen remembered the satisfied smile of the magistrate and the enduring words he said: 'You've penned your last pamphlet, Tom Gobey.'

But today she didn't want to think of her sweetheart's downfall. Today she wanted to remember better times, when they were free to love, free to roam the streets without fear of arrest. Hand in hand they would follow the river out to the sprawling fields, sometimes staying till the sun crept down and the stars came winking into reality. Flat on a blanket, looking up at the sky – two specks of the universe with no hint of their fate. She had lived in the present then, enjoying the moment. Now she was preoccupied with reliving cherished fragments from the past. They say that a hundred lovers down the line, one never forgets one's first love. He was her only love – a love that started on the streets of London and continued to haunt her thoughts.

Sitting on the bed, she closed her eyes. She conjured the time she first saw Tom Gobey. It was winter in the city, the frost sparkled white on the ground. The sky was pale, the atmosphere slate grey. London was alive with the traffic of people, transient faces passing on the street.

Walking backwards around the corner she had bumped unconsciously into the beginning of a new life.

That day had started no different from others – she had worked all morning writing handbills and preparing them for print. After eating a small meal of bread and cheese, she had taken a nap on a bench. Waking refreshed, but somewhat cold, she had put on her coat and begun to collect the pamphlets to be sold on the street. She had stoked the fire and sat for a moment, staring into the flames. She had filled a leather shoulder bag with handbills and braced herself for the pulsing city.

She had wandered along the Strand, calling out to the passing people. It was bitterly cold, her breath steamed in a puffy cloud. The windows of the shops were frosted and just starting to thaw. She sold a pamphlet here, a handbill there. There were the usual amount of mockers, throwing up their hands and rejecting all notions of a better world. She was rebuffed on one side of the road and praised on the other. An aristocrat had cursed her, while a beggar had shaken her hand, 'Good on ya, love. Good on ya. Someone's gotta help the poor, someone's gotta.'

She spun and twisted as she travelled, turning to face the oncoming flux of people. From the distance, she could hear a man calling, a hawker or vendor she thought. Looking down the street, there was no sign of him, but the voice continued in its demanding tone. As she backed around the corner, her shoulder collided with the perpetrator of that noise. 'All men have rights! All men have rights, I say!'

Tom Gobey, who was also backing his way along the street, turned to face her. His arms were full of pamphlets 'Sorry,' he said. 'Sorry. I wasn't looking where I was going.'

'And women,' she smiled, and swept the hair from her face. 'What about women?'

'What's that?'

'Do women have rights?'

For a moment he lost his speech and then he said, 'Some say they do.'

'And what do you say?'

'Yes, women have rights. All people under the sun have rights.'

Already she had warmed to his face, those chocolate, fathomless eyes. 'What about dogs?' She giggled and teased him. 'Do dogs have rights?'

Now he could see she was making merry, and he liked it. 'If I had rights to give, they could have them. All beasts of the world included.'

'And what rights would you be after giving me?'

'What rights do you want?'

'The right to live without prejudice or oppression. To live without squalor in an equal, peaceful world.'

'Granted.'

They laughed, and for a moment the world seemed a more liberated place. They talked for a few minutes, no more, but during that time a great warmth passed between them. It was a meeting of fiery souls and egalitarian minds And they were not blind to the aphrodisiac of passion they saw in each other. They traded handbills and parted on the street, both groggy from the intoxicating encounter.

That afternoon, she sold more pamphlets than she had all week. She was electrified, enthused, oblivious to rejection and hell-bent on liberating the masses. She flitted in and out of the taverns, leaving handbills on the tables, debating politics with the men. The stallholders were not safe from her zealotry – she cajoled them to listen, hushed them when they tried to speak. She won minds that day, and more than a few hearts among the men she encountered.

That night, she went to bed exhausted, but could not sleep. She ran the day backwards and kept finding her thoughts returned to that chance meeting on the corner. Of all the many people she had encountered, it was Tom Gobey that stuck in her mind. Those dark eyes, that gentle smile. Something in his soul that moved her, something that made her want to dance.

She woke the next day with thoughts of his laughter. Sleep-deprived, she dragged herself around all morning, knocking her knees on the furniture and cursing those knocks away. There was much work to be done on the pamphlets, but she couldn't settle to anything, couldn't pin a job down. Frustrated, she filled her bag with handbills and left to sell them on the street.

It was a grey day with the moisture dampening her hair. Crests of mist crept down the alleys and curled over the shop windows. Without conscious effort, she found herself making her way to the Strand. On the corner, she paced up and down, looking for Tom Gobey. She dispensed handbills to kill time, calling out the slogans of revolution. Hours passed without selling a pamphlet. Weary and dispirited, she couldn't seem to drag herself away. Eventually, she wandered home with the disconsolate cries of the starlings ringing out her departure.

For three days she returned to the Strand in the hope he might appear. She cursed herself for being foolish, for building false hopes and dreams. The longer she waited the more desirous she became. And desirous for what? A man she hardly knew, a figment of her imagination? In truth, she could not precisely say why she was waiting, except there was something inexplicable that drew her. Something blinding and altogether beyond the faculty of reason.

Another day on the corner, she stomped to drive out the cold. She called to the passing people and handed out pamphlets, calling through the mizzling rain, searching faces for that dark lad that had touched her. Resigned to failure, she had given up the quest and was about to leave when a voice came mocking behind her. 'Rights for women, women in the rain.'

She turned to the flash of his teeth, his sparkling eyes. No part of him seemed unhappy, no part of him ashamed. He was free in the heart, not bound by inhibition or crushed by the world around him. A man beyond the decree of Church or Government – it was a joy to hear him laugh. 'I read your handbill,' she said, 'I read it well.'

'You did,' he said, still holding his smile. 'And I read yours.'

Now she was smiling and meeting his eyes. 'So the King is an arse, is he?'

'He is.'

'And God is a chimera?'

'Most definitely.' He swept his fingers through his hair and came back at her. 'We need a republic, you say. All monarchy disbanded.'

'We do, sure.'

'Then between us we'll start an English revolution.'

They laughed and stumbled towards each other. For some time

they stood exchanging ideas of liberation. They praised Tom Paine and Joseph Priestley, talking of a new state beyond the hierarchy of Church and Government. They walked together, hardly noticing where they went, or the city around them. Wandering into a tavern, they found a seat in the corner. They spent hours in discussion, never running out of conversation or laughter. Neither one seemed keen on departing, so the day became night with the darkness gathering at the window.

Eventually they went outside, cutting through the damp night air. She might have known him all her life, or in some past life, for the easy converse between them. There was no shyness to prevent her linking his arm, and she did so, feeling a sense of belonging rise inside her. She wished the people passing might think of them as a couple, lovers of some years, questors on life's journey.

Outside her rooms, he kissed her cheek and made off into the night. She stood at the door to watch his departure. He was slowly enveloped by the mist, carried off in a vast swirl. When she could see him no more, his voice came falling through the haze. 'Eileen Dineen! You are as sweet as sweet liberty!'

The next day they walked by the river, and by the river they fell in love. On the banks of the Thames, out from the city, they found bliss in solitude, solace in the passing of the tide. Within the month they were sworn to each other, rebel hearts waging war against all hierarchies. Eileen came to work at Gobey's pamphlet house, and they distributed handbills together on the street. Back to back, leaning on each other, they set about changing the world.

In the summer, they made love in the fields. They would lie with the sun kissing their faces. They'd sit watching the eddying river, departing from the city like something ordained at the world's beginning, something destined until the last day ends.

There was a knock at the door and Eileen was shaken from those blessed days with Gobey. Lying on the bed, she clawed herself back to the present. The maid entered and speedily crossed the room to draw the curtains. A drunken ballad singer was howling on the street. His voice made for melancholy listening – roaring one moment and lamenting the next. He was longing for a love that could never be.

Arms folded, the maid stood smiling by the dressing table. 'Does madam require any help this morning?'

'Madam requires a certain maid to join her for breakfast by the fire. Now Lily, what say you to that, wouldn't that be grand?

'Oh, Miss Eileen, it would be grand – grand indeed.' Lily skipped across the room, closed the door and pulled up a chair alongside the mirror. She pressed her hands between her knees and rocked from side to side. 'Will I go and fetch the breakfast now, Miss Eileen?'

'Sure you may as well, Lily. Or the hunger will be the death of us.'

The maid hurried from the room and danced down the stairs, regaining her composure at the bottom. She lowered her eyes and took a deep breath before entering the kitchen. She piled a plate with eggs and ham, cut some cheese and freshly baked bread from the oven. As she filled the teapot, Mrs Hodgers came from behind and peered over her shoulder, 'Hungry is she, the lady? Eating for two, in the family way, is she?'

'She has a great appetite, Mrs Hodgers.'

'Get out of it,' the old cook scoffed. Her goitre rocked in her throat as she spoke, a smile concealed in the fleshy roundness of her face. 'I knows what you're up to, my girl. You're sharing the food with the lady upstairs, that's what you're doing. And why not, I say, why not grab it, indeed? Fill your boots girl, fill your boots. Just don't get caught, that's all. The master will have you dismissed, God strike me down if he won't. Don't you get caught, now. You hear me, young Lily? Don't get caught, my girl.'

'I won't, Mrs Hodgers.'

'Well, be a good girl then and run along.'

'I will, Mrs Hodgers.'

'And don't forget.'

'Forget what, Mrs Hodgers?'

'When you've done chin-wagging with your ladyship – it's your turn to do the pots.'

'Yes, Mrs Hodgers.'

'Now, I'm going to have meself some liver and bacon, and I don't give a damn who knows it. Liver and bacon I wants, and liver and bacon I shall have. With an egg on top.'

'God bless you, Mrs Hodgers.'

'God bless young Lily.'

Lily slowly climbed the stairs with the breakfast tray. On the landing at the top of the stairs, she encountered Mr Sticks. His suit was entrenched with longstanding grime and his boots were soiled with mud. Leaning against the wall, he cupped his testicles as if assessing their weight, laughing and calling to her 'Cock-a-coming, big-cock-a-coming.'

She stood frozen, unable to move. The waft of the river steamed from his tatty clothes. She rushed for Eileen's bedroom door and tumbled inside, slamming it with her foot. The tray clattered as she placed it down – her face was flushed and her eyes held great fear. She sat and pinched her hands between her knees to stop them shaking.

Eileen sat beside her and took her hand. The fingers were cold and rigid. 'What ever's the matter, Lily? What's happened, my love – what on earth has happened?'

'It's Mr Sticks. He's a filthy dog, a stinking rotter. Nobody likes him, nobody does. He's no friends and no one has a good word to say about him. They say there's nothing he won't stoop to, nothing. Not one little bit of him is good, not one bit.'

Eileen carried a chair across the room and placed it against the door. She knew it wouldn't keep Mr Sticks out if he was determined, but it would help to calm Lily. She hurried back to the fire, 'Don't mind him, now. He'll not come while I'm here. Have some breakfast, love. Warm your hands at the fire. He'll not come now, he'll not come.'

Lily shakily poured the tea, everything she handled shook or rattled. She sat back for a moment and pursed her lips. 'I would like to call him certain things, Miss Eileen, but I wouldn't dare curse in front of you.'

'Curse away, Lily. 'Tis good for the soul, good for the soul, so it is.'

The maid took a deep breath and blinked several times. She seemed more breathless for doing so and put a palm against her chest to restore some balance. She looked at her feet and around the room. Then she said, 'He's a filthy little bugger-shit.'

They shrieked with laughter. 'He's worse than that, Lily. He's a little sack of boiled arses.' Now they were roaring, waving their hands with tears flowing and swatting imaginary flies. They heaped insults on that putrid little man, until they could hardly eat without choking. And every time one looked at the other, they started up again, snorting and hooting and cursing unrestrainedly in cathartic release.

Mr Sticks slunk away from the door and crept down the back stairs. He silently entered the kitchen. Mrs Hodgers was at the hearth, frying on the pan with the smoke drifting around her. A tangy waft hit her nostrils and she crouched to sniff the liver, thinking it might have gone off. She was struck by a sudden epiphany and turned to find Mr Sticks with his penis out of his trousers.

'Mrs Hodgers,' he smiled, tilting his head. 'Pleased to see ya.'

'Good day to you, Mr Sticks.' She wouldn't look down, wouldn't acknowledge his behaviour. Turning away, she shook the pan and the contents sizzled. The fat spat on her hand but she didn't flinch, made no movement from the hearth. She was gratified to hear voices approaching the kitchen – it was the butler, Mr Stanley, and the young lad, Bob Docker. They stopped speaking at the sight of Mr Sticks and passed him, ignoring his existence.

Mr Stanley led the lad to the table, directing him to a chair. They sat stiffly with their arms hanging and their faces morose. They sat in silence – the dignified man with his wild hair sticking out at the sides, and the young lad with his mousy nose twitching, and a hundred questions suppressed inside him. Only when Mrs Hodgers spoke did they look up from the table.

'Will you have some liver and onions, Mr Sticks?' Her throat clogged; she had to drag a cough to clear the passageway. 'Miss Eileen has put some aside for the staff.'

'No,' he said sarcastically, folding himself inside his trousers. 'I'll just stand here by the wall, starving me guts out. Off course I'll have some.'

Mr Sticks sauntered over to the table and sat down with his arms on the top. He had soiled and worn sleeves, his hands had an eggy stench. They could hear him scratching his groin over the crackling fire. He burped and grunted simultaneously, as an offering, and blew the odour around the room. He rubbed his nose with the palm of his hand, until it clicked – higher and higher into the oily folds of his face. The lad took a sidelong glance at him. There was something odd about his cheek – it was swollen on one side.

Mrs Hodgers put down the plates and served the liver, flipping it with a knife. She cut some bread and melted the frozen butter over the fire. They ate in silence, staring at their food. The lad couldn't keep his eyes off Mr Sticks. Mr Stanley caught his attention and shook his head, but young Bob seemed oblivious to any oblique warnings.

Mr Sticks pointed with his fork and spoke without looking up. 'Something wrong, is there? Something wrong with me old face?'

The lad didn't know what to say or where to look. He gawped with his tongue thick in his mouth, often on display when he wasn't talking. He turned to Mr Stanley, who was pulling a strange face. Mrs Hodgers was whispering, but he couldn't make out the words – his ears were ringing, his head was full of unrelated thoughts.

Mr Sticks turned on him and spoke while chewing. 'There must be something wrong, cause while I'm trying to eat, ya keep staring at me. Have I got pickle on me snout, a sword sticking out of me head? What's the interest?'

The lad shook his head.

'Do ya know, I must be going deaf. Coz every time I ask a question, I can't hear a thing ya say. Now listen to me good, boy. This is the last time I'm for asking. What's so special about me face that has yer interest?'

Mrs Hodgers put down her knife and fork, her breathing came thick and fast like an asthmatic's. Mr Stanley stopped eating. 'Nothing,' the lad whispered. 'I was just looking around.'

'Are ya saying that I'm nothing? Not important like, not here – present, sitting, eating? Are ya saying that, are ya? Are ya saying that?'

'No I ain't, sir. I just mean I'm not looking at anything at all.'

Mr Sticks leaned across the table, his eyes fixed on the boy. Young Bob stared back with his tongue filling his mouth, purple and veiny. He had the feeling that if he looked away he would be struck. No one was eating, no one moving. The snow fell at the window.

'Some more liver, Mr Sticks?' Mrs Hodgers left the table and shook the pan. 'Plenty more for the hungry.'

'No,' he turned and looked down at her plate. 'How come you got an egg and we ain't?'

'Would you like me to fry you an egg, a nice fresh egg?' Mrs Hodgers could now see what had taken the boy's interest. Mr Sticks had a jagged scar running down his face – it had been crudely stitched together in a crooked line of overlapping skin. 'It won't take long for an egg or two.'

'Yeah, I've got all day to wait for eggs. Take yer time – bake a cake, a plum pudding. I'll just sit here twiddling me thumbs.'

Mr Sticks stood and his chair scrapped along the stone floor. They could smell him as he swaggered across the room. Climbing the stairs, he had the muscled buttocks of a bull. You could sense his weight on the boards, crossing the next landing.

No one moved until he was lost in the house. A tear ran down the lad's cheek, Mr Stanley reached over to rest a hand on his shoulder. Mrs Hodgers came beside him with the pan and piled food on his plate to restore his spirits. Lily entered the kitchen with two other maids. On hearing that the lad was upset, they ruffled his hair and kissed him. Of all the maids, he loved Lily the most. He had the dream that they would one day marry. How they laughed when he said he had driven Mr Sticks from the kitchen, shown him the door with the threat of his fist. The girls indulged his wild fantasies, until he was so bloated with heroics, he was all for fighting a duel on the street.

CHAPTER 11

Imprisoned in Saffronetti's house, Eileen often dwelled on her childhood in Ireland. She remembered the darkness from her window – how at night, when the candles were blown out, it would creep around the house and nudge against the glass. Darkness that was so dense, it seemed no new day could penetrate it. A darkness that could enter your veins, permeate your bones, infiltrate your mind with its silent presence. Now it seemed that all of Ireland, all those past days, were lost in a backdrop of darkness.

They had lived in Passage West, a small town on the river Lee. Their house was built on a hill, a stone abode overlooking the river. Her father, Michael Dineen, was a blacksmith, a big man with overdeveloped forearms and an underdeveloped heart – for his wife, Maria, had died giving birth to his only daughter. In another life, another destiny, he would have had a house full of children and would have loved them equally in his magnanimous way. But when his wife departed, so did his interest in loving. And thus, he didn't hold or behold another woman in affection for the rest of his life. What love he had left was bestowed on his daughter.

His wife's death changed him. Had Maria survived the birth of their daughter, he would have continued in his normal way – a gregarious man who would often invite visitors to the house, a house of fiddle playing, singing and storytelling, a house of much hospitality and laughter. He was a man who liked to drink, but now would drink no more. Once a great reveller, he came to prefer the company of silence. He began to shy away from social gatherings, avoiding the discourse of men. Habitually quiet, he would haul his large frame around the forge a blacksmith that never sang or whistled, never mumbled expletives or even sighed from exhaustion. To watch him work was like observing a man that was deaf and mute, accustomed to the silence and thoughtful in that quiet domain. Even when shoeing horses or hammering at the anvil, he maintained an impassive exterior, seldom grimacing or straining the muscles of his face.

The father Eileen inherited was aloof and reclusive, reticent in the company of others. She had no concept of the man he had been, who had sung and played the fiddle, danced on the tavern table in the town. The father she knew was too introverted to attend to his own business. As a small girl, he would send her to the front door to collect the payments for his blacksmith work. And before she could properly talk, she knew the price of every job, from shoeing a horse to forging a gate.

While her father was publicly withdrawn, in private he would come alive to play and entertain his daughter. He used to toss her in the air and catch her as she fell. The young Eileen would laugh and bellow for more. 'Again, Daddy,' she would cry. 'Again! Again! Again!' He would continue until he was exhausted, and then he would kiss the tip of her nose.

With Eileen on his knee in front of the fire, he had told her stories. Among those stories, there would always be a tale about her mother, detailing her beauty, describing her gentle ways. To Eileen, her mother became a figment rather than a reality, someone who lived within a tale and thus had an everlasting existence. It was in the soft, confessional tones of her father's voice that her mother came to life – strolling through the barley or calling across the river.

On one such occasion, she was nestled on her father's knee. They were seated at the table and she was rubbing the stubble on his face with her fingertips. She remembered catching his eyes, off-green with a residue of sadness. Even when he was smiling, bestowing love, he was never far from a melancholy thought.

'Daddy,' she said. 'Is Mummy in heaven with God?'

He closed his eyes and opened them. Some seconds passed, then he gasped and shook his head. 'No, my love. She's not. There's no God and no heaven. For if there was, he would never have allowed your mother to die.'

'Then where is she, Daddy? Where has she gone?'

His eyes were wistful and seemingly awash with the Irish Sea. 'She has not gone, my sweetheart. She has not gone.'

'Then where is she? Where is she, Daddy?'

'She's in the rain, the breeze, the stars and the flowers. She's in the air, in thoughts and words and forever in our hearts. Wherever you look, she's there, beside you. Never more than a breath away.'

She didn't understand her father's philosophy – since, when she looked around the house, she couldn't find her mother. And so in her childish mind, she took this to mean there were signs, faces in the knotted furniture and the grainy stone of the walls. After much searching, she discovered her mother's countenance in the bark of a tree, outside the house. The tree became a shrine, where she would speak to her mother of the notable events in her life.

Now a grown woman and confined to a room in Saffronetti's house, she still spoke to her mother. She spoke as if they had shared a lifetime of intimacy, years of conversation and tenderness. As a child, her father had said she resembled her mother, and thus Eileen now sat before the mirror to conjure her mother's presence. She brushed the dark hair from her face and met her own eyes, green and moist with emotion. *Mother*, she said. *'Tis only me, only me. Sure, it's snowing in London, the river is frozen and the air is brittle and cold. Outside you could snap your breath with your fingers, break it like shards of glass. All the clothes in the world couldn't keep you warm and the poor beggars are half-frozen to death on the streets.*

Oh, mother, I am most saddened. For I have not heard from my sweetheart for some time. He is still imprisoned in Botany Bay and I have no word of his existence. Saffronetti has a vicious nature and he will not allow me to write or receive letters. I am worried to death that Tom Gobey has perished, and yet, for some inexplicable reason I believe him to be alive and well. I will never give up on him, never stop thinking of that sweet-natured boy.

How I miss father and our home in Passage West. I still remember climbing the bank and running through the long grass, looking down upon the river, where the boats would sail to Cork harbour. We used to pick apples from

Hickey's orchard, and father would lift me high into the trees, for I was too small to reach them. Such happy times, happy times.

Oh, dear Mother. I fear my best days are behind me. And if it wasn't for you, I don't know who else I should speak to. Methinks there are hard times ahead, but I'll keep faith that my sweetheart will return, and we'll once again love with the passion of young radicals, the force of rebel hearts.

Eileen left the mirror and sat on the bed. Her mind travelled once more to Ireland. It was summer, the sky had darkened and a thunderstorm made its way along the river. The kitchen door was open and the rain crashed against the ground outside. She was kneeling on a chair at the table, playing with an old rag doll. She heard a strange sound, an odd barking. At first she thought it was a dog from the cottages below. Then as she tilted her head, she found it was her father. He had left the forge and was approaching the house, coughing and spluttering as he walked.

When he reached the house, he leaned into the kitchen doorway to catch his breath. His chest was heaving, his eyes were watery and had a strange lucidity, a glassy luminosity. She had never seen him looking so tired, so lacking in energy and purpose. He was a big man, strong and statuesque, always ready for a day's work and never one to rest for long. Now he lumbered into the kitchen with his mouth open, gulping for pockets of air. 'Eileen, my love,' he gasped and wiped his brow with his hand. 'Will you go down to fetch Dr O' Sullivan?'

Eileen left the chair and ran to him. She took his hand, it was lifeless and without warmth or strength. Pressing her thumbs into his calluses, she stared up at his pale face, 'What's wrong, Daddy? Are you poorly?'

'No, no, my love. I'm fine – just an old fever, that's all. But go down to the cottages to fetch the doctor, will you?'

Eileen left in the rain. The sky was black in one corner and darkly bruised everywhere else. A flash of lightning crossed the sky and vanished. Then the thunder boomed and she felt the ground shake beneath her feet. Her thin summer dress was drenched and clinging to her chest and legs. Her father had said there was no God, but for that moment, the child atheist imagined His wrath let loose upon the earth. As the day plunged further into darkness, she thought the world might come to an end.

She ran down the bank to Dock Cottages and returned with the doctor. They entered the kitchen, but her father was not there. They followed the barking sound of his cough to the bedroom and found him in bed. She had never known him to take to his bed in the daytime, and certainly not with his clothes on. He was shivering beneath the blanket, with his large boots poking out. His hair was drenched, his face sweaty.

Dr O'Sullivan stood shaking his head. His plump cheeks were flushed from climbing the bank, his breath not quite returned to normal. While he gathered himself, he didn't take his eyes from his patient and appeared to be forming a diagnosis from across the room. Then, as if suddenly aware of the child's presence, he led Eileen outside and closed the door.

The weeks that passed saw her father often in bed. He would rest for some days, then continue to work, but it was never long before he returned to bed. He developed a habitual cough, a perpetual tiredness. His eyes were never anything other than glossy – they had a frightening refraction, as if the light from another world was passing through him. His clothes grew large and swam about him in loose corrugations. He began to pale, to shrink, to hunch and dodder.

Dr O'Sullivan became a regular visitor to the house. He would place his black bag on the table and take out his medicines, but there was nothing inside the bag that could improve her father. As time went on, the bag was never opened, just placed down and picked up and taken away without hope or remission in his condition. One day, as the doctor was leaving, Eileen had called to him. 'Dr O'Sullivan,' she said, following him to the door, staring up with her honest green eyes. 'Please, sir. Can you tell me what's wrong with my father?'

The doctor crouched to meet her eyes. He put a hand on her shoulder and she might have collapsed under the weight. 'Well, child. You know your father is a very poorly man. He needs lots of rest and lots of fresh air.'

'Will he get better, sir?'

'I hope so.'

'Will he ever stop coughing?'

'Not for a while. Not for a while.'

'But what's wrong with him? What makes him so tired and ready for sleep?'

'He has consumption, child. Consumption.'

The doctor stood upright and sighed. He left the kitchen and closed the door, leaving the child alone with a house full of disease. She knew nothing about consumption, except that it was in her father and possibly crawling the walls and up the chimney and in the mice holes and everywhere she looked and somehow behind all of her thoughts. And on that day, when she closed her eyes and tried to fathom the word *consumption*, a black and formless mist descended, a cold and pitiless chill ran through her.

For a month, her father was powerless to leave his bed. Eileen began to doubt he would ever rise again. It was difficult to imagine him walking and impossible to envisage him hammering at his anvil. She had a terrible compulsion to drag him from the bed and make him toss her in the air like he used to in those glorious, bygone days. But now, he could hardly recognize her. He would sometimes call her Maria, as if his wife had returned in the ghostly form of his daughter.

Then, unexpectedly, an aunt she had never met arrived at the house. Her name was Betty. She was her father's sister, a tall woman with grey hair. In fact, everything about Betty was grey – her eyes, skin, voice and manner. Betty was besotted with Catholicism and would stand in the corner, facing the wall to say the rosary. Eileen had never seen her father pray in the house and this seemed an odd occupation. And while to keep up appearances in the parish, Michael had taken his daughter to mass and gone through the motions of religiosity, they had shared a secret – there was no God, no divine agency .

Betty began cooking and taking over the chores that Eileen couldn't manage. She tended to her brother and was often at his bedside, whispering and nodding and puckering her dry lips. Whenever she left the bedroom, she would stare at Eileen and shake her head, as if all hope of recovery was lost. The house soon fell under the regime of Betty's rules, a creed of harsh laws and austere practices.

There was a correct time to eat, a correct time to sleep, and no time at all for play or laughter.

As well as caring for her brother, Betty also began to care for Eileen. She would comb her hair, usually too hard, with the teeth scratching her scalp. She was heavy-handed and had no idea of her own strength, so that her touch always felt like a push or a jostle. She would bathe Eileen in the tub, scrubbing with a flannel and never failing to get soap in her eyes. Having lost her mother at birth, Eileen was accustomed to looking after herself – but she never said so, and silently suffered these groomings and ablutions with a heavy heart.

One evening, when her father had been coughing all day, Betty came to Eileen at the table. She sat for a moment in silence, then after gathering herself and taking several breaths, she said, 'When your father has gone, you'll come to live with me in London. You'll go to school and be happy and want for nothing at all.'

'Where's Daddy going?'

'To heaven, where he'll be with God.'

'But Daddy said there's no heaven and no God. He said if there was a God, my mummy would still be here.'

Betty sat motionless, not looking at the child, but staring across the room. Her reticence spoke of disapproval, of a deep annoyance that had thrown her into silence. There was disillusionment in her eyes, a stunned disbelief that a Catholic child could have no faith in God. When she was finished brooding, she turned to Eileen, 'We'll see about that,' she said, glaring and tightening her mouth. 'That we will.'

And Eileen did see about it. For the next morning, she was shunted into the corner and made to face the wall. She was handed a set of rosary beads and told to say ten Hail Marys for each bead that passed through her fingers. The child protested. 'I don't want to,' she said. 'I want to play in the fields.'

Betty knelt to face the child. Her face was pale and long, her teeth stained and chipped like broken crockery. Close up, her eyebrows were conjoined and her fine moustache had a film of powder that failed to conceal it 'Now, child, listen to me. Do you want your father to become well?'

Eileen nodded, reluctant to speak.

Betty continued. 'Do you want your father to live, do you?' She nudged Eileen with her elbow, a bony weapon. 'Do you want him to leave the bed, so?"

'I do, sure. I do.'

'Then say your rosary, and with the help of God, your father will be well again.'

Betty turned Eileen into the corner and the child began to pray. She trawled through the rosary, but was not convinced of its power. She tried desperately to imagine a God, but failed to convince herself of His existence. And the nearest thing she could find to a God was not a man, but a woman – the remote sense of her mother as a paragon of goodness. It seemed foolish to pray to her mother – since she could go to the tree and converse with her whenever she liked – and thus she continued to pray to a God that didn't exist, empty words to a fictional creator. She rushed her prayers, mumbling and flicking through the beads to complete the cycle. When she was finished, she spun around to make a speedy getaway, but was once more herded into the corner and made to start again.

But all the prayers in the world could not change things. Her father died and Betty was given charge of the child. Eileen did not wish to live with her aunt, but there was nowhere else for her to go. While Betty thought it her duty to look after the girl, she didn't warm to the task and found it a daily burden. Though she never once struck the child, she never cuddled her either. The relationship was strained, their conversation was always perfunctory and lacking in feeling. If they had spoken the unspoken, both would have preferred to live alone than with each other. And whenever her aunt came close, it was like standing beneath a cool shadow, a tower of contempt.

On an ash-grey day, they boarded a ship for England. The water was murky, it lapped against the side of the boat. Crushed by her father's death, Eileen stood on deck, trying to fathom the events that had befallen her. They sailed out of Cork harbour in the mist, a dreary departure on a damp November morning. By means of intuition, she knew that her links with Ireland were severed , and she would not see the land of her birth again.

CHAPTER 12

Eileen was brought to her aunt's house in Newington Green. The house had three floors and was tidier than any home she had seen in Ireland. There was no clutter – no shoes, books, clothes, newspapers, crockery or ornaments on display. At home, her father would often leave his blacksmith's tools in the kitchen, but here there was nothing leaning against the walls or resting on the furniture. One might have thought the house was deserted, except that the furniture was scrupulously polished and not a speck of dust could be found anywhere. There were no cobwebs in the corners or cupboards, and under the beds the fluff had been expunged, given no time to gather and multiply. Wherever Eileen went in the house, she felt out of place and uncomfortable – as if her presence was a source of untidiness.

She was given a small room with a bed but no furniture. A varnished box stood by the bed, with a bible and a lantern on top. She was handed new clothes that she didn't like, some smock-like dresses that had frills on the hems. Her shoes were clumpy and awkward to walk in, since they were too big and flopped around her feet. Her aunt had said, 'They'll be fitting you snugly in the years to come.'

It became apparent that Betty was something of a miser, opposed to spending of any kind and prone to making things last. If cut thinly, a loaf of bread could last them a week. She used to say a little hunger in the belly was good feeding for the soul, it concentrated prayer and focused the mind on heaven. Though a practised skinflint, Betty was not poor, for she had inherited the house and some small wealth when her husband had died. It seemed her life's preoccupation was to conserve all her assets, monitoring her expenditure like a neurotic accountant.

Life in the house was austere. Eileen was prohibited from play, barred from making noise and disqualified from acquiring any item that required the exchange of money. She was fed an adequate amount of food – enough to maintain weight, prevent illness and malnourishment – but not enough to feed the heart and enliven the spirits. Praying was mandatory in the house and Eileen had her own darkened corner for the saying of the rosary. If Betty was hell-bent on imposing her values, Eileen was already inwardly resisting them and quietly forming her own.

Displaced in the heart of London, it was difficult to comprehend her father's death. She recalled him in the days before his illness, hammering in his forge and carrying her across the fields. His laughter was locked in her memory, his tenderness enmeshed in her heart. He had such rough hands from blacksmithing, but was always gentle when handling his daughter. She longed for Ireland and a time when her father was healthy, a loving refuge in her life. In her dreams, she revisited those blissful days, playing over and over the memories of childhood.

As she grew older, Eileen began to oppose her aunt's regime. She was placed in a school, but was sent home on the first day for blasphemy. She was sent to another school, but fought with a boy who had tugged her hair. That night, she had cried so much and protested, that Betty could not send her back the next day. She was eventually found another school where she began to progress in her studies, but to her aunt's dismay, she was also developing a propensity for rebellion.

One morning at her new school, Eileen was seated around a table with some other girls. The girls were teasing her for being Irish, for not believing in God and having no respect for the King. Though outnumbered, Eileen argued against them, insisting that God was a lie and that the King was just another man, no different from any other, despite his wealth.

Overhearing the conversation, the schoolmistress called Eileen to her desk and asked the class to continue with their reading. The child stood beside her chair. 'Now, Eileen,' said Mary Wollstonecraft, suppressing a smile and trying not to give too much of her heart away. 'In what sense precisely has God offended you?'

'He offends me, Miss, because He doesn't exist and everyone says that He does.'

Mary giggled and stifled the action with her hand. 'How can you be sure that He doesn't exist?'

'If He did, he would never have allowed my mother and father to die.'

Though this came as cheerless news, Mary was more amused than saddened, as there was something about the girl that was unashamedly honest and steadfast in her conviction. Eileen was intriguing, for it was not common for a child to express such rebellious views. 'Well, Eileen, you have killed off God very nicely, but what objection do you have towards the King?'

'The King is too rich, Miss. He has so much land and money, but he doesn't share it. And there are poor men like my father, who had to work so hard as a blacksmith and became ill and died. And there are poorer men and woman and children on the streets with hungry bellies. London is a terrible place for the poor, Miss.'

The mistress now laughed openly. 'Methinks we have an Irish rebel among us. Glory be, a child dissenter.' The mistress parted her arms to embrace the child. 'Miniature republican, most welcome are thee.'

Mary embraced Eileen warm and kindly, rocking her from side to side. Since her mother's early death, Eileen had never been held by a woman – certainly not her aunt. It was only her father who had administered affection, and thus she had no concept of maternal love. In this action of being held, Eileen was deeply moved and had the strange feeling her mother was somehow present in spirit, transmogrified and alive again.

Eileen had never met anyone like Mary Wollstonecraft. She had black worsted stockings and a scarf tied around her head. Her hair was always dishevelled, as if she had stood for too long in the wind, or simply never bothered to comb it. Her nose was straight and her eyes were soft and her lips were exquisitely pretty. To Eileen, she was the most beautiful woman in the world, and indeed, the most unorthodox, for she had a tendency to challenge all points of view. And whenever the mistress addressed the class, Eileen felt she was somehow speaking to her alone, in a direct communion of matched hearts.

Eileen progressed under her tutelage, acquiring great skills in writing and independent thought. Mary took a special interest in the child, nurturing her development and giving her gifts of books and pamphlets. And what started with a hug was to become an enduring friendship, lasting beyond Eileen's schooldays and into her adult life.

Betty did not approve of Mary Wollstonecraft – she was too outspoken, unconventional and rebellious, a bad influence on her niece. Eileen was cluttering up the house with books and pamphlets, attending political meetings and talking provocatively about revolution. She refused to say her rosary and was openly profane, preferring rational discourse to the bible. In Betty's eyes, Eileen had too much education and too little religion, a dangerous imbalance for any woman.

After years of confrontation, they finally parted company. The rift was caused by a memorable incident, one that had driven Eileen from the house. Eileen was now a young woman, publishing pamphlets of a radical nature and earning a small salary for her efforts. It was a cold day in January, the frost crisp on the ground. The streets had a fine layer of ice that had not thawed by the afternoon. Now with the light fading, the temperature was plummeting and a bitter night was to fall on London.

After spending the day working on a pamphlet, Eileen arrived at the house in Newington Green. She was heartened to see the smoke billowing from the chimney – an unusual sight, since her aunt was usually too miserly to build a good fire. Even though Eileen had purchased the coal, Betty would insist on rationing it, on retaining each lump as if it were a hoard of treasure.

But on this day, Eileen entered the house and the heat was overwhelming. She found her aunt standing before a blazing fire, behaving suspiciously. Betty seemed to be at a loss for what to say, or how to act.

''Tis a lovely fire, aunty.'

'It is so. Grand.'

Betty had a half-smile on her face. There was a rare sparkle to her eyes, an unaccustomed ease to her voice. She seemed in no mood for scolding or criticism of any kind. This was all most peculiar – the pleasant tone of her voice, the non-combative stance, the trace of humour in her countenance.

Could it be that her aunt had discovered a newfound congeniality? Eileen doubted this could be possible. Unnerved by the whole affair, she decided to go to her room before her aunt reverted to her old, crabby self. Eileen took the stairs in a quandary, baffled by her aunt's behaviour. When she arrived at her room, there was something altered inside. The room looked different for reasons not immediately apparent. Then, in an unsettling moment, she came to see that her books were gone – all her books, pamphlets, journals and her own writings. Apart from a few belongings, the room looked as vacant as the day she had arrived. It was like peeling back the years and returning to her childhood – parentless and without possession, a child marooned in the city.

Eileen rushed down the stairs and found her aunt still standing before the fire. Her arms were folded, as if braced for some expected attack. 'Where are my books, my pamphlets, my writings?' Eileen was struggling for breath, her head was throbbing at the temples. 'What have you done with them?'

Betty said nothing. She angled her head and nodded towards the fire. Eileen gazed at the hearth and could see the remnants of one of her books, the green cover charred and filthy with ash. 'You've burnt my books! You've burnt my books!'

Her aunt nodded and shuffled into the corner to face the wall. She gathered her rosary beads from beneath her sleeve and began to mumble in prayer. Eileen rushed at Betty and spun her around, 'Why did you do that? What would make you do such a thing?'

Betty briefly opened her eyes and turned again to the wall. The hint of a smile was fixed on her face, not expanding to laughter, nor fading. Lost in prayer, she was miles from converse.

Eileen stood clenching her fists and releasing the tension. Her breath came heavy with choking disbelief. Staring at the fire, a ball of fury engulfed her. She found herself fixating on the poker in the grate, wishing to wield it like a weapon. In all truth, she wanted to crack her aunt's skull into two halves.

But instead she hurtled up the stairs and began to pack her clothes and belongings into a bag. When she had finished, she stood in the doorway to absorb the atmosphere, to acknowledge a farewell to the small room that had been a refuge for most of her life. On the varnished box beside the bed, she noticed the bible that Betty had placed there. Each day, on leaving the house, Eileen would put the bible on the downstairs table, only to find it returned when she next entered her room.

Eileen scooped up the bible and trotted down the stairs. She found her aunt, still praying in the corner, her face inches from the shadowy wall. 'Here's one book you forgot to burn'.

Eileen tossed the bible into the fire, scattering red cinders and hot ash onto the hearth. Betty flinched and became hunched at the shoulders, rounded at the back. Her head hung like a throttled goose and leaned against the wall. Her prayers became louder, desperate and frenetic, as if she were pleading to a God that wouldn't listen.

Eileen left the house and slammed the door behind her. The night had fallen on Newington Green, icy and inhospitable, the frost coating anything that couldn't move. She passed along the street with the house lanterns flickering and glowing in the windows. Her chest was heaving, her stomach tight. A drum in her head was pounding out a momentous rhythm, gathering speed and building to a great din.

On the corner, she hired a carriage – not knowing her destination, nor her plan for the life ahead. She told the coachman to head for the city, seeking asylum among the hordes of people, anonymity in the faceless crowds. Inside the carriage she wept into her hands – wept for the mother she had never known, for the father she dearly loved and for the land she had left behind.

The carriage progressed by the river, through the rookeries and slum dwellings. They passed onto the respectable neighbourhoods of Georgian mansions and boulevards lined with trees. Eventually weary, Eileen rapped on the partition and called for the coachman to stop. She paid him and wandered into the night, seeking shelter from the bitter cold.

In the Strand, she hired some rooms, placing her small bag of belongings on the bed. For the first time since leaving Ireland, she felt truly free. She was glad to be seperated from her aunt, beyond the possibility of any reconciliation. She lit a lantern on her new life and stared into its glow, trying to foretell the future in the dance of a flame.

Detained in Saffronetti's house, she was restless. Eileen stood at the window, her mind travelling to past events, flitting from one incident to another. The snow was melting against the glass. She remembered her glory days with Mary Wollstonecraft, days that were rich with discovery, alive with possibilities.

As a young woman, she had joined the sisterhood that surrounded Mary. Mary was a writer and a philosopher, a supporter of the French Revolution and an advocate of women's rights. From childhood Eileen had proved a fast learner, and now she was an astute analyst of the political realm, writing handbills and pamphlets against the establishment. With God long displaced, she believed reason was the force to liberate the world, the great leveller of humankind.

Eileen recalled a day that had brought joy to her heart. She had been writing a pamphlet and was to meet Mary to discuss the project. They met in a tavern, these trailblazers, inheritors of the enlightenment, liberated from convention and charting their own course through history. It was a cold day in December and the fire was built high. They sat in an alcove by the window, drinking from a single pot of ale and taking turns to swig. Their eyes glistened in the firelight in the early stage of alcohol consumption – their spirits elevated, their minds lucid and vibrant.

Eileen had spread her notes upon the table and they were leaning over them, discussing the pamphlet's theme. Mary's hair was wild and untamed and her headscarf did little to contain the disorder. Though in her early years Eileen had tried to adopt this style (or lack of one), she simply could not bear to have her hair in a tangle. Thus her hair was now long and well combed, with a sheen that held the light. In the likeness of her mother, she had grown most beautiful, and although not vain, she had become accustomed to the stares and advances of men.

The night was closing in around the window. The lanterns from the shops and inns began to ignite along the street. The landlord lit candles on the tables, passing from one to the next and lighting lanterns that were fixed to the walls.

The door of the tavern flung open and the wind sounded over the rooftops – wild and ferocious, at war with London on this winter's day. An old aristocrat bundled inside, slamming the door behind him. The snow followed his entrance, melting before hitting the ground. Gasping from the cold, he clapped his hands together and staggered unceremoniously inside. He was drunk and unapologetic for the fact. He had an audacious self-confidence, an arrogance instilled by a life of privilege and high society. He epitomized excess on two legs – his wig was lavish and ridiculous, powdered and tied with bows. The lapels of his silk jacket were patterned with extravagant sequins. The buckles on his breeches and shoes were polished to look like mirrors.

He staggered to the counter, slammed down some coins and demanded the landlord bring him a drink. When he spoke, his voice filled the room – a voice so loud and dictatorial that it was difficult to ignore. The landlord poured him a small glass of brandy and left the bottle on the counter. Ignoring the glass and taking up the bottle, the aristocrat turned to survey the people in the tavern. There was a couple seated on a bench with their backs to the wall. The man was holding the woman's hand and they were speaking quietly, an intimate exchange between lovers. Further along, four codgers from the lower classes were huddled around a table. They had known each other so long, there was no pressure to amuse or impress – they sat almost motionless, bleating out platitudes and inanities about the weather. To the aristocrat, they were all incomprehensibly dull, monstrously uninteresting to his present state of mind.

Looking for sport, but finding none, his eyes fell upon Eileen and Mary, in the alcove by the window. Bleary-eyed, he stared at them for some time, unable to place them in any sector of society that he knew. He tilted his head to listen – if he was not mistaken, they were having a discussion, talking of politics and literature, art and revolution. And by God, if he was not preposterously drunk or hideously confused, he would have said they were educated – women, educated, oddly dressed and supping from the same mug in a tavern.

The aristocrat swigged from the bottle and his eyes watered in the process. He pushed off the counter and lurched to the table where they were seated. They sensed his swaying approach and turned to look at him. Belching and adjusting his face to normality, he straightened his jaw with his hand. 'What's this?' He said, addressing Mary as the older woman. 'Two wives in conference, planning a revolution?'

Mary had a self-assured smile. 'We're not wives and there's no revolution here, sir. You are presently safe.'

The aristocrat took this as a threat. He drank from the bottle and the brandy glistened on his lips. 'Are you threatening me with revolution?'

'We are not, sir.'

He began to suspect these women were the radicals he had read about in the newspapers. The English Jacobins, they had been called. 'But you are supporters of the French Revolution, are you?'

'We are, sir.'

The aristocrat sneered, a mizzle of spit sprayed the air. 'So, you would have my head chopped off, would you?'

'No, sir. I should think the drink has done enough damage to your head without us tampering with it.'

Eileen sniggered and placed a hand over her mouth to conceal her mirth. The sound drew the aristocrat's attention – he turned and stared in a drunken trance, trying to comprehend what mockery was at hand. He gazed over the papers on the table, pointing with the bottle towards them. 'What's this?' he said, squinting and shutting one eye. 'What's all this?'

Mary gave a knowing look at Eileen and winked. 'It's a draft of a pamphlet. Do you know what a pamphlet is, sir?'

The aristocrat became suddenly inflamed, his face reddened and inflated. He was breathing heavily through his nostrils, much like a bull or some frenetic beast. 'Of course I know what a pamphlet is!' His voice blustered around the tavern and everyone looked up from their conversations.

'Then please tell me, do.'

'I'll tell you what a pamphlet is, madam. A pamphlet is something that a woman should have no hand in, no knowledge of and no pretensions of ever writing.'

'Why so, sir?'

'Women are naturally delicate creatures, more suited to domestic than educational pastimes. They are creatures of sensibility, blown in every direction by emotions and capricious habits. Women know nothing of the world and have no capacity for reason – and thus, under no circumstances, should they be allowed to partake in the printed word. I say they should be allowed to have their thoughts, but to keep those thoughts silent and not impose them on the rest of society.'

The aristocrat was convinced he had won the argument and reduced the women to their rightful place of silent deference. He was not prepared for the fact that few men, far more skilled in the art of argumentation, had succeeded in getting the last word with Mary Wollstonecraft. With great calmness and no loss of temper or composure, she addressed him once again. 'Good sir. You talk of sensibility and reason, faculties you do not possess in your drunken condition. You speak of women being blown in every direction, and yet, you are so bloated with drink, you can hardly stand on your own feet. Do you have a wife, sir?'

'I do.'

'Well, sir. For the sake of your improvement, I suggest you go home to your wife and plead for education, to be schooled in the ways of appropriate conduct, on how to behave in the company of your superiors – namely women.'

The aristocrat was stunned into silence. He had been so expertly corrected, that he couldn't think of anything to say. For a moment he staggered, hopelessly drunk and desperately trying to form a counter argument, but nothing arose in his befuddled head. Thus, to save face, he grumpily made for the door and swung it open, lurching into the snow. But before the door had closed, their laughter fanfared him into the night, mumbling and cursing under his breath.

The women screeched with laughter. They snorted and choked until the tears streamed from their eyes. They cuddled and separated, still laughing, still tickled and unable to stop. Mary took a sip of ale, but meeting Eileen's eyes and finding them full of amusement, she sprayed the liquid out, showering the table and the notes on top.

And all these years later, Eileen was still laughing. Despite being incarcerated and parted from her lover, she could still take pleasure in recalling this event. It was a small incident, but one that would remain with her for the rest of her days. For the moment had not only encapsulated their sisterhood, it had also taught her that laws, conventions and traditions could be mocked and challenged, and new perspectives could be put in their place. A man should have no greater rights than a woman, an aristocrat no more than a beggar – and to this end, she had dedicated her life.

Eileen rested on the bed. She lay back on the pillow and stared at the ceiling. The boards creaked outside her door – it was Mr Sticks on guard duty, ensuring she didn't try to escape. She closed her eyes and began to recall the events that had led to her captivity.

Her ruin came in the year of 1797. England was at war with France and the nation was on high alert for invasion. Fearful of home-grown insurrection, the Government had clamped down on radical groups, banning their meetings and prosecuting their publications. It was a dangerous time to be an atheist reformer, a supporter of the French Revolution. One could be imprisoned for expressing radical views, or be beaten by a Church-and-King mob. Most of the friends of freedom had been silenced – or had retired, emigrated or gone underground.

Gobey had been transported for five years, but he was still alive in her heart. Eileen had fallen on hard times – in this climate of suspicion, the publishing houses would not take her pamphlets for fear of prosecution. She made a scant living from printing her own writings, but it was dangerous work, and she was always looking over her shoulder for a spy or a magistrate.

With little money at her disposal, she had got into rent arrears for her rooms in the Strand. She had been given the final notice to leave and was desperately trying to raise some funds to pay the landlord. She could not go to her aunt, for the door was now permanently closed on any communication. And to her utter heartache, she could not go to her best friend, for Mary Wollstonecraft had sadly died, after giving birth to a daughter.

Mary's death compounded Eileen's troubles. The grief she felt for Mary made her yearn all the more for Gobey, to long for his homecoming. He was never far from her mind, never far from her yearnings.

In contemplative mood, she began to take long walks by the river. She crossed hills and fields and wandered with the wind, blowing with the autumn leaves in no particular direction. Sometimes, she would walk at night, away from the crowded streets to sit beneath the stars. She used to wonder whether Gobey had access to the night sky, to its bright unfathomable clusters.

When the weather was wild, she used to visit a church for shelter. She took comfort from the peace, solace from the surroundings. Though her atheism was still intact, there was something about the church that attracted her. One did not need a God to feel holy – holiness could be found in the silence, in the smell of the incense.

One squally day, after visiting the church, she returned to her rooms and found her possessions on the street. Her books and clothes were strewn around, some children were picking through her belongings. She shooed them off and gathered her things in a pile against the wall. As she entered the building, a squat man was descending the stairs. He was carrying an armful of her pamphlets, and holding some between his teeth. As he leapt off the last step, she accosted him: 'Please, sir. These are my things. Where are you going with my things?'

The man spat the pamphlets onto the ground and dropped the rest in a heap. 'I'm Mr Sticks,' he sneered, the muscles in his thick neck pulsing. 'You ain't paid yer rent, have ya?'

'Well, no, but I, I –'

'Then these ain't your things. They now belong to Master Saffronetti.'

'But these are my books, my clothes'

Mr Sticks pointed his stubby finger like a pistol. 'Have ya paid yer rent?'

'No, but I will. I promise you, I will.'

'Master Saffronetti works with currency, not promises. He owns this house and all the things in it.'

'I will pay the rent. I just need a little time to gather my finances.'

Mr Sticks sniffed and scratched his head. His face had a yellowish tint, his hands were dark and oily. 'There's no time left for ya.'

'I want to speak with Saffronetti. I must see him, I must.'

Mr Sticks stomped over the pamphlets to reach Eileen. He gripped her wrist and tugged her onto the street. Such was his grip, she thought her bones might snap under the tension. He dragged her towards a fine carriage, the large black horses eyeing their approach. A man stood beside the carriage and began to sing – such a strange voice, such an odd enchantment. He was dressed in the most extravagant silk with sparkling embroidery. He was wide at the hips and narrow at the shoulders. So tall, he had to be a man, yet from different angles, he seemed to be girlish – such skin, smooth and hairless. When he saw Eileen he stopped singing mid-flow and his face filled with palpable delight. 'Release her,' he said to Mr Sticks, brushing the hair from his eyes. 'Release her now.'

Mr Sticks let go and Eileen rubbed her throbbing wrist. 'Sir,' she said, trying to fathom the strange form that was Saffronetti, this effeminate man with icy blue eyes. 'I am behind with my rent, but I shall pay you every penny. In the near future, I shall pay you.'

Already smitten, Saffronetti decided he must have her. All that was Eileen Dineen must come into his ownership. He had the pick of the ladies of London, but they were too affected and not like this natural girl that stood before him. 'But when shall you pay?' He blinked and smiled, but most strangely – his eyes did not soften, did not alter from his cold, devouring stare. 'When, I say?'

'Next week,' she said in a panic, to stave off eviction and not knowing where the money might come from, 'I shall pay you next week.'

'And if you don't?'

'I will, I promise that I will'

'You shall pay or go to prison.'

'I shall pay.'

Saffronetti swivelled his head. 'Mr Sticks, the contract.'

Mr Sticks swaggered to the carriage and opened the door. He reached inside, the sound of a latch flicked and a box lid creaked open.

Dipping a quill into a pot of ink, he returned and handed a contract and quill to Eileen. She took them reluctantly, looking between the men, down to Mr Sticks and up to Saffronetti.

She flicked through the pages, trying to absorb the indenture but, close to homelessness, her belongings scattered around her on the street, she could not process the information, the extortionate interest rates that were levied against her. In any case, faced with destitution, she had little choice but to sign. And in all truth, she believed she would make the payment and free herself from Saffronetti's clutches.

Mr Sticks turned around and told her to sign the contract upon his back. She tentatively placed the papers there and etched her signature, handing them to Saffronetti. Mr Sticks snatched the quill from her and helped his master into the carriage. He then joined the coachman at the front with the horses. The vehicle shrugged onwards into the mist that was gathering in the Strand, into the daily bedlam of the city. Eileen stood with her worldly goods scattered around her. She had the feeling of sinking, of being drowned in the quagmire of London.

Staying at a dingy inn, Eileen spent the following days trying to raise the money. She managed to sell a few pamphlets on the street, but in this climate of fear, the publishing houses were too cautious to sell her writings. She worked all week on a fruit stall in Camden Town and managed to borrow some funds from a friend, but it wasn't enough to cover the rent arrears. By the end of the week, there was a shortfall in the intended payment. She hoped this would be enough to keep a roof over her head, but it was not enough for Saffronetti.

Precisely a week after she had signed the contract, a carriage came to the inn to take her away. She was bundled inside by Mr Sticks, weeping and pleading for her freedom. Transported to the grand house in Covent Garden, she demanded to be taken to court, preferring the debtors' prison to this heartless abode. But alas, she was soon to discover that Saffronetti had other plans for her.

CHAPTER 13

Eileen sat at the dressing table She began the humdrum routine of dressing for Saffronetti – squeezing a ring on each finger, fastening a necklace of pearls. When suitably perfumed, powdered and adorned, she sat on the bed and waited. There were no books to read, there was no paper to write on. These things had been confiscated to break her down.

For two years, she had been imprisoned in this way – two years with no news from Tom Gobey. There were times when she presumed him dead, for many convicts had perished in Australia. She would wake at dawn and listen in the silence for him, a whisper, some intimation of his being. Inexplicably, she could sense his spirit had not expired. By some intuition she knew he lived, that his heart was still pulsing somewhere in he universe. She would run her mind down the river, traverse oceans and mountains to land on his shore.

Each day, she was locked in this house of boredom. Kept like an exhibit to be watched and guarded. Countless times she had tried to escape, only to be blocked by Mr Sticks. He was always lurking in an alcove, loitering in the shadows beneath the stairs. When she wandered the rooms, he would appear like a ghost that could pass through walls. It seemed he knew every creak of the house and could chart her whereabouts by instinct. If she took the backstairs, he would take the front, heading her off at the door.

One day, she came down the stairs and found the front door open. Saffronetti was singing in the music room upstairs. She gazed around for Mr Sticks and could hear him cursing in the kitchen below. In a flimsy dress and no shoes, she left the house and went onto the street. She walked calmly down the hill, expecting to be grabbed at any time.

She slipped through an alley and crossed a field. From there, she ran to the bustle of Covent Garden.

Lost in the crowd, she presumed herself safe. With no money or abode, she roamed deeper into the innards of the metropolis – savouring the bliss of anonymity, the joy of camouflage. The smell of the chop houses was overwhelming, the waft of the taverns permeated the streets. How grateful she was for the hordes of people around her. Now she thought, I am a needle in a haystack, a drop in a vast ocean. Here, at last, in sweet freedom.

Those hours in the city were spent roving. She followed a passing group and kept to the crowded markets. It was summer and, sweltering in the sunshine, the windows and doors of the houses were flung open. People were sitting on steps and walls, enjoying any slight breeze that came their way.

By nightfall, she made her way to Whitechapel to find somewhere to rest. The heat had increased and the city was now stifling. She stood on the corner to wait for the road to clear. A carriage approached, and as it veered on the bend, she was lifted up and bundled inside. Manhandled into her seat by Mr Sticks, his imbecilic laughter a ceaseless din.

She sobbed all the way back to the house. Her face in her hands, she did not look at him. Did not want to breathe the same air, share his noxious space. Each moment in his presence she reviled, abhorred, detested. London was spilling free outside the carriage, and it was torturous to adjust to the promise of confinement. She would have rather lived as a lowly dog in the alleys than under the roof of Saffronetti.

That was her only glimpse of freedom in two years – a few snatched hours roaming the city. The days that followed were long and monotonous, drawn-out affairs that lacked purpose, meaning, deed. If not for the servants she would have gone insane long ago – their kindly interaction restored her faith in humanity and provided some outlet for her affections. She came to think of them as family, spoiling them whenever she could, whenever Saffronetti was not around to prevent such actions.

Now she could hear Mr Sticks on the boards outside her room.

She took a deep breath, opened the door and spoke into vacant space. 'Is he ready for me?' He had not yet appeared, but his aroma was present – river mulch, foul odour.

'Not yet, lady.'

Mr Sticks stepped into the doorway. A scar ran from his ear to his mouth – it was stitched with fisherman's gut, a crude, jagged line. Brown stains were smeared on his face, and his clothes looked too tight, at ripping point on his bulging body.

'I want to see him now,' she said, looking away. 'Right now.'

'Your man,' he grunted and sniffed. 'He's a bit handy with a blade, ain't he?'

'What man?'

'I ain't saying nothing.'

She brushed past and made her way down the long corridor. Mr Sticks trailed behind with his thighs chafing, his breath loud and toxic. Saffronetti was singing at the back of the house.

Eileen paced to the music room and entered mid-song. Saffronetti continued to sing stretching a melodic note. The act was effortless, with no loss of breath. Arms out, hands fluttering, his cool lazurite eyes fell upon her. Today his eyes were calm – and if they were not, she knew to be careful, to watch her words.

He fell silent. Outside the refuge of opera he looked bereft, depleted, unstrung. His mood visibly worsened and his mouth drooped. He didn't know what to do with his hands, they swished and parted, running over his thighs to his hips. A simmering agitation pulsed inside of him. No matter how vicious his intentions, he could not shake off the look of boyish innocence.

'What matter . . .' he spoke with a woman's voice, a hint of Italian giving speed to his sentences. All his gestures were grand and exaggerated, conditioned by his years in the opera. 'What matter of importance has impinged on my rehearsals?'

'How long am I to wait?' she said. 'How long am I to wait for your orders?'

He fluttered his eyelashes, which swept his face like black insects. His puff sleeve rustled in a backhanded gesture. 'Is your boudoir, your sulking palace not luxurious enough for the grandest of ladies? Do you not have everything you need for a pampered existence?'

'I have no books to read, no quill to write, no love in my heart for persons present.'

'You may have any number of books, quills and paper – anything you ask for. Do as I say and all your requests shall be fulfilled. Be more free with your affections, more tactile, more animated in my presence. From thenceforward you shall have the newfound freedoms of your desire.'

'I shall not,' she glared at him. Her eyes were prominently green in her powdered face. Her voice was starting to crack. 'I'll not yield to any of your wishes, your proclivities, anything to do with you at all.'

His mouth was fixed in a pout. Saffronetti made a pronounced turn of his head. 'Mr Sticks,' he called. 'Step outside for a moment. And do me the honour of getting yourself bathed, preferably today. Definitely today. In fact, today and tomorrow to see the stench off. You smell like a rat on the bank of the river.'

Mr Sticks left without speaking and Saffronetti beckoned to her. The silence was a taut rope between them. 'Come,' he said, standing with his feet together, hands at his sides. She shuffled a little closer. 'Here,' he pointed to a spot on the carpet where her feet came to rest.

'If I could be granted one letter, one letter to him, and one in return – that's all I ask.'

He whispered. His voice was like seeping gas. 'Shush, shush.'

She closed her eyes in anticipation. He struck her shoulder using both palms. She tumbled backwards over the carpet and dragged herself up at an angle. Her collarbone hung like a broken wing, her arm swung on the hinge of her elbow. She leaned against the wall, crooked and immobilized, her eyes flickering.

Mr Sticks entered to find Saffronetti standing tall, poised and marvellous, as if to begin a performance. He waved his hand like a fluttering bird. 'Take her to that Shapp woman and bring her back to me. Don't let her out of your sight, not for a moment.'

Mr Sticks strutted over and hoisted her onto his shoulder. The oily touch of his hands repulsed her. His eyes had the yellow taint of a lizard. There was white crust in his hair, red inflammation on his scalp that looked like galloping scurvy. He dragged her towards the door, grunting within, belching and blowing the fumes around.

'Wait, place her outside, will you? Step over here for a moment.'

Mr Sticks leaned her against the wall in the hallway and returned to Saffronetti. The master gazed at his scar, the wound infected and oozing pus. He made a long curious examination of its length – it intrigued rather than repulsed him. 'Have you mangled this Gobey fellow yet?'

'Nearly, sir.'

'I want him out of her thoughts.'

'He done me with a razor.'

'Well do him back – cut his throat or something. Do whatever you do.'

'I will, sir. I will.'

'Dump him in the river or somewhere.'

'I will, in the river. I will.'

Saffronetti put his delicate hands together, rubbing his palms and parting them. He stood upright and leaned back as if he might break into song. 'Fetch some opium for the pain.'

'She won't take it, sir. Miss Eileen won't have it. I tried the last time ya done her. She won't touch the stuff. It makes her sick, she says. I could force it down her, but –'

'Not for her! For me!' Saffronetti began to drift, his eyes wandering around the room in search of focus. 'It's for me, for the pain of childhood, the loss of manhood.'

Mr Sticks delivered the opium to Saffronetti then returned to Eileen. He stood over her, slumped against the wall. Raised on tiptoe, he tried to look down her dress. She had a green tinge to her face, a pale sickliness to her skin. He dragged her up and the sudden motion made her yelp. 'Shut up,' he said. 'You're getting on me nerves.' He lifted her in both arms, sucking in her perfume.

At the bottom of the stairs, the servants were arranging flowers in the hallway. They stopped working as Mr Sticks carried her down, barely conscious and unable to acknowledge them. One of her eyes flickered and rolled white. She was lopsided in his arms, pained in the face with a crooked twist to her neck. Mrs Hodgers reached for Lily's hand. 'He's done it again. That poor girl.'

'He has, Mrs Hodgers, he has.'

Once Mr Sticks had left the house, young Bob began to rant and stomp. He was all for fighting and bloodshed, boxing with his miniature fists and kicking out at nothing. All the world's armies wouldn't stop him, until Lily gave him a slap in the face. He stood morose, but not beyond asking questions. 'Why do they say the master's a queer one?'

Lily was flushed and furious, there was sweat in her hair and she couldn't keep still. She looked at Mrs Hodgers, then back at the lad. 'Mind your own. You don't need to know these things.'

'I do – I'll find out anyway.'

'All right, have it your own way. When the master was a boy they cut off his bollocks. Cut them off, so he could sing in the choir, then the opera. That's why he has a girl's voice, can sing so high and stoop so filthy low.'

'There's no need for cursing.' Mrs Hodgers turned to the lad. 'He's a castrato, young Bob. Master Saffronetti is a castrato. He's a male singer who's been tampered with below to preserve his voice. That's all it is, nothing for you to worry about. Now don't you be going around the town talking about such things. You'll get yourself in big trouble that way. Do you hear me? Big trouble.'

'Is he a man or a woman?'

'Hold your tongue now, boy. Hold your tongue.'

It was cold in the carriage, and Eileen shivered beneath a blanket. The pain ran from her shoulder to her neck, creeping down one side of her ribs. Mr Sticks climbed on board and the smell came with him. He slammed the door and it was sealed inside – boiled eggs, stewed vegetables – she couldn't put a name to it. In an imbecilic trance, he looked her up and down. He had no more finesse than an ape slouching in the corner.

Eileen glimpsed her pale reflection in the carriage window. She imagined her mother to be staring back at her – a mother dead for more than twenty years, a mother she had never known. In her usual way she began a conversation, her inward voice a channel between them. *Mother,* she said, *'tis only me, only me. Please give me strength, for I am facing great trials – great trials. I have been abused again, but I shall not fold, not crumble. I shall hold your love and it will protect me, shield me from this cruelty and exploitation. Oh, mother, wherever you may be, please give me strength.*

The carriage traversed the deep snow on the road. The people on the street struggled to keep their balance, sliding and falling down with their arms in the air. The vendors stood around the roadside fires, selling roasted chestnuts, baked potatoes and hot pies, and never ceasing to holler in the sale of those goods.

The carriage slowed, the horses clopped over the ice and stopped. Mr Sticks left the carriage and slammed the door twice – once to close it, and once for the noise. The snow had been cleared outside Donavan's tailor shop, and two lanterns were alight in the window. He entered and took a slow look around – the suits were racked in lines, piles of material were stacked on the floor and hung over work benches. The old tailor was stitching by the fire in his nightdress, a full chamber pot at his feet.

Mr Sneathen heard the door open and made his way to the front of the shop. An awful smell was circulating the room, as if the river had flooded. He saw Mr Sticks and immediately disliked him, doubting he had money, or any idea of what clothes to buy. He stood a foot over him and looked down. 'Hat, scarf, shirt or jacket?'

'None of 'em.'

'Waistcoat or trousers?'

'Nah.'

'Tell me what you want and I'll see if I can find it.'

'I know what I want and I'll find it meself.'

'Please do.' Sneathen stepped aside and stretched out his arm. 'Take a look around and call me when you've decided.'

'I've decided.'

'Tell me, do.'

'I'm looking at it.'

'At what?'

'You.'

'And?'

'I'm having you.'

'Look, I haven't got time for messing around – either buy something or get out.'

'I know ya, don't I?'

'I think not.'

'I do.'

'Look –'

'I saw ya at a molly house in Covent Garden. You're a sodomite, a buggerantoe, ain't ya?'

'Now you watch –'

'Do ya know who my governor is?'

'No, no I don't.'

'It's Master Saffronetti.'

'I fail to see what that has to do with me.'

'Saffronetti is a good friend of Judge Reynolds. And the judge hates bog-house dwellers like you, don't he? Hates ya.'

Sneathen grew pale, the colour drained from his countenance. He might have died on his feet, for he did not move, could not talk. Not one word did he plead in his defence. And when he thought about Judge Reynolds, about the humiliation of the pillory, a street flogging, or a spell of hard labour, he knew he was done for.

He was bundled to the back of the shop in silence. Never had he encountered more smelly hands, a more nauseous tongue. Donavan worked by the firelight, mumbling and replying in a waspish scolding of himself. He continued to work, using his teeth to pull the thread, his long fingers dragging the needle. A moist clicking came from somewhere in the darkness, but it did not interest him, did not stall his progress. Had he looked up, he would have seen the squashed face of his assistant, bent double peering through the mounds of unsold clothes.

CHAPTER 14

The morning broke in grey desolation. A blizzard was blowing in from the west and gaining momentum. The first gusts rolled into the city, blustering against the buildings, whistling through the trees and courtyards. The river stood in petrified silence, a lone dog wandered on the ice. On Fetter Lane, a drunken ballad singer staggered along the road, his voice blowing up and down like washing on a line.

Gobey stirred on the floor of the pamphlet house. After his carriage fall, it hurt to move in any direction. He had a sharp pain in his spine that ran down his leg. His tongue was dry and furry from a lack of fluids. He listened to the drunk wailing outside. It was a song he knew – a song of sea voyage, lost love, forced exile. The story of his life, cut loose in the wind and running away without him.

He braced himself to stand, but didn't attempt it for some time. His teeth chattered, his nose was numb from the cold. Steadman's old fur coat was like a shroud around him. He went to stand, but found that he couldn't. From the hips he lurched forward and sat up, roaring from the effort. He crawled over the boards in slow, painful shunts. He rolled into the wall to urinate, but nothing passed. He heaved until it trickled – sore and forced and stinking. He could have killed for a drink – something to drive the grit away, to get the juices flowing. To quench his thirst, he worked up some spit and swallowed it.

He rolled over and looked to the window. Everything was stark and ashen. He wiped his nose with the back of his hand and couldn't feel his nose or his hand. For want of a better thing to do, he laughed and called out, 'Gobey, my son. Life is a rich mixture.'

There was a flint, a steel block and some tinder in the grate, but no coal or wood. He dragged himself to a pile of pamphlets and tossed them on the hearth. He repeatedly struck the steel with the flint, until some tiny sparks ignited the tinder. He lit the edges of the pamphlets and blew on them to make the flames grow. He morosely watched the fire devour those pamphlets of rebellion. Some were penned by himself and some by his comrade, Johnny Steadman.

When his limbs had warmed, he made an arduous crawl on his elbows to the front door. He jerked it open and the cold rushed over him. He had blurred vision and sore eyelids – black shapes, dots and quavers appeared in the hazy light around him. It took several deep breaths to clear his head, to focus his eyes. A rat scurried over his back and made off leaving tracks in the snow.

He grabbed a fistful of snow and crushed it into his mouth, the ice driving nails into his nervy teeth. He screamed and swallowed, screamed and swallowed. Half out of the doorway, he couldn't find the will to crawl further, and so he rested to think. He put his face in his hands, in search of wisdom.

He slept in the doorway and woke frozen, not knowing how long he had slept. It was his teeth that woke him, rattling like pegs in a bag. Dazed, he looked around and found the noise was coming from his own mouth. The cold stone of his hand touched the cold stone of his face, and there was little benefit from that union. His eyes hurt from the wind that cruelly lashed his face.

He pushed on, zigzagging over the snow on his elbows. The street was deserted and unnaturally quiet. A dog passed and he tried to grab its tail, but it slunk suspiciously away. Across the street, he saw a figure that he vaguely knew. It was Sneathen, the tailor's assistant, struggling through the snow in a sorrowful mood. He'd been crying, his face was wet and smudged, his hair uncommonly ruffled. He had a mangled look about him. The lapels on his jacket were ripped, and one of his shirt cuffs hung raggedly over his hand. His ears were red, as if they'd been tugged.

Gobey called across to him, 'Can you help me, sir?' But the wind picked up and stifled his voice. Sneathen limped on with his head down, oblivious to his cries. A lost cause now, but Gobey hollered again. 'Hey, hey! Won't you help me? Won't you help a man in trouble?'

Gobey shunted over the road, moaning with the effort. The cold snow beneath him was draining his energy, sucking the life out of him. There were sudden gusts that blocked all sound, a deadening at the heart of things. It seemed the world had rolled away and left him to fend for himself. One man in the dead heart of the city, he pushed on. He could see no means of salvation but for a door banging in the wind. He progressed towards the door as if deliverance lay inside.

Crawling like some prehistoric creature, he traversed the road. Head first on his belly, he made a slow ascent of the incline, down some steps to a splintery cellar door. Flipping it open, he crawled inside and closed it behind him. He remained still, adjusting to the dark and trying to see through it. There was an increasing stench of urine all around him. He laughed and mouthed the words, *piss pit*.

The wind blustered on the street. He waited in the dark without moving, listening for a passer-by, someone he might call to his rescue. His thoughts drifted back to the ocean – the creaking ship, the wind ruffling the sails. He tried to conjure the Botany Bay sun, but it wouldn't come to him, wouldn't come to that cellar abode.

Flat on the ground, he spat in the air and shifted to avoid being spattered As he settled again, a sound of heavy breathing crossed the cellar. In a dark corner, a throat rasped and a rattling chest clearance was followed by a bout of spitting. The rustle of clothing, the creaking of knees as if someone was squatting, and then a line of piss rolled over the ground towards him.

He rolled away from the flow and called out, 'Halloa.' Silence in the dark. He called again. 'Halloa, is someone there?'

A hoarse voice croaked back at him. 'Who's that, then? I didn't hear ya come in, who is it?'

For reasons unknown he said, 'It's me, Tom Gobey.'

'Oh, Tom is it? Well, glad to meet ya again. I've missed ya, so I have, sweetheart. Missed ya a good while there. I always miss the best fellows, sure I do. The best are always missed. Never forgotten.'

It was the voice of an old woman, husky and rasping – a pipe smoker with a burnt out larynx. She spoke as if they were friends, yet they had never met. A candle sparked in the corner and she shuffled away to light another. There was a makeshift bed on the floor, covered in straw, oily rags and soiled clothing. She approached with a lantern,

'Where are ya? I'm not seeing ya at all.'

She was tall and bony in a stained dress, her grey hair bunched high. Her struggling breath made a sucking sound, as if her lungs were stuck together.

'I'm down here, lady. On the floor.'

'Lord help us – what are ya doing down there?' She lifted her dress and stepped over him, her genitals mangled, pinched tight to the bone. She lowered herself down. 'I'll do the riding, you wield the crop.'

He pushed her away. 'No, no, no. I'm not up for that, not up for business. I need shelter, I need help.'

The woman stepped aside and stood squinting down at him. She lowered her dress and coughed viciously. The phlegm thickened in her throat, 'Help, ya say?'

'I'm injured, I can't walk. I need to get to Covent Garden.'

'Ya don't want a fucksa then?'

'Not at all.'

'A little one?'

'No thanks.'

'Something else?'

'No, really. Thanks, no.'

'Well,' the old women puffed out her cheeks. 'Ya can't stay here, sir. Not without paying for me time.'

'How much.'

'Call it the King's shilling. I used to ask more, but these days it's a bob, or less or more. Depends, it does – on the nature of the gent, and the nature of the service. On the nature of the weather, on nature itself. Though I don't suppose there'll be many coming out for it today. Not with the snow, not with the cold rattling the old bones.'

He gave her a shilling and she helped to drag him across the floor. She stood upright to look at him – Agnes Hurly, last in a line of Irish rebels crushed by the state. She lit an old newspaper beneath some scraps of wood and coal in the corner. The smoke billowed up the wall and over the ceiling and rolled back down to itch his throat. She handed him a small bottle of opium. He supped a few drops, bitter and lasting on his tongue. He dreamily watched her going about her business, bending for this and searching for that, speaking to herself and over her shoulder at him. The gravelly texture of her words pinged off the walls, as if she spoke each sentence twice.

She creaked open the door and the cold rushed in at them. She hurried from the building, ducking against the wind and snow. The wind growled from the other side of the city – it sounded like the distant roar of cannons on the Channel. She returned with a bottle of rum, shaking it for no apparent reason. She sat him against the wall and dusted down his fur coat. Her fingers were like twigs, her skin was etched with a thousand lines. There were veins on the outside of her hands, blue wormy tendrils that pulsed with life. He turned from her breath – rum, bile and hot-sour spit.

She added some opium to the rum and they finished half the bottle. Kendal Black Drop she called it, brought down from Cumberland by one of her men. She couldn't stop laughing, and the motion brought on a terrible crackle in her chest. A client banged on the door and they fell silent, a gruff voice booming through the woodwork, 'I wants me oats, Agnes!'

'Well go and find an horse then! I'm all out of pottage!'

They laughed together, tears rolling, and pointing at each other. Though utterly haggard and ravaged by disease, she had something of Eileen about her – the Irish way of making merry. Her eyes flashed when she focused, full of cod and mockery for the world they had seen. They were somehow preserved in her ageing body – everything was dying around them, but those eyes would leave two bright stones in the ground.

The man shuffled away from the door, cursing and hollering in the snow. They could hear him shouting on the street. Agnes hooted and struggled to catch her breath, a violent attack gripped her. For some time, she choked and spluttered, and when the bout subsided she reverted to laughter. She laughed when nothing was said or happened, laughed for the sheer sake of laughing. And when he looked at her battered face, full of rapture and foolishness the merriment erupted inside of him.

They passed the day in folly, half-stupefied by opium. When Agnes wasn't choking, coughing, spitting or dying, she was roaring. There were contagious specks of fun in every hoarse cackle, every scrap of hurtling spit. Who could say how long they sat there? For opium time is no ordinary time, it doesn't tick on any clock. They sat. They drank. They talked. By God, they laughed. Tom Gobey with his back against the wall, and Agnes Hurly, cross-legged facing him.

When they fell quiet and were almost sleeping, she arranged for a man to take him to the bone-setter. The cart drew up and the street was virtually deserted, the day given up for vagrants and beggars, doxies and bedlamites – outcasts, wanderers, restless pariahs of the road.

The old horse was knackered on its legs – its shoes were worn, its tail thinning. It had green bile in its nostrils and one of its eyes had been plucked out, or had simply rotted. There were sores on its coat, and its ears were flaky and encased with grey crust. Forlorn and dispirited, it ducked from the wind, trying to dodge the oncoming snow. It was making a noise that didn't sound like a horse, didn't sound like any living creature.

An old man drove the cart, rotund and humorous, with his face braced against the weather. He spat into the road and wiped his mouth on the crook of his arm. Lifting Gobey onto the cart, he spoke incomprehensibly, mumbling and chuckling.

Agnes leaned over the cart. Gobey held her bony hand, the fingers like frail twigs. She stood shivering with the snow in her hair, there was hardly a tooth to rack her mouth. The cart rolled on in creaking motion. A gust of wind raised her clothing, revealing bruised thighs and worn-out genitals, a battered life between her legs. She drifted back towards her home, hunched and soiled like a cave dweller from another age, another species.

The old man drove the cart into the oncoming snow. Head down, the wind struck the crown of his hat. The horse turned away from the squall, blinking and snorting and reluctant to go on. The cart screeched and slid on the packed ice.

Gobey rolled on his side and wrapped the fur collar around his neck. The wind blew powerfully from different directions. The snow settled on him like an inanimate object. The old man cracked his whip and the cart rocked as the pace quickened. They rattled along, and hadn't gone far when the horse stopped. It made a sound like speech, a woman crying. The old man climbed down and worked his way to the front of the horse. He stared into the woeful creature's eyes. He made his way to Gobey. 'Me horse has had it,' he said, choking on the words. 'Had it, good and proper. He can't go no further. Not another inch.'

Gobey leaned up from the back of the cart, 'Is it ill?'

'It's dying, good and proper. Dying.'

The old man gazed at the ground and shook his head. He shunted a forearm across his face to wipe his tears. Feet shifting in the snow, he said, 'I've had that horse for twenty odd summers. Since me wife died I've had that horse. That horse never did me wrong, never did. Me wife was a shitter, but the horse was as good as gold.'

'I'm sorry.'

The old man took a deep breath to compose himself. He looked up and down the street to think for a moment. Then he spoke from the corner of his mouth. 'I'll go and fetch me brother and come back for ya.'

'It's all right' Gobey gestured with his head. 'I'll make me own way from here.'

'But ya can't walk, how will ya?'

'It's all right, I'll get a coach or something. I'll be all right. But if ya can help me down I'll be most grateful.'

The old man nodded. 'Yeah, yeah,' he mumbled. 'Yeah, yeah.'

Lifting Gobey beneath the arms, he dragged him down. Then the old man went in search of his brother who would return to retrieve his horse and cart. 'Luck to ya,' he said as he passed into the night. 'Man and beast, luck to ya.'

Gobey assessed the world from below, gazing along the street with the wind howling. A thick carpet of snow was glistening on the ground, gathering on the sills and ledges of the houses. The black smoke trailed from the chimneys and drifted with the wind. Progressing on his elbows, he shunted past some kids standing at a fire – sweeps and costermongers, with black featureless faces against the illuminating snow. One of them approached him as he dragged himself along. 'What ya doing down there?'

'Swimming the Channel to fight the French.'

'Where'd ya get that furry coat?'

'From a bear.'

'Why don't ya get up and walk?'

'I like the scenery down here.'

The boy slunk off to his friends at the fire. They watched him leaving on his belly, groaning with the strain. Some of them threw snowballs and laughed raucously as he snaked onwards. They thought he was drunk and trying to get home.

He ascended a steep hill, clambering on his belly and levering with his forearms. A doxy passed in a ragged shawl and stood winking, swaying her hips. He closed his eyes and shook his head; she moved on with a tuneless whistle. A dog crossed the road with its tail wagging – it sniffed the top of his head and licked his face until he pushed it away.

Gobey proceeded with his head down, his body shunting along. Coming over the brow of the hill, he began to slide and tumbled off the street towards a large house. He continued to roll until he struck a door that opened, and he fell inside. 'Oh, my word!' The maid put her hands to her face. 'Mrs Hodgers! Mrs Hodgers! Please come, Mrs Hodgers!'

The old cook waddled along the passage. She was breathless, her puffy face blotched. 'Who's this, then? Is this one of your boys, young Lily?'

'No, Mrs Hodgers. I've never seen him.'

'Not that lad from the grocers?'

'No, no. Honestly it ain't.'

'Go and get Mr Stanley and young Bob. Be quick, girl, be quick.'

Mrs Hodgers crouched to take a closer look. His face was gaunt and predominantly blue, nicks and grazes ran over his hands. She knelt and touched his face. 'You poor bugger. You're half-frozen. And look at all these knocks and scrapes, look at them. What's been happening to you, hey? Hey?'

They carried him into the kitchen and placed him on the table. Young Bob and Lily stood silently staring. Mrs Hodgers scattered them by clapping her hands. She lifted Gobey's head and helped him to sip some brandy. 'What's your name, young man?'

'Tom Gobey.'

'And what's been happening to you, Tom?'

'I fell off a carriage, madam. Right on me back.'

'And where was you heading when you came busting through our door?'

'Covent Garden' He looked down at his legs. 'I need to see the bone-setter.'

'And what's wrong with your bones, young fellow?'

'Methinks me legs have gone to sleep, madam. The bone-setter helped with me knee and I was hoping – praying, like – she might do the same with me pegs.'

The old cook waddled away, calling instructions and pointing to the cupboards. Lily appeared with a medicine box and a bowl of hot water. 'Now, sir. Tom, is it?'

'It is.'

'Mrs Hodgers says I must cleanse those wounds on yer hands. Sore as they are, I must do it. I'm sorry if it hurts, but I'll be as gentle as I can, you understand.'

'Most grateful.'

Lily gently treated the abrasions on the back of his hands. She met his dark eyes and stared longer than she should have before turning away. She examined his fingers – all the knuckles were scuffed, one of his thumbs looked broken. She held a cloth to an abrasion on his scalp – it throbbed like an egg about to hatch. With thumb and forefinger, she eased the grit from his earlobes, driving out the dirt beneath the skin. The snow had somehow packed into his pockets. She scooped out two handfuls onto the spitting fire. Very slowly, she applied an ointment to his lips, ran her fingertips across them. She would have kissed them wildly given half the chance.

Flat out and half-slaughtered, he listened to the converse in the kitchen. He could hear them whispering, as they nodded and made discreet gestures that were unknown to him. Mrs Hodgers was at the heart of everything, directing and hushing, beckoning one person and dismissing another. She had a cloth hat on, curls of peppery hair sprouting from the sides. Lily kept staring at him, fiddling with a swab or pouring from a jug – her eyes never left him.

He watched the staff going about their chores beneath the hanging pots. A rich buttery aroma drifted from the pantry, the ashes collapsed in the grate. Their voices dragged his weary thoughts around the room. Then they descended upon him and undressed him. Without permission or forewarning they lifted him by the legs and beneath the armpits. They eased him into a tub of steaming water. Then they gathered around to stare at his tattoo.

Young Bob squinted and wrinkled his nose. He pointed unashamedly at Gobey's back. 'What is it, what's it doing there?'

Mr Stanley shrugged his shoulders. He put a finger to his lips to quieten the boy's intrusive questioning. Gobey looked at them. 'I have to get to Covent Garden. I have to see the bone-setter.'

Mrs Hodgers brushed by them and stood at the tub. She was eating something and took a moment to swallow, patting her chest before speaking. 'Now, Tom – don't you worry. We'll get you to the bone-setter's. The carriage is in use, but when it returns, Mr Stanley will drive you himself. Up the road and round the corner and down the hill.'

'Most grateful, madam.

'Now you eat and drink and rest. The devil himself knows that's what's needed.'

'Thank you kindly.'

'And do one thing for me, will you?'

'Anything at all.'

'Keep quiet. Master Saffronetti won't have strangers in the house. If he finds you, there be trouble, and lots of it – weeping and gnashing of unholy teeth.'

'I'll not say a word.'

They bathed and dressed him, fed him porridge and hot milk that he took in sips. They placed him on a mattress in the room off the pantry, where the smell of fermenting cheese was rife. Young Bob entered tentatively, with a slice of bread and a mug of ale. He watched Gobey eating, noting every sup and mouthful, every pause and effort to swallow. The boy sat on the floor beside him. 'What's that thing on your back?'

'A tattoo.'

'How long did it take?'

'I can't remember.'

'Will it last forever?'

'As long as me, I guess.'

'But if you die and go to heaven, will it last then?'

'I'm not going to heaven.'

'Will it last in hell?'

'I hope I never get to find out.'

The boy stopped to think. Gobey, hoping that was the end of the interrogation, put his head on the pillow and looked up at the ceiling. He closed his eyes and opened them again. A pot was boiling in the kitchen, the water simmered and a lid rattled on top. It was good to hear Lily's laughter. She stood at the door, gazed in and hurried by as he looked at her.

The boy prodded Gobey's shoulder. 'Mrs Hodgers said you're a convict, transported to the land of the sun.'

'I used to be.'

'Did they flog you?'

'Once or twice.'

'Did it bleed all over the shop?'

'That's one way of telling it.'

'Are you a highwayman?'

'Nay – never.'

'Have you got a knife or a pistol?'

'Not at all.'

'What about a sword?'

'I had a pen.'

'You can't kill with a pen.'

'Don't you believe it.'

'But you have killed a man?'

'Not yet.'

'Did he shout and holler and beg?'

Gobey laughed. 'I said I didn't kill anyone. No shouting, hollering or begging – no violence at all.'

'You haven't killed a man.'

'I might start with a boy.'

Bob twitched his nose. His tongue was unavoidable, perpetually on display. 'Then why was you sent there? If you didn't kill anyone, what did you do?'

'I wrote a pamphlet against the King, the Church and the Government.'

'That's only words – words don't murder people.'

'Words are more dangerous than weapons.'

'How's that?'

'They live forever.'

The boy scratched his head, his forehead lined with concentration. A few seconds passed with the underside of his tongue showing a spongy purple. He stood up and went to leave, but decided against it. 'If you were to kill a man,' he said, 'A man you really, really hated – someone who was a rotter, a proper filthy dog – how would you do it?'

Gobey looked away from the boy. Someone was scraping a pot in the kitchen, the fire crackled with sparking wood. Through a gap in the door, he could just make out a pair of hands that were rolling pastry. He met the boy's eyes and held them, held them as if some great truth was to be told. Then he spoke in a whisper. 'I'd take away his sweetheart.'

CHAPTER 15

You could hear the blizzard approaching in the distance. The birds left the trees in scattered flocks, dipping and diving across the river. The first breakaway gales came lifting roof slates and blustering the signs along Fleet Street.

Mr Sticks did not sense the birds fleeing, nor notice the sky, or care about the wind and snow closing in. He stood in the road and violently scratched his scalp. Eileen was injured inside the carriage, asleep. She needed to visit the bone-setter, but first he had a little business to attend to – a small matter concerning the imminent demise of Tom Gobey. The horses snorted and reared as he approached, banging his fist along the carriage and climbing inside.

Eileen woke with the smell of him. His face was moist and unshaven – always unshaven, but never quite a beard. He slumped heavily down in the seat and the wood creaked. A crust was forming on his scarred face, he picked at the scab and flicked it. The carriage shunted forward, rocking sideways in the snow. He fidgeted in his tight suit, pulling and pressing at his crutch. Grimacing, he again scratched his scalp and sucked his fingers like a child.

She glared at him. 'Take me to the bone-setter.'

'Stop whinging.'

'Saffronetti gave you orders.'

I'll take ya when I'm ready. I've got a little business to do, a little someone to do in.'

'Take me now.'

'Nah.' He put a hand down his trousers and left it there. 'One job at a time.'

The snow sprayed against the window, a side wind rocked the

carriage and it lurched and steadied. They drove onto the Thames, sliding on the ice with the horses' hooves clattering as they lost their footing. A grey miasma hung over the river – silent, deserted, godless. The snow-hooded trees lined the banks and, from the higher ground, great spirals rolled across the landscape.

Mr Sticks faced the window, his yellowish complexion reflected in the pane. He lowered the glass to get a better view, scouring the landscape. After a few minutes, he banged on the panel and called the coachman to a halt. He took a short wooden mallet from under the seat and left the carriage with a finger in his nose. Crossing the ice, the snow was in blinding sheets. He pushed on through the squall and clambered up the bank. He stood shielding his eyes, stood for some time scanning the marshes – barren, desolate and unforgiving to all creatures of the earth. From left to right his head moved in a slow arc, back and forth, until he stopped dead. He rolled his shoulders and looked at the sky, up at a faint line of smoke penetrating the snowfall.

He pushed on in the snow, sinking knee-deep and dragging himself out in a vile temper. He stopped to catch his breath. Across the marshes an old house drifted in and out of vision in the snowfall. A trail of smoke puffed from the chimney and was drawn away by a crosswind.

From the side, a strange movement, a flicker caught his eye – something shifting through the snow, moving at speed and pounding the earth. Tall and muscular, a chestnut horse came running across the marshes at him. He had the feeling it was going to run him down, crush his body. On approach, the creature slowed and stood with the snow falling around it. The wind shook its tail. Their eyes locked, a spell thrown on both parties. Then, without warning, the horse reared and kicked up the snow in a spray. It made a hasty departure over the marshland, galloping until only the thud of its hooves could be heard

He stumbled on against the icy snowdrifts. Every now and then, the sound of hooves pounded in the distance. He stopped to listen, tilting his head and licking his lips. Moving on, the wind had a cruel bite to it. There was little in his vision that wasn't white, but his heart felt black – black and hard as obsidian – and all its rhythms were driven by hate.

When he arrived at the house, he gazed through the frosty window. He squatted to listen, then rose with a grimace. He shunted the door with his shoulder and closed it gently on the wind. He gazed around the shabby interior – damp walls, strewn newspapers, old saddles and tangled rope. He took the groaning stairs and stood at the door, listening to the fire crackling behind it. He gently turned the handle and slipped inside. The ashes were crimson in the grate. Steadman was asleep in the chair, the old dog peered up from his feet.

The coachman climbed down from his seat, the wind lashing his face. He staggered along the side of the carriage, tapped on the door and opened it with a creak. 'Please, mam. Can I come in? I'm freezing half to death, and God knows when Mr Sticks will be back.'

'Do come in, John.'

He climbed inside and closed the door. He sat opposite, staring pityingly at Eileen – her face drained of colour, her hands bone white. The wind howled down the river like a fleeing banshee, rocking the carriage and spooking the horses.

'I'm sorry for your trouble, mam.'

'Thank you, John.'

'You know if I could do anything, I would. I'd take you to the bone-setter, right now. It's just Mr Sticks. He won't listen, there's no talking to him. He's an odd article, a deviant creature. No one will go against him.'

'Sure, I know it well.'

'We're very sorry for the way you're treated, mam. Master Saffronetti's too cruel and all of us are against it. Mrs Hodgers says he should be strung up and left for rot and rat feed.'

'Bless Mrs Hodgers.'

'Bless you, mam.'

Eileen smiled. Her face was pale and pained. Her breath came heavy, in slow laboured gasps. 'Where's he got to, John? What business can he have in this weather – out on the marshes, out in the snow? What could need mending, what use for a mallet?'

'I fear it's not for mending, but for a-breaking, mam.'

A breeze rattled the carriage windows, the horses danced and tossed their heads. Eileen turned and winced with the movement. Her collarbone throbbed and the pain ran into her arm. 'Oh, John, where has Mr Sticks got to?'

'God knows, mam.'

'Do you think something has happened to him?'

'I hope so, mam.'

The wind crossed the marshes with an unholy growl, a warning of its growing power. The ice creaked as if someone had crossed it, but no one was there. Something frightened the horses and they tramped about, whinnying and dragging their hooves. 'What was that, John?'

'What, mam?'

'A scream, I thought I heard a scream.'

'It's only the wind, mam. Only the wind.'

They waited in the biting cold, their breath puffing before them. They tapped their feet, jiggled their legs and rubbed their hands for warmth. They listened to the melancholy squeals of the ice, the disconsolate howl of the wind. 'He's here now, mam. I can see him coming.'

The coachman left the carriage and took up his seat above the horses. He pulled his hat over his ears and raised his collar. Spattered with blood, Mr Sticks came wandering through the snow with his mallet, wandering like one from a slaughterhouse, or some forsaken place of carnage. He called up to the coachman, 'Fetter Lane.'

'Fetter Lane?'

'Yeah, get a move on.'

'She's in a bad way, Mr Sticks. She's as pale as a ghost, shaking all over. She needs to see the bone-setter.'

'Did ya hear what I said?'

'Yeah, but –'

'Just drive will ya. Shut yer mouth and drive'

He climbed inside the carriage and slid the mallet beneath the seat. He looked long and hard at her face, then slumped down with his thumb in his ear. He tried to nudge her foot, but she shifted away. The blood trickled beneath his sleeve and dripped off his fingers.

The wind followed them along the river, the wheels crunching over the brittle surface. They dodged the driftwood and the frozen boats lodged in the ice. The snow scudded from the hills, crossing the fields in heavy drifts. The cattle grouped in the distance, half-frozen with nowhere to shelter. A peal of church bells sounded from a nearby town.

They rose on a ramp and left the river. Hitting the streets in skids, they slid and rolled onto a fresh carpet of snow.

On Fetter Lane, the road was beaten into a slippery packed surface. The carriage wheels locked and they came to a standstill. Mr Sticks left the carriage with his mallet. Pacing in the road, he made a slow inspection of the surrounding buildings. He came to a house with the door ajar, the lock bashed and splintered. He stepped inside and sniffed at the air – a pile of paper had been burnt in the grate, ash was spilt on the floor. He plunged his hands into the ashes; slightly warm, he thought, a hint of flame – the vestiges of Tom Gobey.

He checked all the rooms, kicked holes in the doors. Swinging the mallet, he pounded the pamphlets around the house, dragging them under his boots, until they were torn and besmirched. He stomped a chair to pieces, shattered the legs and backrest. He drove his elbow through the windows, and when there was nothing left to smash, he upturned a table and hurled it against the wall.

He strolled out into the street with a little man swagger. He danced down some steps and jerked open the cellar door. 'Aggie! Ya old slag heap! Where are ya? Speak to me, Aggie. Speak to me, now.'

Asleep on her feet, Agnes Hurly stirred. She reached for the opium, but didn't get the chance to imbibe. He shoved her against the wall. 'Come here, ya old trollop.'

'Good to see ya, Mr Sticks.'

'What's good about it?'

'Oh, just to see yer face and all.'

She wriggled under his arm and moved from the candlelight. She turned to face him, straightened her hair and tried to smile. He charged and forced her against the cellar door. She was bent, buckled, contorted and half-choked – abused, pinched and pawed. When he stepped away and fastened his trousers, there was hardly a breath inside her. Upside down against the wall, she toppled onto the ground. She called out as he was leaving, 'It's a shilling, Mr Sticks. Not much for me trouble.'

'For what?'

'To keep me fed and watered.'

'Ya ain't worth it.'

Boarding the carriage he was sweating, almost smouldering with the heat. 'Now ya can have yer bone-setter,' he said. 'Now ya can have her.'

The carriage made a staggered journey, slowing when the snow thickened and speeding when it dispersed. They drove through the coal smoke that gathered in the road and above the houses, spilling like a black ocean around the city.

They stopped at the bone-setter's. The snow was blowing sideways along the road, drifting in blinding sheets. When the wind changed direction, he lifted her out of the carriage. He flung her over his shoulder and she screamed in pain. 'Shut up,' he said. 'Shut yer row.'

He shuffled up the staircase and swung her into a chair. She screamed again, and he went to strike her, but thought better of it. When she grew silent, he slowly lowered his hand, scratching his groin as if he was infested. He slumped beside her, the chair creaking beneath him. She took long gasping breaths, until the room came into focus.

Seated opposite, parted by a few chairs, a man and woman gazed at her. They took in her pale drawn face, the crooked angle of her body. The man had a boot removed; his ankle and foot were swollen, a blue misshapen block. He gazed at the injury to monitor its swelling. The woman had something wrong with her arm, which she supported at the elbow. She sat without moving her head – her face was smudged as if she'd been crying and wiping the tears with dirty hands. She flickered her eyes at Eileen, who returned the gesture to acknowledge a sisterhood of suffering.

Mr Sticks stared at the woman, up and down. He tried to gauge the shape of her body. Then without warning, he sprung from the chair, gripped the woman by the arm and marched her to the staircase. 'Go on, get out! This lady's first.' He pointed to Eileen, 'She's first for treatment. Go on, get off home.'

The woman stood for a moment in shock – hair dishevelled, hands shaking and hanging before her. Tears filled her eyes and she winced from the pain of her injury. She couldn't think of anything to say and when she did, she was too struck by fear to say it. She flashed him a glance and left by the stairs. When she got to the bottom, she began cursing and took those curses onto the street.

Mr Sticks crossed the waiting room and stood over the seated man. 'On yer way.' The man looked up at him. His face hardened and he passed his boot from hand to hand. 'I ain't going nowhere, mate.'

'You are.'

'I ain't.'

Eileen called in pleading tones. 'Let him be, I can wait. It's no trouble, no trouble at all. Let the poor man be. We'll all be seen in good time. Please, no fighting – there's no need for fighting. Let the man be.'

Mr Sticks gazed dreamily towards her. For a moment, he seemed to listen. He closed his eyes and opened them again. Then he made a vicious grab for the man's nose. The man pulled away, but was clasped by the jaw. 'Up! Now! Right now, or I'll mash you up! Ya got five seconds' He began counting. 'One . . . two . . .'

The man struggled from the chair. Leaning on the backrest he swayed and held onto the wall. He breathlessly limped to the stairs, hopped a few steps and rested with his hand on the rail. When he had caught his breath, he turned back, cursing and making threatening gestures with his boot. Mr Sticks skipped down the stairs and kicked him in the face. The man tumbled backwards, crashing and bumping all the way down – it sounded like ten men collapsing on the stairs, limbs flailing against the woodwork. He clambered to stand, then lurched outside, spitting fragments of teeth like hailstones.

Mrs Shapp came hurriedly from her room at the sound of the commotion. She looked around for her patients – the woman with the injured arm, the man with the swollen foot. She could hear cries on the street, someone moaning. Eileen was seated with her face in her hands – she'd been crying, her collarbone was dislodged. Her shoulder hung crookedly like a snapped branch. The bone-setter beckoned, 'Come this way, my love.'

Mr Sticks rounded the banister. Eyes roused and jaundiced, his lips were like wet snails. He gazed at the bone-setter – her smooth ivory skin, the white sheen of her hair. She stood a good foot above him. His thoughts went beneath her gown. 'She ain't going nowhere without me.'

'My patients are treated alone.'

'I go where she goes.'

'Then take her home. Return her to your master in the state in which he left her. I work alone, to no audience, or not at all. Either leave her with me, or leave the premises.'

He took a moment to ponder. He rolled his head on his trunk neck. 'Make it quick,' he snorted. 'Fix her up.' He slumped into the creaking chair and cupped his balls.

The bone-setter helped Eileen into the room. Once inside, she turned the key in the door. She led her to a bench at the window. 'He's been at you again.'

Eileen tried to smile, but couldn't quite manage it. 'He has, sure he knows where to strike me.'

'He's a brute and a coward.'

'True enough.'

The bone-setter stood back to survey the damage, closing one eye and tilting her head. She took a step to the left and two to the right. Her gown was long and flowing, flared at the sleeves, which swished when she moved. She put a hand on Eileen's back, the other on her shoulder. 'Straighten your spine. Sit upright, relax for me. Let yourself go. Even if it hurts, try not to flinch. I want you to think of a river – close your eyes – can you do that for me?'

'Yes'

'I want you to imagine the sound of water on the rocks. Listen for the flow, the gush. Can you hear it now?'

'I can.'

'Listen for the birds, pick out their melodies from the trees.'

'I hear them.'

'Now here comes the mist rolling off the hills. Can you see it?

'Great clouds –'

With a sudden jerk, Mrs Shapp manipulated Eileen's shoulder. There was a loud click, then the bone-setter lay her down to rest, touching her eyes closed. 'Tom Gobey has been here.'

Eileen bolted upright. The bone-setter put a finger to her lips. 'Shussssh. He has come after all these years.'

'It cannot be. My Tom – my Gobey, my sweetheart – was here?'

'Yes.'

'Back from the land of the sun?'

'In person.'

'Coffee eyes, raven hair – my boy, my boy has come?'

'Yes, yes, yes.'

The boards creaked on the landing as Mr Sticks came to the door. He jerked the handle and called out, banging with his fist. He shunted the panel with his knee and tried the handle again. 'Open the door, or I'll bring it down. I'll kick the thing in. Ya got five seconds and I'm coming. One . . . two . . .'

The bone-setter helped Eileen to stand. 'Look, your Gobey will return. I can arrange a meeting for you. When can you come again?'

'I don't know, I'm not free to –'

'Give me a day.'

'Friday, this coming Friday.'

The bone-setter swept over and unlocked the door. Mr Sticks pushed his way inside. 'Where the hell is she?' Eileen stood adjusting her clothing, then leaned forward and kissed the bone-setter, who whispered, 'On Friday you shall meet Tom Gobey.'

His squat frame came between them. He looked from one woman to the other. There was something going on he didn't like, couldn't understand. He pushed the bone-setter and she stumbled back to regain her balance. He gripped Eileen by the elbow and forced her towards the door. As he turned, the bone-setter called out to him, 'Little fellow, there's a fee to pay, little fellow.'

He spun to stare at her. He could feel silent laughter between the women. They were not smiling, but their eyes were moist and glistening in some amusement. His face felt hot and prickly. Hands sweating, a great source of humiliation gushed inside of him. Never had he been called such a thing – *little fellow*. He tried to think of the business at hand, but couldn't move on from the jibe. He stood between them, the helpless butt of some feminine jest. What am I, he thought – a dwarf, one of the little fucking people?

He turned violently to Eileen, then back to the bone-setter. His tongue flashed over his lips and he spoke through gritted teeth: 'I'll pay ya, don't worry about that. I'll pay ya, all right.'

'Make sure you do. If your master's going to beat a lady, he should at least pay for the mending.'

Head down, he shoved Eileen from the room and led her along the hallway. The bone-setter called out to him, 'Don't fall in the snow, little fellow. You might need someone to fix your bones.' He didn't look back, he couldn't think straight in his present rage. They went hurriedly down the staircase and outside into the falling snow. He gripped her arm and marched her through a group of people, scattering them.

In the carriage he would not look at her. Stiff and motionless, he sat upright against the window, his breath smudged against the glass. The scar on his cheek was inflamed and all the more gruesome in the reflection. Outside, the snow fluttered in a blue tinge, in the pale remnants of daylight. The night crept up like a cat on a bird, slinking around corners, lurking behind walls and seeping along the ice of the river. If the night was running out to the estuary, the wind was turning back on itself, flexing like a great muscle and heading for London, spoiling for a fight.

CHAPTER 16

Saffronetti was most agitated on this evening. He stood naked in his room, wild and frenetic. For all his wealth, he could not make Eileen bow to his wishes. She had been imprisoned and beaten, but still showed no sign of submission. Whatever he said, she was inclined to the opposite. If he reached for her hand, she would tug it away. If he touched her hair, she would flinch as if he were some freak of nature, some abomination.

He stomped in frustration. In his warped thinking, he believed the demise of Tom Gobey would make her warm to him. With no sweetheart to hold dear, she would somehow be more susceptible to his persuasion. If he could obliterate her options, she would have no choice but to veer his way. He was growing increasingly weary of her rejections, and the more she ignored him, the more he loathed himself – a loathing that was unforgiving in its intensity. He so much wanted to be adored, as he was in his days at the opera, when the ladies would fall at his feet.

The colourless advance of frost on the window, the relentless fall of the night outside. Saffronetti crossed the room as if entering a stage. Sweeping past the fire, he spun for an encore, an imagined outpouring of adoration. In his mind there were flowers thrown, the audience calling his name. But when he opened his eyes, there was little to please him – the lavish room where silence gathered, the deserted bed with crumpled sheets, a single glass on the cabinet, the gritty dregs of claret inside.

He lifted the crystal decanter, filled his glass and drank with a sloppy, sucking greed. He added opium from a phial, a reckless dose for an insatiable appetite. It was never enough and never could be – his being begged for excess and he wandered the room in search of it. Little did he find. In the corner, he downed his claret and flittered back to the decanter. He filled his glass and gulped more and more, like a drunk from one of his own operas. A song came to him, but faded away before he could recall the first line.

His slender hands dropped unwittingly to his groin, and his thoughts flew back to his childhood in Rome, back to the day of his mutilation. It had been a sweltering day, with the breeze lifting his hair through the open window. He was bathing in a hot tub, the steam rising over his face. He remembered his parents were pacing in the hallway, waiting for someone. He was somewhat puzzled about the anticipated guest. Outside on the street his friends were playing – young Farinelli and Senesino were running and laughing along the dusty road. One of them must have been carrying a stick, for he could hear it scraping the church wall as they ran. A dog was chasing them, panting and barking in a frenzy. Eventually, their voices faded to birdsong among the cypresses, ghostly whispers among the trees.

Then, standing in the doorway, he saw the barber, Mr Nicolini. He was wiping the sweat from his bald head with a handkerchief, his forearms glistening. This powerful man with a wet moustache and unforgiving eyes had come to the house. Why had Mr Nicolini come to the house, when his hair had been cut last week? Now the barber sat beside the tub, stroked his head and bid him, 'Drink this, young Saffronetti. Drink.'

He embarked that day upon a lasting habit, a lifetime's addiction. His first taste of opium, his first vision of paradise. He briefly struggled in the tub, but Nicolini pressed his thumbs into the boy's jugular. Soon he was barely aware of the razor unfolding, hardly conscious of the slice between his legs. The barber departed with the boy's testicles in his hand, like a demigod who had stolen the power of creation.

That single vicious act spawned wicked intentions in the boy. For the two small testicles he lost, a mountain of disenchantment grew inside of him. His life became a bereavement, a constant lament for his lost manhood. Neither dog nor bitch, he lived in a half-baked androgyny, a mourning Hermaphroditus.

And now, fleeing those memories, he could find no satisfaction. He went to the desk to find some small amusement, something to snap or smash. His lips were stained from the wine, a ruby mess on his chin. Dribbling and infuriated by his laxity, he wiped his mouth with the back of his hand. Then, to forget the whole ugly business, he spun, round and round, with his arms aloft. Careening across the room, he collapsed on the bed. Bewildered, he ran his hands over his naked, hairless body, those fleshy, womanly hips. He writhed and sang with a shrill, whipping voice that echoed around the room.

In the room along the corridor, Eileen waited in the dark for his visit. She could hear him striking walls and bumping furniture, the heavy rush of his feet. He rattled the poker, or some metal implement, along the hearth and a glass shattered. There was a bang and a crash, a large weighty object toppled in his room. Then he wept hysterically, louder and louder, until the weeping distorted into song, a wrung-out lament.

The wind howled outside, the snow drifted at the window. She turned in the bed and stopped to listen – there was no sound from his room. Then he came thudding across the floor and his door swung open. He roamed over the landing in a fit of distress, moaning like a child fleeing a nightmare. His voice warbled outside, she closed her eyes and stayed motionless. She threw herself into the role of death and would not wake for him.

But before shutting her body down, she communed with her mother, in the way she had done since childhood, an inner voice in the wilderness of night. *Dear mother, 'tis only me, only me. On this eve, the devil himself does visit my room. Please teach me the guise of death, the marbled coolness beyond feeling and emotion. May the serenity of the grave take me for the next hour. Oh mother, may I join your long, peaceful sleep.*

The door creaked and Saffronetti stepped inside. He stood over her, trying to adjust to the darkness. She was perfection, aesthetically exquisite everything he might have been as a fully fledged woman, but he was not even a fully fledged man. He stood at the bedside and studied her pale face – a corpse on a slab, she would not move for him. He clutched at her hand, but it flopped lifelessly down. He kissed her lips – hard stone, tense and unforgiving – nothing he could do to make them pliable. She was death in a nightdress, the draw of her breath undetectable, the lids of her eyes sealed like a tomb. He bucked and shunted his way on top of her, but nothing stirred. The wind bashed up against the window and somersaulted down the road. They lay like dead fish on a beach, given up to the fate of the elements, lost to the will of the tide.

Mr Sticks had returned from the bone-setter's in a disgruntled temper. Mrs Shapp had humiliated him. He would not forget that transgression. One way or another he would get even, this week or the next – the time span didn't matter – for a grudge would fester inside and be more vicious for the wait. If someone would have asked him, *How are you today, Mr Sticks?* he would have replied in all honesty, *I'm in a cunt of a mood, a cunt of a mood.*

He loitered on the stairs as the servants worked below in the kitchen. They were ignoring him – denying his existence, belittling his importance. He coughed to make a noise, but no one looked up. To gain their attention, he slapped his hands against the wall, making a drum roll. 'Here I am,' he called down to them. 'Here I am.'

Mr Stanley came from the pantry with a jug. He didn't nod or gesture, or acknowledge the arrival of the visitor. He calmly crossed the room, put the jug on the table and continued with his next task. Mrs Hodgers was at the range with her back to the servants. She took a pan by the handle and shook the contents. There was not a sound in the kitchen she didn't recognize – a maid folding the linen, one cutting the cheese and another cleaning the cutlery. She knew only too well that Mr Sticks was scratching his scalp on the stairs – and she hoped that was all he was scratching.

He jumped the last few steps and landed flat on his feet with a clatter. 'Here I am, then.'

Mrs Hodgers called over her shoulder. 'A good evening to you, Mr Sticks.'

'What's good about it?'

'Well. There's a blizzard blowing outside, the snow's a-falling and the wind's a-blowing, but it's lovely and warm in here. Warm with the fire and the heat of good friends.'

'What friends?'

'All us staff.'

'I ain't got any friends.'

''Course you have.'

'I ain't.'

'They're all around you, Mr Sticks. Take a look'

Mrs Hodgers swept a hand across the room. Mr Stanley opened a drawer and began rummaging for something. He picked up a candle and placed it back down. He did the same with a pen, a doorknob and a piece of string. There was not much in the drawer he didn't handle in the seconds that passed. The maids busied themselves – they polished and cleaned, tidied things that didn't need tidying. Two of them left the kitchen in a hurry and took the stairs, shoulder to shoulder.

Mr Sticks followed behind them and lifted their dresses, 'Wooooh.' He made a kind of animal noise that sent them fleeing. He turned to find Lily halfway across the kitchen, frozen under his stare. He came up to her, pinching her sides, then felt her bottom. 'Friends are we?'

Gripping her arm he pulled her towards him. The scar on his cheek was crusty and inflamed, starting to fester. Mrs Hodgers stepped forward from the range, 'Would eel pie and gravy do you, Mr Sticks? A nice bit of pastry?'

He released Lily to consider the option of food. She slunk away to the wall, pressing her back against it. She looked over at Mr Stanley. Their eyes met and he looked at his feet. He shook his head, seething inside. She thought he might say something, but he put his hand in the drawer and shifted the objects around.

Mr Sticks turned to Mrs Hodgers. 'No, I don't want no pie. I'll just hang around starving me guts out.' The old cook tried to speak, but he started up again. 'Don't worry about me – me guts thinks me throat's been cut.'

'Well, be seated then,' she waved a hand. 'I'll dish up the grub now. And plenty of it for a hungry man.'

He dragged the chair from under the table and slumped sullenly down. He drew the mucus through his nostrils and swallowed in a motion that was visible in his throat. Mr Stanley stared angrily at the back of his head .

Mr Sticks stared at Lily standing up against the wall. She gazed all around the kitchen and back at him. He was still staring, as if through her clothes. She thought he had a terrible lust in his yellow eyes.

Sitting in the room off the pantry, young Bob was plying Tom Gobey with questions. The conversation in the kitchen suddenly halted. The door was ajar and the boy peeped through to assess the situation. He spotted Lily, stiff as a pole against the wall. Mr Stanley was standing with no particular purpose. His hands were shifting in the drawer.

A low voice cursed in the kitchen and the boy turned back to Gobey. 'Bastard hell, it's him. I really hate him. He's a right proper –'

'Now, now – you've a tongue like a devil. What's the trouble, lad?'

'Mister-bastard-Sticks is here.'

Gobey's face drained of colour, and he rolled from the mattress onto the floor. He looked to the window, but it was too narrow to squeeze through, and the room was stark with no place to hide. There was nothing he could use as weapon, only a large spoon. He picked it up and put it down. He tried to stand, but his legs wouldn't support him. He crawled around on his elbows looking for his boots in the shadows.

Mr Sticks leaned into his supper and made a sucking sound with his tongue. His lips were wet, his nose shining with grease. He took savage bites of his pie, humming loudly as he chewed. For no good reason, he thumped his elbow up and down on the table. The dishes shook until a single plate journeyed over the surface – it stopped at the edge and he thumped again, sending it crashing to the ground.

Something caught his attention near the pantry – a white face peered like a barn owl through the door. He crooked his finger, 'Come here.' The boy withdrew. 'Come here, I said, ya little-rat.'

The boy slowly crossed the kitchen floor, the plate fragments cracking under his feet. Mr Sticks continued to crook his finger, 'Come here.' He placed his knife and fork down, a mash of pastry working in his mouth. He dragged the boy onto his lap and held him. Young Bob was as stiff as a corpse.

Mrs Hodgers drifted over with the baking dish, 'More pie, Mr Sticks. You must be hungry, you must be. More pie, plenty more pie.'

He kissed the boy's ear with a loud smack 'Yer pie tastes of cow shit,' he said. 'Worse than dung.'

Mrs Hodgers crashed the dish on the table. 'Come on, now. None of that old caper.'

Mr Stanley could take no more and jumped the stairs three at a time. Along the corridor and up more stairs into the house, he stopped to listen for the master singing, but all was quiet at his bedchamber. He rapped against the door and Saffronetti appeared in his nightgown. He sobbed and moaned, half out of his mind on opium. His eyes were blue swirling orbs, they drifted in his head like fleeing jelly fish. 'What is it?' he wept. 'What do you want?'

'Most sorry to disturb you, sir, but it's Mr Sticks. He's interfering with the young boy, Bob Docker. Please come, sir – please do.'

'What boy?' Saffronetti stopped weeping and tried to concentrate for a second. 'What boy is this?'

'Bob Docker, the boy who works for you, sir. Mr Sticks is harming him. It's just not right, not natural. You're the only one, sir. The only one who can stop him. He won't listen to anyone but you, sir. Please, sir. Will you come, sir?'

Saffronetti's hands went limp at the wrists, he looked as if he was swaying on a rope. His girlish face was moist and smudged with white powder, the gooey insects of his eyelashes glistened. 'Misery,' he sobbed. 'Mutilation and misery. That's all I have. That's all I've ever known.'

The door slammed. The breeze swept Mr Stanley's face. He stood for a moment to gather his thoughts, then he sprinted down the stairs to his room. He pulled a trunk from beneath the bed and rummaged inside for a bayonet, sliding the weapon up his sleeve. The blade was cool against his forearm.

He entered the kitchen in a red faced fluster. Young Bob was sitting away from the table, Mrs Hodgers was stroking his cheek. The boy looked as if he'd been caught in the rain, his hair was tousled and his face wet. Mr Sticks finished his pie and gruffly belched, blowing the stench over at Lily. She was still standing against the wall, pushing against the brick and mortar.

Mr Sticks stood with his hand on his groin, rocking up and down.

Lily made an attempt to flee, but he stood in her way. 'Where ya going? Don't be going when I got something for ya.'

'I've a job for Miss Eileen, a job upstairs'

She tried to round the table, but was blocked at the other side. His beefy hand manacled her wrist. 'I got a job for ya downstairs, something to show ya.'

Mrs Hodgers rushed at him. 'Smoked ham, Mr Sticks? A lovely bit of smoked ham.'

'Ram it.'

Mr Stanley surged forward. 'Stop! Enough!' He looked as if he might burst into tears. 'Let the girl be, let her alone.'

Mr Sticks spun around, licking his lips and squinting. He released Lily's wrist and looked up at the butler. It was possibly the first time he had heard him speak – a weak voice, unconvincing and brittle. 'You ain't gonna stop me.'

'Please let her be.'

'I'll do ya in, good and proper.'

'Do what you will to me, but let the girl be.'

Saffronetti stumbled on the stairs in a haze, the tears glistening on his cheeks. His nightgown was tied with a silk belt. He stepped groggily into the kitchen and looked around at everyone. 'Mr Sticks,' he whinged like a spoilt girl. 'I'm out of opium, get me some opium. I must have it, I must. As fast as you can, off to the cupboard – now, now, now.'

Mr Sticks led the master into the upper part of the house. By the time they reached the corridor, Saffronetti had started to sing – a delicate lament that he transformed into a requiem, a disconsolate drone. He stopped mid-song and turned in anguish. 'Tom Gobey! What news of the fellow? Have you found him yet, what news?'

'I'm on his trail, sir. On his trail. He was down at Fetter Lane. I'll get him for sure.'

'She'll not yield whilst he's alive. Do him in, you must do him in.'

'He's done for, sir. I'll mash his head.'

Saffronetti stood in the dim light of the corridor, he swayed in distress and rocked with the jitters. A trickle of saliva hung a foot from his mouth; he swiped at it, but it stuck to his hand in a string. He angrily fled into the bedchamber, slamming the door. From inside he screamed out at Mr Sticks. 'Opium! Opium! Opium! Now! Now! Now!'

Gobey listened to the sounds of the kitchen – the servants talking quietly, the rattle of pots on the range, the sporadic crackle of the fire. He was flat on the floor, looking up at the ceiling. There was no movement in his legs, no sensation in his calves. In his toes there was a tingle of life. His feet were stone cold, like bloodless trotters on a butcher's slab.

Mrs Hodgers trundled in with a bowl of soup. 'Now, our Tom. We'll have you off to the bone-setter's in the morning. When the blizzard's gone, we'll set you on your way. How does that sound?'

'It sounds good, madam.'

She placed the bowl on the floor beside him, holding her lower back and grimacing as she rose. She went to the cupboard and returned with a blanket. Her knees creaked as she walked. She tossed the blanket over him and went to leave. He called after her, 'Madam. Can you tell me something, something about Mr Sticks?'

'What do you want to know?'

'Who is he?'

'He's a man gone bad. From head to toe – bad, bad, bad. Not a good bone in his body.'

'What does he do here?'

'He works for Master Saffronetti.'

'As what?'

'Debt collector and God knows what else.'

'Does he have reason to do people in?'

'Mr Sticks don't need reasons for anything. He does whatever he wants, whenever he wants to. In his head, he owns this city. From Edgware to Tyburn – every inch of every manor, cesspit and grand hall – it all belongs to him. Some things are best left alone. Mr Sticks is one of them. Place him on an island, sail him out to sea.'

'How does a man go so wrong?'

'God, knows, it starts young. They say his mother gave birth and left him on the cobbles. He was reared by the streets, and no good can come of that. As a boy he worked in the courtyard slaughterhouses. I used to know the governor of those houses. Old man Figgis was his name. And do you know what he told me?'

'I don't.'

'He told me the boy didn't kill the animals in the usual way.'

'No?'

'No, no, he didn't. He didn't use a blade.'

'What did he use?'

'A mallet.'

'And why would he do that?'

'They say – and don't quote me on the gospel – they say that he liked to bash them up first.'

The old cook left the room and quietly closed the door. He tried to sleep with the wind brushing the window, whirling in the trees. He could hear a voice, a wailing songster with the shrill cry of a child. He closed his eyes on that dark river melody, closed his eyes to shut out the night. If by some means of miraculous levitation Gobey would have hovered through the ceiling, through the many floorboards, he would have landed in the arms of his sweetheart. And yet, in his present state, she had never seemed further away.

Oblivious to his presence below, Eileen was resting in bed. The bone-setter had worked wonders with her shoulder, and there was just a dull ache running through her arm now. The experience had left her sleepy and exhausted. Lily was sitting on the bed, chattering in her usual way – from one topic to another in a tireless loop of digression. But Eileen could not concentrate, she was overwhelmed with the news of her sweetheart's return. Over and over, she ran his image through her mind. She could think of little else – Tom Gobey back in London, alive and for the loving. Now all she wanted to do was sleep and dream of him –picturing how he was when he had won her heart all those years ago.

The lanterns flickered in the window. The blizzard was blowing outside, rolling off the river in all directions. They could hear Saffronetti sweeping about his room, haunting the night with his presence. 'Oh, Miss Eileen, what a day we've had. There's you injured again and us all running from Mr Sticks.'

'A man gone to rot.'

'He is, he is.'

'And that's not the all of it. You wouldn't believe the handsome fella who's landed at our door. Mrs Hodgers says he's fallen from a carriage. He's got injured legs and he ain't walking at all.'

'Poor thing.'

'He's downstairs resting on the floor. Come and see him, Miss, do. He's a sight for sore eyes.'

'I'll not, Lily. I'm too tired, my love.'

'Oh, do come, Miss. He's a fine fella.'

'I'm sure he is, but I'm too weary to move.' Eileen closed her eyes and breathed heavily through her nose. Her words were starting to slur, 'Wish him well for me. Wish him well.'

Lily tucked in the sheets around the bed, took up a lantern and left the room. The wind howled and seemed to wrap around the house, a draught touched her legs from the servant's quarters below. The sound of someone's breath startled her, from the shadows a figure passed along the banister. She thought it was young Bob, up to one of his pranks. She called out and waited for his laughter, but none came.

Lily came down the stairs three at a time, rushing along the corridor into her room. She slammed the door and turned the key in a single action. The other maids were sleeping, their heads above the covers. Mr Sticks sprinted up the stairs, pushed his back against the door and slid down to sit. She climbed into bed with her clothes on, pulling the covers over her head and humming to drown out his presence.

He sat slumped against the door, cocking his head and listening for any sound – the shuffle of undergarments, the fall of her drawers. Rising up, he tried to peer through the keyhole, but it was blocked with the key. From his jacket, he took a piece of coal and started to chew it. His lips turned black, he spat the fragments onto his boots. He viciously scratched his scalp and grimaced, as if someone else was inflicting the pain.

The house was silent, the servants sleeping. He passed the old cook's room and pressed his rump against the door. He creakily farted against it, and Mrs Hodgers let out a muffled cry: 'And a good night to you, Mr Sticks.'

He pushed off.

At Mr Stanley's door, he stood for a moment – he knew the lad was inside and wished to get at him. He tried the handle, but the door was locked. He slouched away disgruntled, rolling his shoulders like a tormented beast. He took out his penis and walked along the corridor, up and down, before returning it to his trousers. He slid down the stairs on his bottom, bumping onto the ground. He sat aimlessly where he had landed. For a few minutes, he slapped his hands against the wall – just to hear the noise, just to feel the sting. At the end of his drumming, there was no more reason to the evening than there had ever been – the nights were long and lonely, restless hours to wander in search of his soul.

He opened the front door and stood looking out. The snow was drifting in a side flurry. Everything stood blue in the darkness. The wind blustered, toppling a post in the distance, it made a shrill ripping sound. He wandered out without a coat, with only his lust to keep him warm. He trudged into the blizzard, out to find the welcoming lights of the brothels – home from home for this misfit of the night.

CHAPTER 17

Covent Garden bustled with carriages, veering round bends and sliding sideways on the ice. A band of hawkers came hollering from the river and hollering through the alleys, where their voices reverberated off the walls. The tavern revellers spilled onto the street, drunks fighting and women weeping.

It was just another day in the city, but not for Tom Gobey. He was lying face down on his stomach and waiting for the bone-setter to treat him. She had paced the room in contemplation. Several times she had approached him, but then had suddenly veered off. She seemed to be waiting for some external inspiration, some mystical knowledge to guide her hand. A vision in her flowing gown, she looked like some enchantress from the dark ages – someone who might invoke a spell, divine the future in a glint of glass.

After several manipulations, now she stood over him, imposing in her stature. Then she placed one hand on the other and made an almighty jolt at the base of his spine. 'Up!' she said. 'Rise! Take up thy legs and walk. Stand tall. Walk, Tom Gobey, walk. There's nothing to stop you walking.'

He couldn't say she had done anything significant to warrant such a command. She had shunted him this way and that, jerked his head and pressed along his spine. He had been turned once or twice, had his knees pushed up and stretched down again. On his belly, she had twisted his neck. On his back, she had thumped his shoulders. What business she had massaging his feet he didn't know. All of this did not amount to much, yet here she was commanding him to walk.

She crossed the room and beckoned to him. 'Up – come now to me. Walk you must, tall and proud.'

He got dressed, slipped on his boots and sat on the edge of the bench. The blood ran through his legs like a drainpipe – it made a slow trickle into his feet. His toes prickled when he swivelled his ankles, his calves were stiff and wooden. When he swung his legs, the knees creaked. When he stepped down, the room seemed to sway. He took a shaky step, almost falling. Two more – then he paused to look over at her. She was laughing, nodding her head and wagging a finger. As he approached, she extended her arms to receive him.

She sat him on the bench and placed a hand on his knee. The heat from her palm penetrated inside, ran up his thigh and remained there. She took up his leg and worked it like a pump, but he stopped her. 'Has she been here, my Eileen?'

'She has.'

'She's injured?'

'Indeed.'

'This fellow beats her?'

'A sad truth.'

'And did you tell her I was back, looking for her and all?'

'I did.'

She worked with her head down. He placed a hand on her shoulder. 'What did she say of me homecoming?'

The bone-setter rose in a slow, deliberate way, pushing up from the knee. She stepped back and met his watery gaze. 'She'll come on Friday – love is not lost.'

He expelled an almighty gasp, a loud exclamation – half-laughter, half-catcall. He shook his head and the tears spilled down his cheeks. He dabbed them with the back of his hand, sniffing and rubbing his face to gather himself. He closed his eyes to concentrate, counted on his fingers. 'What day is it, what day? I've lost all sense of time. I can't think straight, can't think at all. Me mind's left me behind. It's run away without me.'

'Monday – today is Monday'

'Four nights. Only four nights and I'll see her. My girl, my Eileen.'

'Go steady.'

'I've been going steady for seven years. Seven years on a stinking colony – half a world and a rocking ocean between us. There's not enough time for steady.'

'You need to be careful, she's not free to come and go.'

'My girl.'

'She's not free, I say.'

'Friday, when the cock crows.'

He thanked her wholeheartedly, rocked slowly across the room and slid on his fur coat. She led him to the door, carefully observing his progress. He tried to pay her, but again she refused a fee. She took his hand. 'Take plenty rest, now. Stretch your spine and walk each day. Bend backwards for the body, look forwards for the mind. There's no lasting damage, love is a cure for all ills.'

He made a wobbly descent on the stairs, his leg muscles taut, causing him to shuffle. His head felt too high off the floor, as if he had shinned up a pole and suddenly looked down. At the bottom of the staircase, he called back to where she was standing. 'Thank you, thank you. For all you've done. For all you have done for us.'

It was bitterly cold outside, a smattering of snowflakes drifted in the wind. If a little stiff, his gait improved as he travelled. He thought it was the joy in his heart that was driving him, the joy that he would soon meet his sweetheart. Giddy with love, he could not stop smiling on the street, and smiling in such a way that people tended to smile back at him. How he wanted to share his good fortune with someone, anyone who might listen to his tale. In his blissful mood, he was eager to return to Johnny Steadman to celebrate.

Traversing the snow, a small boy stopped him. 'Hallo, sir.'

'Hello, son.'

The boy seemed to feed off Gobey's enthusiasm. 'I'm going to see me old grandma,' he exclaimed. As if the news might be important to a stranger.

'And I'm going to see me sweetheart.'

'Is she pretty?'

'She is, son. Prettiest girl in all London town.'

'Does ya love her?'

'Every scrap, every strand of her hair.'

Gobey walked on in laughter, he didn't mind the cold and felt refreshed in its embrace. At a junction, some men were clearing the snow to let a carriage pass. He nodded at one of the men and the fellow raised his hand as a greeting.

He came down a winding street and cut through a short alley. His memories of Eileen returned with great vividness – he could see her hair, inhale her scent. He conjured her voice in that lilting tone in which the Irish sometimes speak – more like a song than a mere sentence. She was closer now, closer than she had been for seven years, he could almost taste her existence. He longed for the day when they might again sell pamphlets on the street – back to back, leaning on each other to take on the world.

Gobey turned a corner to face a travelling press gang and stopped in his tracks. Shifting in a line, they hadn't seen him. Armed with poles, pistols and cudgels, they scrutinized everyone that passed. They pointed to the younger men and dismissed the codgers and consumptive beggars at the roadside. They surrounded a tavern and began peering through the window.

Gobey slipped into a cloistered passage, leaning into the shadows. He waited for them to pass, but they didn't appear. He thought they must be clearing the shops and taverns. Someone roared, then they surged from the street, snarling and wielding clubs, falling over each other to get at him. He scrambled through a wooden gate and lost his footing. Sliding on the cobbles, he came down a slope and crashed through a rotten fence. He passed through several gates and crawled through a tunnel of brick rubble, coming out in a snowy field. Behind a large oak, carved with names and slogans, he stood listening for the men – he could hear their voices in the wind, their weapons clattering over the walls.

They chased him over a bridge and back onto the street. The ground was glistening with glassy ice, a carriage sprayed it into the air. As the carriage approached, he tried to cling to the rail, but he couldn't get a grip. He ascended a hill and saw an abandoned cart in the road. He boarded the cart and pushed off with his foot, picking up speed on the way down. The press gang followed him, cursing and hollering and throwing bottles in his direction. The cart ran to ground in the snow, and he clambered off and made his way into a cobbled alley that smelt of animal blood. He turned a corner, crouched behind a pile of crates, until the men passed on the street – rattling chains around a stick, running cudgels over the railings.

He passed through a tight passage and crossed a frosty field. Along a narrow path, down a slope and over a wall, he found a range of winding alleys that had him lost. Randomly selecting one, he came to a shambolic sprawl of houses. He squatted to catch his breath, his ears drummed and vibrated. He could still distinguish the agitated shouts, the distant grunts of the men running through the alleys.

Gobey climbed onto an outhouse roof and slid off the other side. A dog approached and started barking, wagging its tail and jumping up in a playful mood. He pushed it away – a dog with one eye and foul breath, no teeth to cause damage. He squeezed through a broken fence, leaving the dog whining and scratching behind him.

He wandered into a courtyard where a spire rose above the houses. Stumbling through an alley, he came to a crumbling church whose stained glass windows were cracked and smashed. He wearily climbed the steps and turned the ring handle to swing open the splintery door. He stepped inside to wallow in the peace – the empty pews, the echo of his footsteps, the intoxicating smell of the wood.

Gobey left the church and stood in the grey cold air. Going down the steps, he made his way back to the courtyard. He felt dizzy, his vision clouded. He leaned against the wall with the cold penetrating his bones. The snowflakes thawed in his hair and trickled down his forehead. He closed his eyes and might have slept on the spot, but for the voices of the press gang echoing through the alleys.

Opening his eyes, a duck waddled by in the snow. Gobey pushed off the wall and followed it through the open door of a house. The bird was swept up by a woman, who seemed unsurprised to find him standing there. She had a sizeable wart on her forehead, her face was heavily powdered, the hair piled high on her head. It was difficult to distinguish a person beneath the embellishment. Her dress puffed out to touch both walls in the hallway. He smiled, went to offer some excuse for entering, but she cut him short. 'Welcome, deary.' Her voice had a rusty creak to it. 'Glad you could make one of our special days. Are you the friend that Daisy told me about?'

'I am.' He could think of nothing else to explain his presence. 'I am a friend.'

The woman stared intently. 'All good friends here, all good friends.' Her lips were thin and had been adorned with rouge to accentuate them. It gave her a gummy expression that suggested few teeth.

'Thank you.' He was not sure how long he could play this game. 'Most kind, madam. Most kind.'

She squinted to examine his face. In his fur coat, he might have been blown in from the wilderness. The woman laughed. 'Say, will you come and join us then, deary?'

'I will, madam. I will.'

Laughter trailed from a room off the hallway. The duck fluttered from her arms and wandered off in a limping waddle. She led Gobey inside and the conversation halted. Three women sat at a table, tipping glasses and gulping wine. Their wigs were towers of powdered colour, decorated with cheap jewels. The layers of make-up made it impossible to determine their age. The woman with the wart introduced herself as Mary and sat him down. Then, one by one, the other women offered their hands to be kissed. There was Alice to his left – prone to excitement and fidgeting in her chair, she winked and giggled for no good reason. Seated opposite, Julie and Rosie had claret-stained lips – they touched cheeks and linked arms like lovers.

Someone handed him a glass and they raised a toast. 'To all the pretty flowers.' He drank some and felt instantly comforted. Once he had finished the wine, his legs ached less, a gradual process of restoration swept over him. He looked at his glass and it was full again.

The day passed in an alcoholic blur. The women were loud and boisterous they slapped each other and kissed to make amends. They swigged from the bottle, filled their glasses until the wine spilled over the table. Never had he seen so much snuff consumed – in great snorts, they emptied three boxes and were looking for more. They sat coughing and choking with their eyes red and streaming, and this it seemed was pleasure to them – the accustomed way to spend a day.

After hours of wild antics the room fell silent. The woman with the wart was seated next to Gobey, her elbow on the table, her face drunkenly resting on her hand. She met his eyes, 'So, deary, have you done this before?'

Slaughtered by the drink, he struggled to speak. 'Done what?'

'You know, met with groups like ours?'

'I've met with many groups, madam.'

'Like ours?'

'All sorts.'

'Are you sure?' Her voice had taken on an interrogative tone. He could sense the drink gone sour, an irritable surge in her. She closed her eyes and the lids had been dabbed with white powder. 'I'm not convinced, deary.'

'About what?'

'That you've come here for dressing.'

'Dressing?' He sat upright in the chair, lifted his glass to drink, but instead put it down. He felt strangely sober, his feet came to life beneath the table. 'I think we might be at cross odds.'

'You've been here for ages, and there's not a frock in sight, deary.'

He gazed around the table and it dawned on him. Behind the puff, pout and powder, the women were all men. The day was all about dressing, and it was his turn to transform himself. His mind racing, he gazed around the table at the hairy ears, the crab apple throats and the square chins. He stood up, 'I'll just get changed,' he said. 'Back soon.'

He left the room and walked coolly down the hall, his laughter echoing off the ceiling. The ducks scattered as he passed, some padding ahead of him. He came out into the snow, holding his gut and roaring. He turned to find four faces, powdered and grotesque, peering from the window like ghosts. He called out to them, 'Fair thee well, sweet ladies!' Whatever way they lived their lives, there was no harm in them, nothing vicious in these men. If the French Revolution had failed, the quest for liberty was still flourishing in the oddest of places. Libertines and libertarians; better them than a room full of lords, Tories or clergy – then he would truly have to watch his tongue, keep his back against the wall.

Unable to walk straight for laughing he turned into an alley with his voice echoing around the walls. 'Freedom! He called to no one in particular. 'Freedom!' He leaned against a post to collect himself, then continued on through the snow. Beyond the alleys, the thundering carriages could be heard, scattering slush and grit, like the peppered spray of musket fire. On the thoroughfare, a group of shabby doxies called out to him. 'Hey, mister! Fancy a grab of something?'

'Freedom to you, ladies – freedom.'

He trudged into the clutches of the city, embracing him like a lost child. He passed the opium dens, with the blue smoke rising from the cellars. There was a terrible hullabaloo coming from the bawdy houses, where a band of drunken men were in full song. The grand carriages sailed by, the starched aristocrats at the windows. They picked at their hair and tussled their silk cravats, surveying the streets as an unruly theatre. In the drunken hour, he loved them all – each and every one. He opened his heart to any frail bird, any half-starved cat, that happened to be passing. He loved all creation, because his sweetheart was once again to enter his world.

He passed through a snaking alley and stumbled out the other side. The press gang that had pursued him was seated on a bench outside a tavern. They were smoking and passing a bottle around, engrossed in some plan that had them cursing and gritting their teeth. He turned on his heels and walked slowly away. It wasn't until he clambered over a wall that he heard them charging towards him. Still laughing, he crossed a field with the sheep scattering in bewilderment. He took a dirt track where the snow hadn't settled on the stony path. He scrambled down a grassy hill and slipped through a railing into a sprawling enclosure where the earth was lumpy and half-dug. He continued over the waste ground, the coal smoke pervading the atmosphere.

He crossed that land and did not look back. Climbing a railing, he passed through a shallow coppice, with the trees bare and looking frail in the grip of winter. For a mile, he walked on a meandering path and could no longer sense the men behind him. Giggling and mocking, he called over his shoulder, 'Freedom to you, gentlemen! May your warring hearts know peace!'

He travelled in an arc and came back into the city's nooks and alleys. In a little crush of a store, he bought some provisions that he carried in a sack. He swung it from one shoulder to the other, making a slow trudge down to Blackfriars Bridge. The Thames was still frozen, the boats were ice-docked, slanting sideways with the masts sticking out. Pockets of smoke drifted from the chestnut stands, where a few people stood around to keep warm, spitting and stomping their feet.

Still half-drunk, he hired a carriage to take him downriver. He wearily climbed inside, feeling sick in the stomach and aching in the legs. Whatever way he shifted, his back hurt. His feet were frozen and he rotated his ankles to restore the blood circulation. The air had the brittle quality of frozen particles – it hurt to breathe, needling his throat and ossifying his lungs. He rested his head against the window and gazed out. The fields had a furry coat of snow, a lone bird glided above them, stark and ominous in the pale sky.

The coachman cracked the whip and drove the horses on. Lost at times in blinding snow, they followed the ghostly trail of the river. Out past the virginal fields and the snow-covered trees, the sheep were standing motionless in a distant haze.

Arriving at his destination, Gobey paid the coachman on the ice. He stood to watch the carriage turn, skidding and veering back towards the city. Once it had departed, there was no other sound than the wind. He stumbled on with his ears full of gusts, unable to hear his feet crunch, the laboured flow of his breath. He walked until the old house came into view, that ghostly abode barely visible in the crosswind. It struck him as odd that there was no smoke coming from the chimney.

A line of mist was rolling off the river, creeping inland and growing dense. Hands stinging from the cold, he trudged on with his head down. He came to the front of the house and stood for a moment to listen. The wind dropped and the dull thudding of hooves came from the distance. It grew louder and faster until a horse appeared with steam blasting from its nostrils. He stepped forward, but the creature backed away. They stood for a moment contemplating each other; the horse shook its head and Gobey made a creeping advance, 'There, boy. Me and you are friends. Friends from the river.'

The horse trotted out of reach. The wind picked up and it suddenly took off, kicking up the snow. He watched its wild journey eastward, following the river as if it were chasing the wind off the face of the earth.

He cupped his hands and hollered. 'Freedom! Freedom!' The wind snatched his voice and obliterated the sound. The sky was all about snow, whirling in soft fragments and sheeting in great drifts.

He turned to face the old house, which seemed to lean into the oncoming wind to stop it falling. The windows shook and rattled as he pushed against the door. 'Well, well, Johnny! Are ya well, matey? Are ya well?'

He stopped to listen – no reply, no movement, only the wind roaming like a ghost on the marshes. He gazed around the sprouting plants, the strewn newspapers and old saddles. On the stairs he called out again, making his way along the landing. The door was ajar and he peered inside to find no fire, no glowing embers in the grate. Something moved, a chattering sound crossed the room towards him. He passed the old dog, splayed in an awkward posture and staring in the most pathetic way. The poor creature was resting in its own mess. 'Halloa, Johnny – where you hiding?'

Something rattled and he slowly followed the vibration to find Steadman slumped in the corner. The furniture was scattered about, his wooden leg was on the other side of the room. He looked blind drunk, his teeth were dancing with a clatter. 'Hey-ho, Johnny, why didn't you take the old dog out? Have a few drinks by all means, but don't forget the old hound.'

Gobey steered around a toppled chair to stand over him. Steadman was quivering, crying and shaking his head. He waved his hand. 'I ain't drunk, I ain't drunk. Me foot's been smashed, me foot and all the dog's paws.'

CHAPTER 18

The visit of Mr Sticks had caused devastation in the house. He had pulverized the limbs of both man and beast, leaving Gobey to attend to the injured. Where there had once been the raucous sound of Steadman's voice, now an unnatural calm reigned.

A day passed with no improvement in Steadman's condition. Gobey diligently watched over him, tending to his needs and trying to get his fever to abate. He tried to regale him with jokes and laughter, but Steadman struggled to hold a smile. He winced and denied he was suffering, but it was etched in his eyes. Sometimes it was like staring at a man gone mad, lost and bewildered and trying to keep focused on the world around him.

Gobey knelt by him where he lay bedded on the floor. He fed him a spoon of brandy, his throat rising and falling as he swallowed. His lips were blue and he spoke with a metallic croak: 'Sort the dog out. See to him, my son. See to him.'

'The dog's fine.'

'I can't hear him breathing.'

'He breathes.'

He removed Steadman's sock. The foot was smashed flat. The bones were crushed, the toes like bloody pulp. Beyond repairing by the bone-setter, there was nothing solid to manipulate. He cleaned the wounds and bound the foot as best he could.

Steadman stared, eyes fixed in a watery glaze. 'Tell me straight, son, no messing. What state's the dog in?'

'Not great, Johnny.'

'Will he walk again?'

'No, matey.'

They sat for some time without converse, gazing at the fire and over at the old dog. The hound lay flat like a platypus, unable to move with its squashed paws on the boards. Lost in thought the men fell grave and silent. They hardly moved lest it should break their contemplation. They blinked and sighed and did little else before the firelight, one man thinking on another man's sorrow.

Gobey glanced over at Steadman to find him weeping, shaking at the shoulders with his mouth downturned. He put his palms to his face, his speech inaudible behind his hands. He dropped his hands to speak, his beard wet and glistening. 'Will you do it?'

'Do what, matey?'

'The decent thing'

'What thing's that?'

'For old Plato, to see him off.'

Gobey stood up and dragged the air through his nostrils, exhaling in a deep breath. Three times he repeated the action until his head cleared. 'If that's what you want.'

'It is.'

'Now?'

'Yeah, now.'

Gobey lifted the dog and it whimpered. He crossed the room and placed it gently with its master. Steadman dropped his head among the fur, he thumbed its velvety ears and inhaled that old biscuity aroma. 'Over there,' he said. 'In the cupboard by the window – top shelf'

Gobey collected a heavy cudgel from the cupboard, gathered up the dog and made for the door. Steadman was uttering incomprehensible cries as if to call him back. He ignored them. He left quietly on the stairs and went out into the glaring snow. He placed the dog on the ground and returned to the house for a spade. When he came out, the dog was wagging its tail. He approached from behind to avoid its eyes. Two-handed he raised the cudgel and screamed as it swung down.

Some time passed with no sign of Gobey. Steadman roused himself on the floor, rubbed his eyes with his fists. He'd been crying and sleeping and crying in his sleep. The heavy drag of boots on the stairs, then the door swung open. The fire spat a smoking missile onto the boards beside him; he snuffed it with his hand. 'Is that you, Gobey?'

'It is.' He backed inside and turned around with the dog in his arms. 'I couldn't do it. Not yet, not now. We'll take him with us – me, you and the old dog. If things get worse, I'll do the deed, but not now. Not when there's light in his eyes.'

He crossed the room and carefully placed the dog down, its tail sweeping the floor. Steadman drew it onto his lap and kissed its snout. He spoke a strange dialect, an age-old language that the dog seemed to understand. They conversed for some time in this way, the master mumbling and the hound groaning in response.

Soon after, Steadman was writhing in agony. The pain in his foot drew the colour from his face – even his beard looked parched and fossilized. His foot was throbbing through the bandage, lifting off the floor.

In a small bottle, Gobey made a concoction of opium, wine and brandy. He administered it to Steadman, then the old dog. They soon fell quiet, man and beast resting in some otherworldly oblivion. Gobey went to the window. The horse was wandering in the snow. He tapped the glass and the creature looked up at him; it stood motionless like a grand sculptured shadow. He called over his shoulder to Steadman on the floor. 'Got anything to feed a horse?'

'You what?'

'That horse is back, a real beauty.'

'What horse?'

'The horse I freed on the river.'

'There's a sack of oats in the corner.'

Gobey filled a large bowl and went outside. The horse shook its head and lifted its hooves. It had a strange way of staring at him. He approached and it trotted a short distance away, looking back to check his whereabouts. He put the bowl on the ground and went into the house. He watched from the window as it fed, rolling its long tongue and keeping a peripheral eye on guard. When it had finished, it galloped over the marshes, disappearing out of vision with its breath trailing behind it. He could hear its hooves drumming, a rhythmic pulse that travelled in his head long after the horse had gone.

From the rooms downstairs he gathered a rope, reins, bridle, saddle and stirrups. There was some kind of harness that he hadn't seen before, but it was too knotted and rotten for use. He carried what he had upstairs and sat by the fire untangling the reins. 'We're getting out before Sticks returns.'

'I ain't going nowhere. Not with me smashed foot and peg leg'

'We're all going – me, you and the old dog.'

'How'll we cross the marshes?'

'On horseback, matey. On horseback.'

'You'll never catch it, not in a million years. That thing's wild, it won't come to you.'

'I can and it will.'

'A penny says you won't?'

Gobey spat in his hand and they slapped palms and shook on the wager. 'I can hear that penny jingling into me pocket.'

Steadman laughed. 'It will jingle louder coming out.'

Gobey boiled three eggs and mashed them to feed the dog. He fried a fish and tried to share it with Steadman, but he wouldn't eat. When dog and master were sleeping, he took a chair and sat by the window. The snow drifted on the marshes, the day was grey and desolate. No birds called, the river was silent in a grip of ice. He gazed between the distant trees for a sign of the horse, scanning the horizon for a flicker of movement. He stood to leave and noticed the horse in front of the house, looking up.

Gobey went outside and crouched in the snow. The horse faced him; there was a stand-off between them. He waited in that motionless stance until the creature fell calm. He eased a rope from his shoulder and took a slow, stooping walk towards the colt. 'There, there, boy. I won't hurt you. Never would I hurt you.'

Steadman rested on the floor, his back against the wall, one arm around Plato. He was reading a book and simultaneously pressing the dog's ear between thumb and forefinger. A spray of snow hit the window and fell down. He looked up, then back to his reading. The pane rattled again, then he heard Gobey calling from outside: 'Hey, hey, Johnny! Johnny, ahoy!'

He closed his book and turned to the dog. 'What's he after, what's he up to now?' He attached the wooden limb to his stump and clambered upright. He slowly worked his way around the room – his hands slapped the wall, his pole tapped the boards. He dragged open the window and leaned out into the cold air. The horse was saddled and standing calmly below. Gobey called up to him, 'How about that, then?'

'Well, I never.'

'Well, I did.'

'You've gone and tamed the bugger.'

'Good and proper.'

Gobey came into the house and ran up the stairs. He took a bottle from the table, pulled the cork with his teeth and spat it into the fire. He took a swig and joined Steadman after closing the window. 'Here,' he pressed the nozzle to his mate's lips and helped him drink, 'A celebration's in order.'

'You trickster, how'd you manage that?'

'A little coaxiorum.'

'A gentle touch.'

'A little opium in its oats.'

'Never.'

'Oh yeah.'

They laughed and roared and passed the bottle between them. For a short while Steadman came back to life. They stood for some time at the window. The first signs of nightfall had struck the slate sky. A shadow crossed the marshes like a giant hand and a bank of cloud was drifting from the river. They stood until their reflections crept into the glass and stared back at them. Steadman leaned crookedly, his long hair swept back, his plaited beard resting on his shoulder.

'One penny you owe me'

Steadman hopped to keep his balance and giggled hoarsely with sparkling eyes. As he searched his pockets, his peg leg tapped the boards. He leant on Gobey's shoulder. His smashed foot was starting to smell, growing sweet and sickly.

'You're all right there, matey. I'll not take your money. It's only a bit of fun, a lark is all.'

'You will.'

'I won't.'

'No, no,' he insisted. He rummaged for the coin and passed it over. 'A wager's a wager – fair's fair. You tamed that horse, for sure. Never let it be said I reneged on a bet. Johnny Steadman always honours his bets.' As they turned from the window, he didn't notice Gobey drop the coin back into his pocket.

They crossed the room with Steadman leaning into his mate. He flopped down among the blankets and cushions on the floor. Gobey poured two mugs of wine and joined him, with the dog resting between them. The men stared at the fire as if it might go somewhere. They sat in silence, too weary for speech, too far gone for laughter or song.

Steadman slowly keeled over in a slumber, his breath rattled. He looked frail by the firelight, bony like a half-starved child. He seemed to be shrinking in his clothes, retreating from visibility. He slept like one who had no intention of rising.

Goby turned on his back and tried to sleep. The fire hissed and crackled. Outside, the horse was stomping around in the snow – it danced a few steps and grew still. From the distance, an eerie howling travelled with the wind, out along the river and away beyond the marshes. Gobey could not say what beast had made that sound, or what warped nature had spawned it. Steadman lifted his head like a man rising from the grave. 'Leave me, leave me, leave me,' he said. 'Leave me be.' He fell back to sleep as if a ghost had spoken through him.

The next morning a pale sun hung over the house. Gobey stirred and thought of Eileen. Three more days and he would see her again – seventy-two hours to wait. He sat up and moved around the room to keep warm. Steadman's breath was rasping in his throat, crackling in his chest. He was pale and gaunt, the skin shrinking on his withered bones. One of his eyes was twitching.

Gobey lit the fire using twisted newspaper, building it with kindling and coal. Overnight, he had squashed snow into a pot to boil for tea. He took the bread from his provisions sack, placed the loaf under his arm and cut it upwards with the slices falling on the table. He skewered the thick wedges and toasted them on the fire.

For some time he sat at the table, dreamily watching the snowfall at the window. If his eyes were open, they felt half-closed. He ate his way through a third of the bread, then pushed it away to avoid temptation. He looked over at the dog, its back arched with stiffness. Steadman was sleeping next to it, but facing away.

Gobey crossed the room. 'Come on, old Plato, we'll take you out for your business.' He knelt to find that the dog had died. He crouched down to Steadman and gently shook him. 'Johnny, I'm sorry – so sorry. The old dog's gone. He's gone, matey. He's slipped away in the night.'

Steadman's eyes opened as if he hadn't slept – it took him a moment to comprehend the situation. Then he rubbed his face, covering it with both hands. Sobbing and heaving, he gazed around the room. He sat upright and cradled the dog, nosing its fur and ears. After a short while, he set the dog aside and rested his face back in his hands.

Gobey carried the dog outside. He dug a hole by a tree near the house. He had to take a pick to the frozen earth. He helped Steadman down the stairs, hopping on his pole and grunting in pain. They stood with the wind in their hair, leaning into each other. The landscape was bleak with a fresh layer of snow blowing in from the river. From the post where it was tethered, the horse turned to watch the makeshift interment. Not a prayer did they offer – they stood, two men in the Age of Reason with no God, no faith in an afterlife.

Steadman broke the silence in the cold morning air, his words blew across the marshes. 'How I loved thee, my faithful hound.' And Gobey, not knowing what to think about the whole sad business, closed his eyes and said, 'Long live the Revolution, and all the dogs of the world.'

They buried Plato deep in the earth. The topsoil was frozen, but the earth beneath was clayey and had something of the river in its smell. Steadman cut a lock of his hair and tossed it onto the grave – seconds later, the wind had scattered it, the fine strands sticking to the snow. 'Nothing stays where you left it,' he said. 'Nothing stays.' He hobbled to the bare tree and rested his forehead against the bark.

Gobey put a hand on his shoulder. 'We have to leave, Sticks will be after us. We have to make a move, matey.' He helped Steadman into the saddle and walked the horse away. They crossed the marshes with the wind against them, the snow in a heavy angled fall. They came onto the frozen river and passed through a creeping veil of mist. Gobey mounted the horse with his mate behind. They clattered over the ice with the hooves echoing. An eel catcher stood among his baskets and watched them pass.

They left the river at London Bridge and clopped slowly through to Cheapside. The doxies stood in a line, swigging gin; they cursed and called across the street. An old aristocrat with a wig walked among them. He lifted their dresses, eyeing the goods. Gobey slapped him on top of the head as they passed, and Steadman roared with laughter. Further on, they bought a pie from a street vendor , eating on the move, the crumbs trailing behind in the snow.

All along Bishopsgate they were accosted by vendors, calling and beckoning and walking beside the horse. A lad tried to sell them a piglet, holding up the creature to be examined. The creature pissed down the boy's sleeve and it ran under his shirt. Gobey ruffled the lad's hair. 'We're travelling light, sonny, travelling light.'

At Houndsditch, they rented an old slanted house with an old slanted barn attached at the back. The landlord brought some grain and straw and broke the ice in the trough for the horse to drink. Gobey lit a fire and put some bedding in front of it, helped Steadman down to rest and covered him with blankets. Again he tried to make him eat, but he was beyond the exertion of chewing.

Gobey left him sleeping and went for some provisions. On his return, he found Steadman groaning and thrashing among the blankets. 'The old dog's back, my son. He's kipping on the floor, the old dog's kipping on the floor.'

'Johnny, the dog's dead. He's gone.'

'He's over there.'

'He's not, matey. He's dead in the ground.'

'He spoke to me.'

'What did he say?'

'See you on the marshes, with the wind in the trees.'

'It's all right. It's going to be all right. You've got a fever, that's all. It will pass, I'll fix you something to see it through.'

'But the old dog spoke to me.'

'I know, matey.'

'He spoke to me.'

'I know.'

Gobey mixed some wine and opium in a bowl. He stirred it with his finger and licked the sticky contents. He tilted Steadman's head for him to drink. His eyes were half-crazed, staring into space as if something was out there – out there, but only known to him. 'See you on the marshes, with the wind in the trees.'

'You will, matey. You will.'

He unravelled Steadman's foot bandage, releasing a wild stench. The toes were stuck together in a mash of bone and gristle, a green tinge rose into the bloated leg. Gobey turned away, covered his mate in blankets and slipped on his fur coat.

'Hey!' Steadman called to him. 'Where you going?'

'I'll not be long, just rest now.'

'Where you going?'

'Just out. I'll be back in two ticks.'

'But the dog –'

'I know, I know, matey.'

Steadman rose from the blankets, his face awash with sweat. The glossy balls of his eyes rolled in the firelight. He was like a crazed prophet let loose on the world. 'Let him in,' he said. 'The dog's scratching, let the old dog in. He's doofing to come in. Can't you hear him doofing?'

Gobey opened the door and there was nothing out there – nothing but the wind and the snow and the black night stretching before him. He stepped out beneath the stars, the phosphorescent blue haze of the sky. He turned back to his mate by the fire. Steadman was staring to where planets implode and galaxies climb the ladders of gas and dust from this world to the next. His eyes held the great unknown, unfathomable as the minds of migrating whales beneath the ocean.

CHAPTER 19

Dr Capper was drunk in bed, slurring amorous words in the ear of his mistress. It was dark, and he could barely distinguish Maud's face from the pillow. He tried to kiss her, but his lips smothered her nose. He couldn't tell if she was asleep or not, and didn't much care for the difference. She was breathing at least, a good start to proceedings. He tried to mount her, but she rolled away in a sleepy bout of sighs. Downstairs the front door rapped and someone was bellowing and waking all the neighbours.

He groggily rose from the bed, staggered against the wall and pushed off. He scrambled around looking for his breeches and found them rumpled on the floor. He lit a candle on the windowsill, blinking from the light like a chick just hatched from an egg. It took some time to get his shirt on, to pull on his jacket. He repeatedly tried to squash his large feet into Maud's shoes before locating his own.

He bustled down the stairs and unbolted the front door, 'What in God's name are you after, man?'

'I'm Tom Gobey, sir. Are you Dr Capper?'

'The very same.'

'Sorry to disturb you, sir. I wouldn't have come, but it's most urgent. Me friend, it's his leg. It's swelling from the bone. Methinks there's poison in it, black blood.'

'How did you find me?'

'I tried the house across the street. Your wife said you'd be here.'

Dr Capper closed his eyes and shuddered. His hair was grey and blustery with curls. The best part of his face was red, including his ears. His shirt was bursting with the force of expanding flab, a ledge of fat wobbled as he turned. 'You better come inside,' he said, leading the way. 'This friend of yours – he has a disease, I presume?'

'No, sir.'

'Then how's his leg gone bad?'

'Someone smashed it with a mallet.'

'A charming business, I'm sure. What a rich world we live in.'

'He's in urgent need, having visions and all, sir.'

'It will cost you.' Gobey reached for his money belt, but the doctor put out his hand. 'When the job's done.'

Capper shrank at the sight of his mistress on the stairs. Her nightdress was tangled, barely covering her knees. She was half his age, a quarter of his body mass. She sleepily rubbed her eyes, squinting through the candlelight. 'What is it, Richard, who bangs at the door?'

He tried to eclipse her presence by standing in front of her. 'An urgent case, that's all. Go back to bed, petal. I'll return shortly when the job's done.'

She blearily made her way up the stairs, mumbling something as she closed the door. Capper went into an adjoining room and splashed water on his face. He appeared with a towel in his hands, looking around him. 'There it is,' he said, gathering a hard case and a floppy bag with straps. 'Lead the way, my man.'

Gobey had hired a carriage that was waiting when they came outside. The night air was bitterly cold and every breath cut a grey mass before them. Capper ducked his head and scrambled on board with his knees tearing at his breeches. Gobey joined him, squeezing down against the doctor, with little room to stretch his legs. Capper looked across the street to his own house, where his wife was standing at the window, coolly staring. He sheepishly waved, but she didn't acknowledge his existence. 'A difficult matter, you understand.'

'I'd say it would be.'

'Now . . .' The doctor slapped his hands on his sizeable knees. 'Tell me about this leg. The one your friend has.'

'Tell you what?'

'Colour, what colour?

'Greenish and it smells a bit.'

The doctor raised his eyebrows. His breath was heavy at all times, and it seemed a few sentences might knock him out. He gasped and spoke breathlessly. 'Size, shape, thickness?'

'It's bloated, more two legs than one.'

'Pus, discharge, maturation?'

'There's stuff leaking from the toes.'

'Mmmm.'

Gobey leaned forward to look at him. He smelt of drink, a stale odour leaking through his pores. He seemed to be making notes in his head, mulling over the facts. 'Will he be all right, me mate? He means a lot to me.'

'Mate or otherwise, it won't change the odds.'

'The odds?'

'Damaged bone, chance of poisoning, possible gangrene.'

'Sounds bad.'

'Bad it might be.'

The night air was crisply present in the carriage, a hoary frost glistened on the windows. The pitch-blackness of the backstreets gave way to the bluish light of the open road. Clusters of stars lit the sky. Coming into Cheapside it was snowing on one side of the street. They left the carriage and crossed into the snowfall.

They entered the house and found Steadman writhing among his bedding on the floor. Saturated in sweat, he was roasting from a fever, his eyes wildly unfocused and darting around the room. Gobey knelt and took his hand. 'This is the doctor, Johnny. He's here to help you, to make you well.'

'The old dog's back.'

'I know, matey. I know.'

The doctor removed his jacket and placed it on the table. His face was flushed, his breath laboured. He took scissors from his bag and cut Steadman's breeches to examine the leg. It was bloated, misshapen, greatly discoloured. He held the foot, shook it at the ankle. Up and down he pressed with his fingers and watched for results. He spoke without looking up. 'Get me a sack of sawdust, a long rope, two bottles of brandy, some flour and opium tincture.'

'I've got opium.'

'Then fetch me the rest. Go to the tavern on the corner and ask for George – George the landlord. Tell him it's a leg job and you need two strong men. Tell him I sent you.'

Gobey went out into the cold night air. A few lanterns were shimmering from the houses along the street. The carriage was waiting across the road, the coachman smoking a pipe inside. He pulled down the window and called out, his breath blue before him. 'He be done yet?'

'Not yet.'

'How long he be?'

'Not sure, not sure what he's doing.'

Gobey walked into the oncoming snow, which swirled across the shafts of lantern light. He entered the tavern and the heat struck his face. A knotty branch of a tree cracked and smoked on the fire. The tavern was deserted but for two old men drinking at a table. They turned to look at him, one of them nodding as he passed. 'A dirty old night.'

'It is.'

'Filthy as hell.'

The door opened behind him, the fire flattened and rose again. A burly man entered, carrying a huge log that he dropped with a crash. He shoved it with his boot to the hearth then stood with his foot on it. Gobey turned to him. 'I'm looking for George the landlord.'

'Who be asking?'

'Dr Capper sent me.'

'Oh, yeah.'

'It's a leg job.'

The man crossed the room and went behind the counter. Gobey called to him again. 'I need some –'

'I know what you need.'

The man began to load a sack, collecting things from an adjacent room. He stopped for a moment to scratch his head. 'Brandy, how many bottles?'

'Two.'

He leant over the counter to shake Gobey's hand. 'I'm George.'

'Tom Gobey.'

'You done this before?'

'Done what?'

The landlord took a deep breath, it whistled through his teeth coming out. He dragged a sack of sawdust into the middle of the room, then peered over at the old men. He strolled over to their table and stood observing their conversation. They carried on talking without a sense of his presence. 'Which of youse,' he pointed from one to the other. 'Which of youse buggers is coming with me?'

One of them cleared his throat and coughed into his hand. The fire sizzled in a peculiar fashion and the men turned to look at it. They turned back on themselves, supping in silence and deep in their thoughts. 'The doctor needs some help.'

One of the men made a gummy smile – two teeth, one upstairs and one down. They slotted into place as he spoke. 'And I need a good woman.'

'There's free grog for the helper.'

'Not a chance.'

'Free grog and a place in heaven.'

'Nay.'

'You'll not help a man in trouble?'

'Not on this night.'

Immovable as oaks, he turned from their indifference. He rolled the sack of sawdust up his leg and onto his shoulder, heading towards the door. Gobey collected the rope, the brandy bottles and some flour packs from the counter. On the street they turned away from the wind, walking the short distance in silence. They went inside and found Steadman flat on the table in the centre of the room. He was staring at the ceiling, gibbering and dribbling spit. The doctor turned breathlessly to face them. 'Only you, George?'

'Only me, sir. Them buggers won't shift.'

'You it is, then.'

The landlord went about his business, cutting the rope into equal lengths. Capper tapped one of the bottles that Gobey was carrying. 'Get it down your chum, as much as possible, but don't make him sick. I mustn't have him sick.' He clasped the other bottle and took himself into the corner. Half-obscured in the shadows, he drank greedily, wiping his mouth with the back of his hand. Then he called over to Gobey, 'It's coming off, above the knee.'

'You what?'

'Your friend's leg, it's coming off.'

'But he's only got one.'

'It's a leg or a life.'

'There must be something –'

'One or the other.'

Gobey sat at the table and lifted Steadman's head, helping him to drink. He took a swig himself, then another and tried to smile, but every scrap of his face was taut – one of his eyes started to flicker. Steadman looked up at him. His beard was like the rusty chain of an old ship. 'They going to bleed me, drain me blood?'

'Something like that. You'll be fine by the morning. Fresh as a daisy.'

'What about the night?'

'You'll be fine.'

When Steadman was fed enough drink, he threw back his head and launched into a lewd song. Capper saw this and staggered over, opening his bag. The landlord was the only sober person in the house; he tore some rags and stuffed them in his ears. He tied the rope around Steadman's wrist and nodded for Gobey to do the same. They stood with slack in the rope, waiting for the doctor – he was swigging at the brandy and belching.

Capper flipped open his case and took out a leather tourniquet. He measured four fingers above Steadman's knee, and as he tightened the cord, the patient broke into song:

> I'm on the ropes again, my son.
> I'm on the ropes again.
> I'm drunk as a skunk, in a right old funk –
> I'm on the ropes again.

The doctor nodded and they restrained Steadman's arms. He turned a surgical knife in his hand, then hacked at the flesh. The blood sprayed up the wall, the roars were deafening, too loud and disorientating for that small room. Steadman bellowed, shunted and writhed, and they had to pin him down.

Capper stepped back from the table. He put down the knife and took up a saw, driving it in steady motion until the leg flopped off. He crouched to catch his breath, wheezing and sucking at the air. Once revived he sprinkled flour on the wound and tightly bound the stump with a white dressing.

Still roaring, Steadman wriggled on the table. Capper slapped his face to calm him. Then without curse or warning, Gobey struck the doctor on the jaw, knocking him against the wall. They stood in silence, sweating and breathless and staring at each other. 'Done,' said the doctor. 'It's over.' He staggered to the table, swigged from the bottle and handed it around.

They sprinkled sawdust over the floor to absorb the blood. The landlord untied the ropes from Steadman's wrists and tossed them in the corner. They passed the bottle and all three of them drank. They leaned on the walls and pushed off again, restless and unable to settle. They scratched their heads and looked at their hands. They paced up and down and couldn't stop sighing. Steadman was silent now, but their ears were still ringing from his earlier shouts.

The doctor was exhausted and packed his bag without cleaning the instruments. Paid in full, he clasped the bottle and made for the door. He was wet and soiled, his shirt splattered with blood. He left with the landlord – weary men heading for the oblivion of drink.

They left the room peaceful behind them. Steadman was twisted on the table, staring vaguely at the ceiling, no size at all without his legs. His face was pimpled with sweat. Gobey placed Steadman next to the fire. He gathered the severed leg in a blanket, removed it to the barn and returned.

Steadman moaned in front of the fire, calling out in a strange gibbering speech. He rummaged beneath the blankets for his missing leg. He shouted at no one in particular. 'Giz it back, giz it back.'

Somewhere along the street, a clock chimed midnight. Gobey sat with the intolerable groans of Steadman filling his head. For half a man, he made one hell of a noise – he rasped and ground his teeth, pointing and stuttering. He called for the old dog and waited for an answer.

Gobey mixed some opium with wine, swallowing it in one gulp. Draped in a blanket he stood at the back door. The horse sensed his presence and began to clop around the barn. He made his way inside and hooked a lantern on a beam. He petted the creature. 'We're friends now, boy. Friends for life.'

He went inside and found Steadman sleeping with his mouth wide open. He looked peaceful, as if nothing had happened. It was easy to imagine there had been no doctor, no butchery. It was only the scattered sawdust that brought the night's atrocity back to life.

Later that night, Steadman was delirious and moaning constantly. Gobey bedded down across the room, but it was difficult to sleep with the noise. And even in his dreams – skating on the river, rocking on a ship's deck, or kissing Eileen against a tree – he could still hear the discordant cries. The night proceeded in a series of naps and sudden awakenings. If only Steadman would fart and laugh in his usual way, all might seem well. But he didn't – he just gasped and moaned and sweated, and called out strange things that had no relevance.

At dawn, Steadman's breath became a rattle, a pebble in a bucket. Each exhalation made a rasp and a whistle. In the dim light, he looked like an old man, gurgling through his open mouth. He had the pallor of marshland mist – boggy eyes, mud skin, a black tide running through him.

Later that morning, Gobey woke from the noise on the street – a clopping dance of hooves, a carriage rocking and an old creaking barrow on the hill. A man was shouting in the distance, driving a herd of pigs through an enclosure. The sweeps were running their brushes up against a wall. The world was in motion outside the window, but inside the silence deepened. He groggily stood and crossed the room to Steadman. He crouched and touched the marbled coolness of his skin, fingering his straggly beard. He held him closely and leaned back to look at him – the crooked shape of his mouth, the blank eyes that would never blink again.

He lifted Steadman to the barn. He was light in his arms. He had never been a well-covered man, was always more bone than flesh, but now he was portable. Gobey put the body in a sack, along with the severed leg. In whatever state, he would take him home – back to the marshes where he belonged.

They rode into the bright morning light, Tom Gobey and his silent friend tied to the saddle behind him. The wind carried the noise from Bedlam around the London Wall, a warped echo of voices following them down to the river.

On the way to London Bridge, he tied the horse to a post and made his way to a beer stall. The vendor was one of these chatty Londoners who would tell you their life story, but Gobey didn't have the will to listen. He paid the man, took the beer and raised a toast to his late friend. He turned to face the horse and found Steadman gone.

He dropped his beer and looked frantically up and down the street. The morning haze obscured his vision, the trodden snow glared in the dazzling light. He turned to the vendor for some explanation, but the man simply shook his head. Gobey looked back towards Houndsditch and spotted a barrow turning a corner. He jumped on the horse and galloped over the track marks left in the snow. He dismounted and asked a boy to look after the horse. The boy had a leery face and pranced in a cocky manner. 'Why should I?' He spat over his shoulder. 'You ain't me boss.'

'I'll pay you.'

'Good as gold.'

Gobey followed the trail through an alley to a courtyard and a tannery with steamed-up windows. The fumes drifted acridly around the square, and a brown liquid seeped under the door, forming a pool in the snow. Opposite, the clattering hammer of a blacksmith echoed off the buildings and bounced around the courtyard. The seething hiss of metal going into water brought a sudden pause for silence – the birds sang beyond the buildings, the barrow boys cried on the street.

He passed a bakery with the powdered faces of the girls looking up – they were slapping dough around a bench. The aroma of fresh bread followed him into a narrow passageway. Further along, a diminutive figure was shoving a barrow through the snow. The plait of Steadman's beard was hanging down, bouncing onto the wheel. He roared along the alley. 'Hey, you! Stop, there! Stop, now!'

He approached with his fist clenched, and an old lady turned to face him. Half-bald and shrivelled, her lips were wrinkled from pipe smoke. Most of her fingers were grazed, as if they had been scraped along a wall. He looked over the contents of her barrow – old shoes, tangled rope, planks of wood, piles of old newspaper.

She stood waiting with no sign of speech. He stepped forward. 'This belongs to me.' *This. This thing. This object you covet, my dead mate.* The old lady made no protest, nor did she attempt to stop him. Gobey gathered Steadman's long beard and folded it out of sight. His face glowed inside the sack. He fastened it,, lifted the body and left with his friend in his drooping arms. He felt sick and dizzy. He could smell dough, blood and treacle, all mixed with the nauseous waft from the tannery.

Two girls came laughing from the bakery and stopped at the sight of him. He wandered towards them with his teeth showing, his face in a snarl. They would have said he was sobbing, but there were no tears, no sound. His waxy eyes washed over them, and they returned to the shop and closed the door with a jingle.

The boy guarding the horse saw him coming and stood mesmerized at his desolate form. Even after being paid, he stood to watch Gobey lay the sack over the saddle. He had never seen a man fling himself so strangely upon a horse – a kind of folding of lifeless limbs, a reckless tumbling. He watched him ride like a ghost through the city – untouched by the surroundings, unmoved by events.

Gobey rode towards the river. The coffee houses were loud and full, the noise tremendous behind the windows. The coal fumes hovered over the rooftops to form a bank of cloud, another world above the city. The alleys were full of shadowy figures, leaning against the walls. The carriages sprayed the slush across the streets, hoards of people were traipsing through the snow.

He rode the horse steadily onto the frozen Thames. Some children were skating up and down, whirling in circles. The stall vendors hollered and beckoned, shaking their chestnuts on crate lids and holding up steaming hot pies. There were tents erected, barrels rolled out to sell beer. Coaches were speeding between Westminster and Temple with the revellers hanging out of the windows. Beyond the puppet booths, horses were raced for wagering men, drinking and swaying and slapping hands to seal deals.

Gobey steered the horse around the frozen boats, the projecting stakes and beams. There was no getting away from thoughts of his dead friend. Steadman was one of these fellows who always had something to say. Now here was jolly Johnny, dead as hoar frost, silent as rust.

He geed the horse and it gathered pace, with its hooves clattering down the river. The ice cracked and creaked behind them. They travelled headlong into the icy wind, passing through the mist. They drove onto the marshes, kicking up the snow behind them. They came to the old house, half-wrecked by the elements and sloping against the skyline.

He buried Steadman in his fur coat, nose to snout with the old dog. He couldn't face going back into the house. It wouldn't be the same without Steadman's laughter. He stood gazing over the marshes and for a split second he was struck by the cycle of birth and death that comes to all people.

He nuzzled the horse for some comfort and could hear the thud of its heart. The wind passed over them and trailed off to the river. He wept and felt the power of weeping, and the depth of raw pain. On hands and knees, he spat and cursed and lay face down in the snow. Wild and furious, he rose with the certainty of one thing – before the sun went down, he would clash with Mr Sticks.

CHAPTER 20

Outside the gunsmith's, a swirl of snow blew across the street. Gobey tethered the horse and watched the people floundering in the snow. The traders pushed their barrows along with the wheels creaking. Two dogs were fighting over some offal in a dark alley. An old woman was shouting at them, shooing them off.

He entered the shop with a jangle of bells above the door. He slowly walked the length of the counter, gazing at the weaponry and not really knowing one gun from another. From behind the counter, the gunsmith faced him. There was lead shot wedged in the gaps of his discoloured teeth. His face was pockmarked from the spray of musket fire, and most of his fingers were stumps. 'Welcome, sir, welcome. Welcome to the best gunnery in town. We've got it all here - precision bores, straight barrels, silver hammers, carved handles. And not just any old cock, but quality gear. Fine metal, class weapons in your hand. Name your fancy, just name it.'

'I need a weapon.'

'How about a blunderbuss?'

'Too big, too heavy.'

'A musket, methinks.' The gunsmith pinched some pellets from a jar and chewed down on them. Either the lead or his teeth were cracking in his mouth. He shuffled forward 'A long-barrelled, keen bored distance shooter. Get it up against your shoulder and fire away.'

'A pistol, I think.'

'Good choice, good choice. A duelling pistol. Long in barrel, fast in hammer, tight in grip. Chestnut, charcoal, slate-grey, tan-brown.'

At the back of the shop, a portly man stood listening from behind the rifle rack. His breeches were stretched across his behind, a line of sweat ran under his gusset. So broad were his feet that the buckles were lopsided on his boots, hanging over the insteps. He watched Gobey at the counter – he had seen that face before and not liked it the first time. Now he was getting palpitations, an inexplicable surge of fury. He closed his eyes and listened to Gobey's voice. By the time he opened them, a shared past was recalled, bitterly remembered.

The man bustled out of the shop and slammed the door behind him. Staggering in the snow, he spat on the horse as he passed. He wobbled across the street into the tavern, shoving by the tables. 'It's him, it's him! Him who done us up!' He huddled with a group of men, speaking through their fingers. Then, all standing at once, their combined weight rocked the boards the length of the room.

The gunsmith leaned further across the counter. Gobey could smell his breath, stale and vinegary. He beckoned with his smoke-stained hands. 'You want something special, a work of art?'

'Anything that fires, anything at all.'

The man dipped beneath the counter like a gannet into water. Shifting boxes and discarding firearms, he didn't appear for some minutes. Then he slowly rose, his mangled face soiled with gun oil. He held a pistol, long and sleek, raised it to the ceiling and brought it down on the glass. He spun it around and watched it rotate – he couldn't take his eyes from it. 'See that?' he nodded. 'That's a masterpiece. God's own hand at work You see it?'

'I see it.'

'Note the long nozzle.'

'I do.'

'You like it?'

'Should do the job.'

'The hammer's heavy for certain contact. You'll have no blockage, no backfire with this boy.'

'Glad to hear it.'

'You won't need a second shot.'

'I can't afford one.'

'Do you know what I call it?'

'I don't.'

'The bishop, boss of the diocese.'

The man swept up the pistol and turned away to a workbench. The back of his jacket was covered with iron filings, and both elbows were showing through the worn material. A short time passed, then he swivelled to the counter with a cloth bag, pulling on the cord. 'Rod, balls, powder and pistol. Loaded to high heaven.'

Gobey felt a terrible rush of adrenaline. He had a good mind to leave the shop without the pistol. 'Here we go, then,' his voice trembled. 'Let's have it, then.'

The man handed it to him. 'God bless the bishop.'

'May the bishop bless me.'

Gobey paid him and left the gunsmith's, slipping the pistol into a saddlebag. He mounted and made a slow clop down to Piccadilly, where the snow was cleared in piles by the roadside. He passed a group of perfumed aristocrats, their sickly fragrance shipped in from France and incongruous among the neighbourhood smells. The snow fell in soft drifts; purblind, he squinted through it. He steered around the barrows and the children sitting in the road. His chest ached for Johnny Steadman. No matter how far he travelled – North Star, ocean blue, mountain peak – the sadness would never leave him.

At Covent Garden, he stopped at the large house where he had spent the night. He dismounted, walked the horse across the road and stood behind it. Someone had spat on its head; he wiped it off with a rag, whispering to the creature. Coming over the hill, he saw Lily, the maid who had tended his wounds. She was struggling to balance, slipping in the snow. He slid the pistol inside his belt, covered it with his jacket. 'Halloa,' he called to her as she approached.

She looked up and a smile struck her face. 'Is it Tom, the one who couldn't walk?'

'It is.'

'Well I never, in all the world. Look how straight you are, how your legs have mended.'

He took her arm and steered her behind the horse. She could feel all his fingers, the arch of his thumb. 'Lily, can you tell me if Mr Sticks is at home?'

'He was when I went out.'

'What room does he use?'

'He ain't got a room. He just hangs about waiting for the master's orders.'

'Can you get him to come out for me?'

Lily pulled away and looked over her shoulder. 'Now listen here, Tom. You've got no business with him. He ain't one of these men to go messing with. I'll tell you that much. Whatever you want, forget it. There's no good to come out of Mr Sticks.'

'I'm desperate to meet him.'

'Well, don't be.'

'I am.'

'What's the game, what you up to?'

'Not much.'

'You are, I can tell. You're going to fight with him. I can see it in your eyes. You mustn't, you really mustn't.'

'There'll be no fighting.'

'Then what business do you have? You haven't come here to shake his hand, I know that much.'

Gobey opened his jacket and revealed the pistol. His eyes ran watery in the breeze. 'He killed me friend, Johnny. Me good friend and his old dog. If I don't come for him, he'll come for me.'

'I'll not send him out, no good will come of it.'

Lily crossed the road, ignoring his calls. She went carefully down the incline and into the side door of the kitchen. Young Bob Docker was seated at the table, buttering bread and eating it in large gulps. A pan was boiling over the fire, but he was paying no attention to it. 'Where's Mrs Hodgers?' She stood beside him. 'Where is she?'

'She's . . .' His mouth was full of tongue and doughy sludge. 'She's . . . I don't know where she is.'

'Have you seen Mr Sticks this morning?'

'No . . . I ain't . . . And I don't want to see him . . . And when I do, I'll knock his block off with this.'

The boy held up the butter knife and Lily snatched it. She slammed it on the table. 'What's wrong with everyone today! All I hear is violence! Now stop stuffing your face and take that pan from the fire. You'll have the whole house burnt down.'

She left by the stairs and went onto the landing. She called out, but the old cook didn't reply. There was a shuffle in one of the rooms, someone was emptying a coal scuttle into the hearth. She rushed inside and Mr Sticks skipped around her, blocking the doorway. He was chewing coal, the black fragments dotted his teeth and gums. He fiddled with his trousers. 'Wanna see the cock crow, wanna see it rise?'

'No, I don't.'

'Well you're gonna.'

'Please, Mr Sticks. Let me go.'

'Not until I've cocked ya.'

'I've something important to tell you.'

'You ain't.'

'I have, I really have. It's about one of your friends.'

'I ain't got none.'

'It's true,' she pleaded. 'There's someone outside to see you.'

He pushed her against the window, ran his fingers through her hair. The gritty specks on his lips felt sharp against her neck. He shook her head and jeered into her face. 'No one wants to see me.'

'He's outside! Waiting for you!'

He laughed and spat at the pane above her, the black saliva drizzling down the glass. He ran his hand across her face, squashing her nose. 'Who is? Who's outside, waiting for me?'

'Tom Gobey!'

He shunted back and slipped on the floor, his trousers tangled at his ankles. He clambered to his feet, fastened his belt and rushed out of the room. Leaping halfway down the stairs, he sprung onto the next landing. Young Bob watched silently as he surged into the kitchen. 'Where's me tools?'

'What?'

'Me tools, where the hell are they?'

The boy pointed to the cupboard, and Mr Sticks threw open the doors. He dropped to his knees, scattering pots and pans around the kitchen. He left with a mallet raised to his shoulder. He gnawed his top lip and sucked through his teeth.

From across the street Gobey watched the door slowly open. Mr Sticks stepped outside. They stood, pensive and motionless, inspecting each other. Two carriages passed between them on the road. When the way cleared, Mr Sticks had gone. Gobey drew the pistol, his breath smoked before him. A church bell rang in the distance, a dog barked on the hill. He gazed over at the house, along the railings and down the steps.

Gobey moved away from the horse. The wind brushed his face, making him shut his eyes. Struck from the side, he went down in the snow, the pistol skittering away from him. From the ground, through the horse's legs, he could see the weapon, but a shower of boots drove him down. He rolled in a ball for protection, someone kicked the soles of his feet and a sack came over his head. He was bundled into a carriage and shunted across the floor. Curled in a ball, he felt the wheels start rolling, the vehicle jerk away. Someone tied his hands in front of him, removed his money belt

They travelled for some time, but he couldn't tell in what direction. The sack was coarse against his face, letting in little light. He listened to the voices on the street and tried to conjure the location – the hawkers were calling, their cries echoed around the walls and courtyards. The carriage wheels locked and freed on the ice, he thought they were briefly on the river, coming off the other end. They continued for miles on a road without turning. He could sense the city falling away behind them – distant voices, inn banter, tavern song, the far-flung rumble of carriage traffic. They stopped and the coachman climbed down to open a creaking gate. They left the road, crossed a field and ascended a hill. He could smell the soil, the mush of leaves.

A bottle was glugged in the carriage, the whisky fumes drifted around him. There were two men inside, laughing and joking and spitting out of the window. They were Londoners – south of the river. They used him as a footrest, roughly resting their boots on his head and shoulders. He remained still, stifling coughs and stemming his breath.

The carriage slowed, shuddered and rocked to a halt. They shunted him out, onto the ground, rolling him over with their boots. Another carriage pulled up behind, with the horses panting and the men alighting from the vehicle. Gobey clambered to his feet, someone tugged the sack from his head. He stood blinking, gazing at the men – five or six hefty uglies. They had new boots, tapered jackets and fine breeches. Two stood out from the gang – a tall flabby man with a drooping chin, his features lost in the colonizing fat of his head. Smiling cockily, the other man munched on a ball of tobacco, the juice dribbling down his jacket in a brown streak.

The flabby man stepped forward and poked Gobey's chest. 'Remember me? I'm sure ya do – ya must do. I'm Blangerd, and this is Mr Topper.'

'I don't know you. There must be some mistake.'

Blangerd scratched his head, his lips were taut and protruding. 'There's no mistake. We met before, didn't we?'

'I can't recall.'

'We met on the dock. Ya stole me money belt and threw me whip in the river.'

'I stole nothing.'

Gobey leaned back against the carriage, grateful that no one was behind him. His stomach churned and his legs were quivering, the metallic taste of saliva slid into his throat. He furtively searched for an escape route, but could see no obvious way of shaking off the men. The fields were thick with snow, rising to the sky – the woods stood stark with bare trees. From the other side of the carriage, he heard the distinctive whinnying of his own horse. He tried to locate its position, to assess the distance between them.

The sack went over his head, and the men tied him to the back of the vehicle. They climbed inside and he could hear them laughing. They set off, leaving the other carriage behind. He was seated on a ledge, his legs dangling above the ground.

Gobey removed the sack, tossing it into a bush. Nightfall was seeping through the pines, touching down on the wooded undergrowth. The darkness crept along the path and the stars appeared like a random tossing of dice. His trembling kept him awake, his jaw shuddering as he hummed involuntarily. He tried to use his teeth to free his bound wrists, but they chattered off the rope. Tugging and twisting, he tried to free his hands, until friction burns scarred his wrists. He spoke to his horse which was trailing behind on a rein. When he whispered, it rolled its soft eyes and nodded in some strange benediction to him.

They turned off a rocky road and travelled along a track with hedges on either side. They passed a lake with the ice sparkling on the surface. There was movement out in the middle, something glowing in the dark. He thought it might be swans, waiting for the lake to thaw.

They came to a large manor house, surrounded by sprawling acres of land. The windows were lit with lanterns. When the carriage stopped, the servants came running from all directions. Blangerd shooed them away, shouting orders for the cook across the courtyard.

They manacled Gobey at the wrists and ankles, led him to an old barn away from the house. They shoved him inside and locked the door. The darkness seemed absolute, perpetual – the world might have ended beneath the blanket of night. Jangling in his chains, he shuffled through the dark and slumped on the ground. He gathered some hay that was scattered about him, placing it over his limbs to drive out the cold. He moaned without knowing he was moaning.

Outside, an owl hooted and another replied in a haunting echo. The rats scurried among the grain, squealing and bickering in the dark. A rattle of shackles came from across the barn. Someone climbed to their feet and jangled closer to him. A lantern was uncovered and the silhouette of a huge man stood above him. 'Brother in chains.'

CHAPTER 21

The barn was cold and inhospitable. The man inside was an African, also chained and somewhat accustomed to those chains. His wrists and ankles were pale and calloused from years of imprisonment. Resigned to his fate, he was unmoved by his predicament. He took deep measured breaths, each one precious in a life where everything else had been taken away. He knew that barn intimately, like the gnarled fingers of his own hand. From one corner to the other, he could count the paces without crossing that space. There was not a place in the dirt where his feet had not trodden

He stood over Gobey and they listened to the wind shaking the treetops. An owl glided through the forest to land on the barn. They heard its claws scratch on the roof.

The African loomed over him, his face obscured by the lantern light. He tilted his head to listen. 'Owls,' said Gobey. 'Night birds, winter spirits.'

The African came closer – a big man, leaner than he should have been. His clothes were ragged sackcloth, tailored by his own hands. He held the lantern to his face, revealing the scored lines of his tribal marks – a noble disfigurement. He crouched with his knees cracking like nuts. 'Brother,' he said. 'We have crossed the same path. I have not forgotten you.'

Gobey squinted in the dim light of the barn. The air was blue around the lantern. He took some time to fathom the African. 'We've met, you say.'

'You remember me. Some time ago, I was on the dock. I am Okoye.'

'Tom Gobey.'

'You quarrelled with the slavers.'

'And look where it got me.'

'You tried to help me.'

'I remember.' Gobey's eyes sparkled in the darkness. 'You were being flogged.'

The African smiled with great gaps between his teeth. There were notches in his head, marks where the skin had hardened and the hair fallen out. He sniffed and nodded. 'One day, I hope to live in freedom.'

'One day, I hope you get the chance.'

The African lit some candles and placed them in a circle around them. The barn was strewn with grain and straw, cowpats and husks of dung among the hay. There were sacks and crates stacked in the corner, where the rats flipped and ran up the walls.

The African stood tall, looking down at Gobey. Scattering the hay, he stooped to look closer, shutting one eye. He gasped, shook his head and gasped again, flaring his nostrils. 'These are very bad men.'

'I seem to attract them.'

'You are very tired.'

'I am,' Gobey nodded. 'Most weary indeed. Me head thinks me body's sleeping.'

The African laughed. 'Then you must rest. Take good rest.'

'I will, I will.'

Gobey rolled over and closed his eyes. Sore and fatigued, he could barely move without discomfort. The room spun and the mice were squealing in his head – they scratched among the straw. He slept for an hour and woke to the odd sound of his own humming, a vibration in his ears. He didn't know where he was or, for a moment, how he'd got there. The fire crackled, the shadows of the flames whipped over the beams. The African knelt and helped him to drink from a cup – a warm beefy, fragrant liquid. It soothed his throat and cleared his nasal passages. He couldn't say what it was, and didn't much care.

He sat up and the weight of his chains almost brought him down again. He took the cup and drank unaided, sip after sip in slow succession. His face was stiff from the cold, stony and hard. His ears were not fully sounding the world around him – things were muffled, slightly delayed in transmission.

The African looked him up and down. 'Good,' he said. 'Much improved, much rested.' He sat at the fire and gazed across at his large feet, his bulging calves each side of the shinbones. The smoke drifted into his face, but he didn't flinch or choke or make any attempt to avoid it.

They smiled and nodded – men enslaved – they shared the same bruises, had cracked the same bones. Both had been rocked on the ocean, sent to lands afar. Both had incessantly dreamed of their native land.

'So, Tom Gobey. We find ourselves in a little trouble.'

'We do, Okoye. We do.'

They laughed wholeheartedly. They drank the African's broth, the fire smoke drifting around them. They spoke with the ease of old friends, talking of their lives before confinement. They spoke as men without caste – nothing but honesty passed between them, nothing they said was misunderstood.

Lost in conversation, the African suddenly held up a finger. His speech tailed off a falling away like a soft wind. Some voices crept slowly into the night and drifted along the outside of the barn. The door unlocked and swung open with a shudder. Two slavers entered with a lantern on a string, carrying the strong odour of stale whisky on their breath.

Topper sniffed and spat. The men passed a flask between them, they drank and winced as they swallowed. Blangerd turned to Gobey, 'Found a friend, have ya?'

'Looks like.'

The men stood without purpose or guile, hypnotized by the fire. For a moment, they didn't seem much inclined for violence as they drank under the spell of the flames. Then Blangerd beckoned with his podgy hand. 'Come with me, Blackjack – the women want amusing.'

The African rose slowly and shuffled in a peculiar way. Before the men arrived, he had been walking without any problem – now he sluggishly crossed the barn. Head down, he plodded past the sacks of grain, tramping the hay to reach them. They took an arm each and tried to rush him, but he hung heavy on them. They shoved him outside, slammed the door and locked it.

Blangerd horsewhipped his legs, but the slave didn't flinch, nothing changed in his demeanour. They shoved him as best they could across the courtyard, yelping insults and tugging at his hair. They spoke nonsense into his face, their fiery breath a repulsive invasion. Their hands clasped his throat and shook his head like fruit on a tree. They peered into his eyes, but he simply closed them – they thumbed them open and he closed them again.

The women were seated in an arc, with colourful drinks and fruit on a low table. In anticipation of the slave's arrival, they couldn't keep still – they twiddled their ringlets, adjusting the feathers in their hair. Their long floral dresses trailed on the carpet. They talked over and across each other – it was difficult to hear any one voice in the room. The collective volume made a tremendous uproar.

The African stood in the doorway, crouching beneath the frame. They gazed up at him, and a current of laughter shot between them. Their bare arms prickled with goosebumps, their voices ebbed to a low hum. Blangerd's wife, Celia, clapped her hands with excitement.

The African kept his head bowed and his eyes averted. He could smell them, like the waft of boar downwind from a stream – the hunter's nose, sharp and responsive Blangerd shoved Okoye from behind and he stumbled into the room to stand before them.

The women squealed and wriggled ecstatically before the slave. Glancing down, he could feel their tense expectancy, their electrically charged movements. He listened to their chatter – words of no particular meaning. They flitted from one subject to the next without taking their eyes from him – his chiselled face, his broad shoulders, his lean legs. They laughed, shrieked and tittered. They might have carried on like this, but for Celia clapping her hands. They looked to her as if she might deliver a speech. She pointed to the slave. 'Blackjack,' she commanded. 'Walk to the hearth and back again.'

The slave didn't move. The women grew silent. Celia sensed their awkward presence around her – someone feigning a cough, someone shifting their feet on the carpet. When the slave's inaction became intolerable, she went to call again, but saw he was moving, after all – moving in a sleepy manner. 'There,' she waved her hand. 'What do you think of that, ladies?'

The women scrutinized his painstaking journey across the room. Each slow step had them twitchy and uncomfortable in their seats. They looked to each other, then back to the slave, and seconds passed without them speaking. It was such a test to their patience that Celia called out, 'Blackjack. Stop now. That's enough, come back.'

The African stood still while the women chattered, but he was listening to the men in the other room. Behind him, they were discussing Gobey in black, unholy words – 'Dead meat, worm meal.'

The women left their chairs and walked around the slave. They touched the back of his neck and examined their fingers for staining. They tugged his hair, thumbed his lips and nostrils, gazed intently at his teeth. Up and down, they scrutinized his body. He endured their advances, slowly bending or shifting as required. Their perfume was overpowering, turning his stomach and making him giddy.

When the women had tired of his presence, Celia clapped her hands for him to be taken away. The men staggered into the room, steadied themselves and tried to stand upright, leaning against each other like toppled posts. They shoved the African from the room, tugging his smock to make him go faster. Outside, they kicked his rump, cursing into his face and pinching his ears. He didn't yelp or make any discernible effort to speak. Whatever the insult, whatever the blow, it washed over him, and he kept to his slow way of moving. They slapped the back of his neck and tried to poke a finger in his eye, but he kept turning away.

Kicking at the back of his legs, they brought him to his knees. He stumbled forward, gripping Blangerd, and the slaver panicked to get him off. Together they reeled and stumbled until the African suddenly pushed away. He rose slowly and with great dignity looked down upon them. Inside his fist he held a key, carefully selected from a ring on Blangerd's belt.

Gobey stirred from sleeping, hearing their laughter approaching, their drunken voices in the night. The slow jig of the African's chains crossed the courtyard, then the barn door creaked open. They shoved Okoye inside, slamming and locking the door. He stood motionless, staring at the ground. When the men departed, he began walking in his usual manner.

Gobey watched him in the firelight. Nimble in his chains, lifting and dragging them as he moved, the African crossed the barn and was lost in the shadows. He bent down and his knees creaked, he pounded something, grinding it with some makeshift pestle. After snapping some twigs and tying them together, he made a four-legged frame with a long shaft. He returned, placed the frame over the fire and hooked a pot on it, stirring the ingredients with a wooden spoon. A short time later, he poured the contents into a bowl and handed it to Gobey.

Gobey sipped and swallowed. 'What is it?'

'Soup.'

'What kind of soup?'

'A very delicious soup.'

'What kind?'

'One made from rats.'

They passed the bowl back and forth. The African produced a biscuit and halved it. They ate without speaking, crunching down on the brittle husk with the fire crackling and hissing. The horses in a nearby stable shuffled and neighed – their piss crashed against the ground. A carriage arrived at the house and left, with the women singing their goodbyes.

Gobey spoke across the fire. 'I suppose they'll take me to the magistrate in the morning. Have me up for stealing the money belt.'

The African shook his head with some certainty. 'You will not go to the magistrate.'

'What makes you say that?'

'They are waiting.'

'Waiting? Waiting for what?'

'For the ice to leave the lake.'

Gobey sat up, groaning from the effort. 'When the ice leaves the lake? What does that mean?'

'I have heard the men talking.'

'About me?'

'About you.'

The African broke some sticks and placed them on the fire. He closed his eyes for a few seconds, his face morose and drooping at the mouth.

Gobey pressed him again. 'Do they have a plan for me?'

'They have a plan.'

'Tell me, do.'

The African sat motionless for a moment. Then he pointed across the barn without looking up. Gobey ran his eyes over the sacks of grain, the stacked boxes, a heap of firewood. He looked back to Okoye, who was still pointing with his head down. Again, he followed the line of his finger to the wall, until he noticed a large rusty anchor. 'What of it?' Gobey tried to gain his full attention. 'What about it?'

The African nodded, running his hand backwards over his scalp. He drew his knees against his chest and peered over the top of them. His large hands were limp, like broken wings. It took a long time for him to speak, and then he eventually said, 'You are going in the lake.'

The African withdrew from the fire, making himself scarce among the shadows, breaking twigs and snaring rats. Through some feat of magic, he managed to stifle his chains, holding them and gathering the links. In the corner, he sat with his legs crossed, a low chant vibrating through the barn.

Gobey rolled in the hay and closed his eyes while the guards paced around the barn with a lantern. He tried to sleep, but couldn't keep still. He tossed in his chains, and each time he settled, the African's murmurs came drifting through the smoky air. The wind howled in the distance. Then, like a landing of starlings on the roof, the rain came spraying.

He thought of Eileen and choked, wept into his hands. He could hear owls calling across the lake, their cries reverberating over the ice. The rain was constant, pounding the mud and sluicing away in pools. Again, he tried to sleep, but couldn't quell the pandemonium of his mind. And he knew, beyond all doubt, there was nothing in the wind, out among the stars – Gods, spells or talisman – nothing in the power of man to stop the next day coming.

CHAPTER 22

Saffronetti was on the verge of a tantrum. For days Eileen Dineen had been defying his orders, ignoring his pleas. She would not look at him, would not acknowledge his existence. It was driving him wild and further into the refuge of opium. He wanted all the things he couldn't have – love, manhood, revived fame.

He stood with his legs together, arms stretched like one crucified He looked to the ceiling as if to the heavens, as if some greater power might look favourably upon him.

None did.

He flung a chair across the room, kicked another that toppled backwards. Throwing a plate down, he jumped upon it until it broke. He ran across the bed in a mad dash to get nowhere. He stepped down and stood close to the wall, mumbling into the cold stone. He flitted from one place to another, visiting all corners of the room. He tugged the curtain and pulled it down, draping himself and twirling until dizzy. He crawled under the bed for a new perspective. He began to sing, but the altered acoustics did not please him. He crawled out and rolled over the broken plate, weeping and protesting as if someone had forced him to crawl there.

In the room along the landing, Eileen Dineen stood gazing at the mirror. She was always aware of Saffronetti's movements. He fell silent, and couldn't fall far enough for her liking. From downstairs someone was shrieking, she thought it was Lily, larking about with the boy. She listened for laughter, but heard some strangled form of her name.

She tried the door expecting it to be locked, but Mr Sticks was sometimes negligent and had not locked it. She went onto the landing and paced along to listen at Saffronetti's door. He struck the walls and crashed into the furniture. She pictured the scene inside – boot marks on the bed, handprints on the mirror, carnage all around – Saffronetti beleaguered in despair, not a shred of hope to cling to.

She skipped down the back stairs and along the corridor to the front entrance of the house. The servants were gathered in the hallway. Mr Stanley stood in front of the boy, trying to shield his eyes. Mrs Hodgers was wrestling with Mr Sticks, swaying on her short legs. He had Lily pushed against the banister and was working through her underwear.

'You!' Eileen screamed, leaving the staircase. 'You evil bastard!'

Mr Sticks turned towards her. Eileen swung a punch that crashed down against his mouth, sending one of his teeth flying. The stained incisor clipped the banister and landed on Saffronetti's shoe as he appeared on the stairs. He looked down at the tooth, then at the group standing below. 'What's going on in my house? Why is everyone gathered like a revolutionary mob?'

He came inelegantly down the stairs to join them. His white suit was soiled in many places, and a crust had gathered at the corners of his mouth. The stale odour of his breath travelled down the hall like leaking gas. 'Well,' he said. 'Am I to be ignored in my own house?'

The servants looked to Miss Eileen, her face wild and flushed. She shook her throbbing fist and pointed to Mr Sticks. 'That bastard's been touching my maid.' Saffronetti's head darted like a bird between them. She could see he had taken opium, but wasn't stupefied – he'd been crying as usual, drenched in dejection, and there was a slant of cruelty in his eyes. 'Mr Sticks,' she said, lowering her voice and speaking more calmly, 'Has been forcing himself on young Lily.'

Saffronetti approached the maid, who recoiled before him. He lifted her dress. Her thighs were bruised and her underwear ripped, and she had finger marks all over her legs. He turned abruptly to the old cook. 'Get rid of her and find me another.'

Mrs Hodgers gasped and looked to the servants with her mouth still open. She shuffled her feet, waved her arms, the goitre seemed to fill her throat. 'Oh, no! Not Lily! Please, not Lily, sir. She's a good girl, such a good girl. She's never been any trouble, never. God knows she's no trouble at all. Never has been, never will be.'

'Find me an ugly maid. One that Mr Sticks will not bother.

Perhaps an old girl like yourself. One that has dried up a bit, has nothing to offer a man. Get me one of those.'

'With the greatest respect, sir, the greatest respect. It won't make no difference to Mr Sticks. He don't care whether they're young or old, chick or child. It's all the same to him. All the same, night or day – no one in the house is safe. If you don't mind me saying, he's not what you would call *natural* in the way of loving. All doors are open to him.'

'Don't lecture me in the way of things natural. Get rid of the maid, or you'll find yourself joining her. Do you understand? I'll have you all replaced, each and every one of you.'

Saffronetti went back upstairs, adjusting his sleeves. He flicked his hair and spoke over the banister. 'Have her out by nightfall.'

Mrs Hodgers embraced Lily and they swayed from side to side. The maid was inconsolable. She buried her face on the old cook's shoulder and muffled a garbled account of the day's events. Eileen gathered the group and led them towards the kitchen. Mr Sticks was left behind, standing aimlessly in the hallway leaning against the wall. His tongue poked through the newly formed gap in his teeth.

The boy broke free to confront Mr Sticks. 'You horrible-bastard! You short-arsed little dwarf!'

Mr Sticks tilted his head in a dreamy state of vacancy. It took a few seconds for him to acknowledge the insult – *horrible bastard, short little dwarf.* Insulted by a boy who runs errands, a boy without position or esteem. He approached young Bob to do damage, but was called away by the master. On the stairs, his face was a numb mask, his teeth grinding. Up he climbed with his muscled shoulders, his mastiff neck tense. Pointing at the boy without speaking, he was unable to disguise the fury in his blood.

That night, on the eve of Lily's departure, Eileen crept along the landing. She slipped inside Saffronetti's room and picked up a ring from the bureau. From the drawers, she took gems, lockets and a pearl necklace of bluish-grey. On the cabinet she found a pocket watch, a silver pendant and, among the bed sheets, a purple brooch like a large ladybird. She wrapped them in a newspaper and left with the parcel under her arm.

She entered the kitchen, dimly lit with candles. There was a lantern on the table, shimmering behind a red glass. The night held black at the window as if someone had painted it there – static, obsidian, impenetrable – a night with no give, no forgiveness.

Lily sat huddled with the servants who were trying to console her. Eileen crossed the room and tucked the parcel into her pocket. 'What is it, Miss?'

'Hush,' she put a finger to her lips. 'Tell no one – no one at all.'

'Yes, Miss.'

'Good girl.'

She knelt to kiss the maid's forehead, to stroke her long, unkempt hair. They embraced and let go, then embraced again. They smiled with wet puffy faces, eyes that were half-red from crying. They made vows and promises that unknown to them would never be fulfilled.

Like a band of weary mourners, they drifted onto the street and stood in a queue to say their goodbyes. One by one they embraced the maid and turned away.

The carriage left with Lily visible at the window. They stood sobbing at the roadside, none more so than young Bob Docker. He wept into his hands and cursed at the ground, dragging his feet and twisting his shoulders. He spat and tried to talk, but no words came out. Eileen put her arm around him. 'Oh, sweetheart. Don't fret, now. She'll come back to visit, she's promised to. She'll be back very soon, I'm sure.'

The boy looked up at her. His face was wet and embittered. 'I love her, Miss. I love Lily so much, I've always loved her.'

She kissed his forehead. 'We all do, sweetheart. We all do.'

'It's that Mr Sticks. It's his fault. I hate him, Miss. I really hate him.'

'We all do, sweetheart. We all do.'

That evening, the boy went sulkily to his bed and sobbed in the darkness. He couldn't sleep with the wind bashing the window. He rolled over and back again, over and over, until the covers were tangled on his feet.

Mr Stanley retired for the night and found him sitting on the bed, face in hands. He tousled the lad's hair. 'What's the matter, boy?'

'Nothing. Nothing at all.'

'Now come on. It's me you're talking to. I've known you long enough to know when something's wrong. You've got the miseries, I can see it.'

'I miss Lily.'

'All of us do, boy. Each and every one of us.'

'But I love her.'

'Love, you say.'

'I know she's older and I'm only a boy, but I love Lily with all me heart.'

Mr Stanley stood up, stretched his arms and yawned in a way that wasn't a yawn. His mouth opened and made a noise, but there was no real tiredness in him. 'Young fellow,' he said, 'It's getting late, we have a busy day tomorrow. We're a maid down and have plenty of work to do. You go to bed now and have a good rest, things will seem better in the morning.'

The boy got into bed, turned over, closed his eyes and listened to the wind. One of his legs was twitching beneath the covers. He thought he could smell the river, the wild old Thames. Then he was drifting, a bottomless fall to the land of Nod.

Eileen woke and listlessly swung out of bed. Her dreams were a blur of some distant past. The rain pebbled the window and she gradually stirred to full consciousness. She dressed speedily and somewhat nervously. She had waited so long for this day, and now hardly knew how to approach it. Today, she would meet her sweetheart at the bone-setter's, but first must dislodge a bone. She swept the room for a suitable instrument. She opened a drawer in the bureau and rocked it up and down. Placing her fingers over the edge, she closed her eyes and considered the crushing of them. She pulled away to find another method of destruction – something tolerable, something quick.

She wandered to the shelf and lifted an ornamental vase. She clasped it to her breast, and held it as if cradling a child. She raised it with both hands, but couldn't think of how, or where to strike. She placed it down and considered how a chair might be used to crack a bone.

She stood with her back against the wall, breathing heavily. Unable to inflict the injury, she knew Saffronetti would oblige if provoked. She got dressed and went to find him, but he wasn't in his bedchamber. Rushing through the house, she ran into Mrs Hodgers leaving one of the rooms. 'What ever's the matter, Miss Eileen? Heavens above, what's wrong?'

'Where's the master, where is he?'

'Why he's gone out, taken the carriage.'

She paced along the corridor, with the old cook following. She trotted down the stairs and made for the front door, but Mr Sticks blocked the way. 'Where ya going?'

'Out.'

'No, you ain't. Not without the master's permission, you ain't.'

Mrs Hodgers coaxed her into the drawing room and sat her down, leaving when she seemed calmer. Eileen waited in the armchair, staring at the fire and listening to life on the street – the wheels of the coaches going over the hill, some passing men laughing.

She paced the room to look for a bludgeoning tool. She took up the poker and measured a blow against her forearm, but instead threw it at the fire, scattering the ash. She caught sight of her pale face in the mirror and stared at her reflection. Her face looked wild and alien.

The master's peremptory voice could be heard on the street as the horses came to a halt outside. He was hardly inside the front door when she reared on him: 'You bastard! Reinstate my maid, you bastard!' He brushed past without acknowledging her, flicking his hair. He marched on, ignoring her pleas and waving his hand dismissively. She thundered behind him and he started to sing, with his voice ringing off the walls.

'You call yourself a man. A man has hair on his chin, balls to swing, a cock to work a woman.'

He turned, so incensed he could barely breathe. He charged and struck her shoulder. She spun into the wall, banging her head and flopping down. He kicked her with his dainty shoes, cracking his toes. Wincing, he kicked again, over and over, like a demented child.

She cradled her head, the room whirled into darkness. She curled in a ball with her chin tucked in, but he continued to kick and dance upon her. Then it all stopped. Saffronetti staggered breathlessly away from her. He ascended the stairs, moaning and weeping and calling out to the servants. Eileen remained motionless on the floor.

Mr Sticks came down the stairs and lifted Eileen in his arms. He marched purposefully from the house, jostling the servants aside. They followed him onto the street, mumbling behind their hands and nudging each other.

Mr Sticks flung open the carriage door and shoved Eileen inside. She could smell his soiled hands, his filthy clothes. Her collarbone was dislocated, there were footprints on her dress, her hair was sticky with blood. She glanced through the window and Young Bob was staring back at her. He raised his hand and tried to smile, but his eyes were wild and murderous .

Mr Sticks sauntered to the front of the carriage. He took the coachman's seat, geed the horses with a curse, and they shuffled to life. Jerking the reins, he cursed once more and the wheels began to creak through the slushy mud.

The old cook put her arm around the boy, whose face was pale and sweaty. 'Mother of God,' she said. 'You look unwell, young Bob. Whatever's the matter?'

The boy would not look at her – his eyes had a deadness, a blank stare. 'I'm going to get him,' he said. 'Do him in.'

'Do who in?'

The boy ignored her and left her embrace, pointing at something across the road. He wandered like one fresh from sleep, half-dreaming and unsteady as he walked. He crouched down and rose with a sleek pistol in his hand.

Mrs Hodgers coughed and hollered. 'Hey, me lad. Be careful with that. Bring it to me. Bring it to me, now.' She shuffled into the road, yelling and waving her arms.

The boy was oblivious to her cries. He ran and clung onto the back of the moving carriage and was swept away. Mr Stanley pleaded for him to drop the weapon, but the boy was determined in this rare show of disobedience. He departed in the London mist, their strident calls falling on deaf ears.

The carriage hurtled into Covent Garden, awash with mud and horse dung. The road was coloured from the overspill of a tannery, the greasy mud glistened with iridescent shades. They drove through the coal smoke into the aroma of coffee houses.

They arrived at the bone-setter's in a mizzling rain. Mr Sticks climbed down and swung the carriage door open, dragging Eileen towards him, tearing her dress and rolling her over. Her face was a pale moon, a creamy white flan of suffering. He stood her against the vehicle, her shoulder crooked, her head drooping. He gripped her under the armpit, and bundled her through the doorway like a sack of coal.

The boy waited at the back of the carriage. He waited in the rain with the city wild about him. He didn't know what day it was, or what duties he should be attending at the house. Nor did he care. He held the pistol tight – it felt like some strange talisman that might alter the future, rearrange the past.

An hour later, he was still waiting, pale and shivering in the cold atmosphere. Then came voices. Miss Eileen, her arm in a sling, climbed into the carriage. Mr Sticks rolled his shoulders, revolved his head and spun to close the door with his heel.

The bone-setter limped onto the street. It was hard to distinguish her eyes among her swollen head. Her face was horribly beaten, a misshapen mass. She was hunched like a puppet, one arm hanging below the other. Her knuckles were grazed, the fingers bent and disfigured.

Mr Sticks shoved her with his fist. 'Get him down to that river, ya hear me?' She nodded with her face to the ground and leaned against a lamp post. He shook her by the hair until her lips wobbled. 'You get him down to that river.'

He jerked himself onto the carriage and shook the reins. They started out against the wind, the spray of drizzle, the horses clopping through the sludge. They made a slow rocking passage down to the Thames, which was still frozen but starting to thaw. The river was deserted, strewn with debris and trampled vegetables on the ice. The cart traffic was a low hum among the distant cries of barrow boys.

They crossed the ice and settled beneath the arch of a bridge. The horses were agitated, their eyes darkly sorrowful. The boy crouched on the back of the carriage, waiting in the cold.

CHAPTER 23

The dawn arrived with crashing rain. Thunder rumbled and the barn shook as if under cannon fire. Tom Gobey woke with a jolt. He was aching all over. His clothes were damp and provided little warmth.

The African sat by the fire, the smoke billowing around his face. He'd been sitting there all evening. His skin blue in the first light of dawn, he seemed to be sleeping with his eyes open.

Gobey sat up. 'The rain's here.'

The African remained still with his eyes hooded. After a few minutes, he took a stick and unhooked a pot from the fire. He stirred the ingredients round and round. He stared into the pot as if the heavens had dropped there. He eventually transferred the contents to a bowl and handed it to Gobey.

'I can't,' he said, waving it away. His hands were shaking, his eyes were watery. The percolations of his gut brought bile to his throat. He stared across to the old rusty anchor and was close to weeping.

They sat in silence, hunched like old men over the fire. A gust of wind swept by the barn, a whoosh of rain struck the mud outside. The mice scurried in the shadows.

Gobey quaked, shuddered and wept into his hands. 'If only I could see her, one last time. Just for a minute, one minute – one last time.'

The African sat motionless in his chains. He mumbled something incomprehensible – a chant or a mantra – once, twice, thrice. Then he spoke in a whisper. 'You will see her. You will see your sweetheart.'

'I've no faith.'

'You will see her again. One day, one day.'

They heard voices on the path, boots in the mud, a cough and a spit. Someone was cursing – cursing the rain. The creaking wheels of a barrow travelled around the barn. The door swung open, the men ducked inside in their long coats, their faces wet and shiny, their hair and noses dripping. Blangerd and Topper stepped forward with a miserable band of men. The fire flattened and rose as the wind passed through, scattering ash in a mist.

They stood over Gobey, looking down. Lifting him by the elbows, he buckled at the knees and they had to prop him upright. They smelt of stale whisky and sweat. The other men wrestled the anchor onto the barrow – it crashed down with the dust flying.

The men wheeled the anchor outside. Blangerd and Topper stood in the barn each side of Gobey, wiping their feet in the straw, freeing the mud from their boots. They passed a whisky bottle between them and drank greedily. Shuffling about, bored with the waiting, they had nothing much to say, other than to curse the rain.

After a while, a muffled voice came from outside – a roar from the distance, it rose three times, then faded. The men led Gobey by the arms and he turned back to Okoye. 'All the luck in the world,' he said. 'All the luck in the world to you.' But the African didn't look at him – he remained stationary, transfixed by the drama of the fire.

They went outside and braced themselves against the rain. Gobey was stiff with fear and his balls had shrunk to small stones. His thoughts were random – Eileen's green eyes, Steadman's laughter, his faithful horse loose on the marshes and pounding away. He was distracted by inconsequential things – rain dripping from the branches, a magpie chirping in the undergrowth, a flock of geese spearing overhead towards some new horizon.

They passed in front of the manor house and rose on a mud-drenched hill. Below on the lake, a boat was attached to the pier. A pellicle of ice partially covered the water, the rain sheeted across the surface.

They led him onto the boat and sat down. The vessel swayed, nosing into the water with the weight of the anchor. Blangerd rowed out, the blotchy airbags of his cheeks growing florid. Topper rolled a ball of tobacco under his top lip, mocking Gobey in an ape-like gesture, showing his teeth and giggling with his mouth full. There was nothing to do but look away – look away and try not to leave this world with that lasting image.

Once out in the middle of the lake, Blangerd stopped rowing. The water slapped against the sides, spilling onto their feet. They worked Gobey to the front of the boat, unlocking the shackles on his ankles. Topper fed the chain through the eye of the anchor and secured the manacles. The men moved behind him. Blangerd raised the oar, then a voice boomed across the water.

The African was on the bank, calling out to them. He had used the stolen key to unshackle himself, and had sneaked out of the barn through a broken panel that he worked loose. Now he stood behind Blangerd's wife, Celia, his hands around her throat. She was in her nightdress, splattered with mud from crossing the hill, and barely able to stand. They could hear her sobbing from the bank.

The African called again, 'Unchain Tom Gobey! Unchain that man, or I'll choke her like a chicken!'

The men stood silently with the boat rocking – it was the first time they'd heard the slave speak. His face glistened silver in the rain, his shoulders looked colossal above her. He gripped her tighter with his bony hands and she screamed.

Blangerd undid the manacles and shouted across the water, 'He's free! I've set him free! Let her go now – let her go!'

Blangerd held up his hands in surrender. Gobey took the key from him, clamped one leg each of the men and secured the irons to the anchor. He shoved them to the end of the boat and sat to take up the oars. As he started to row the boat tilted, the anchor slipped overboard and the men hurtled with it – arms flailing, screaming and thrashing around. He scrambled to reach them, but they had gone beneath the surface. He stood in the rain with the boat see-sawing, only foam to mark the spot of their departure.

He sat until the boat steadied, until his breath grew calm. Celia was hysterical, shrieking and howling from the bank. He tried not to listen. He rowed with the overhead clouds blowing in a colossal line, a vast migration reflecting on the water. His mind inhabited the bottom of the lake – its silent screams, blubbery men with billowing faces.

He abandoned the boat at the shore, crossed the pier and looked back over the lake for any movement. Nothing stirred. Celia fled back to the house, wailing her husband's name, as if he might rise from the lake like a drowned Lazarus.

He and Okoye crossed the hill and made their way back to the stables. Gobey saddled his own horse. 'Can you ride, Okoye?

'Most well.'

The African returned the money belt that Gobey had so regrettably acquired those few days ago. They rode the gravel track from the manor house, side by side. They came to a lane with the rain sieving through the hedgerows. Puddles formed in pools by the roadside, shimmering with their warped reflection. There was still snow on the hills, beneath the trees and in the sheltered woods that were steaming from the rain. They stopped to drink from a trough, sitting down to rest with the horses drooling beside them.

The thud of hooves came from the distance – dogs barking, men shouting in a way that could only mean trouble. Gobey and Okoye geed the horses – kicking with their heels and jerking on the reins they rode on, until they could no longer hear the men. For some miles they rode without stopping, passaging cottages and fields and dense woodlands.

Slowing to a clop, they passed around a bend, weary and half-starved from their captivity. Up ahead, a group of men stood casually by the roadside. They were gathered in a circle, oblivious to the approaching riders, laughing and jeering at each other and standing in a puddle.

Gobey and Okoye rode slowly towards the men, who turned to look at them. One of them raised his hand and Gobey did the same. The man smiled and waved in a friendly manner. Then, without warning, he raised a musket from beside his leg and fired at them in a great blast of smoke, jolting at the shoulder.

The horses reared and bucked, and the riders turned them around and began to flee. The men were shouting and firing in their direction. The pellets whistled over their heads, fragments showering their shoulders.

Low in their saddles, ducking from side to side, they kicked at the horses. They took a bend and rode into a dip on the road. A party of men on horseback was approaching, the gunfire was all around them. Gobey and Okoye crossed a field, gathering speed and momentum.

Heads down, they rode without looking back, travelling for miles, until they could no longer hear the guns, smell the sulphurous powder.

They quietly approached a farmhouse. The adjacent barn was derelict, a burnt out pyre of charred cattle bones and reeking flesh. A sheep skull was skewered on a fence pole like a totem of a lost tribe. They passed a narrow track with sloping fields each side, they veered into the woods and climbed on a steep bank. Up through the undergrowth, they followed a cart track where the trees had been coppiced and turf fires were left smouldering in a circle.

They followed the path with no sense of direction. Deeper into the woods, they crossed a felled tree with the roots upturned. They passed a peat bog, an eggy stench all around them. They rose on an escarpment, leaning back on the horses and geeing them up. Haggard and exhausted, they were slumped in the saddle like corpse riders, men dead or not far from death.

The rain drove them into a cave to shelter. They dismounted, leading the horses inside. They clapped their hands, blew on them and stamped their feet. The African wandered back into the shadows, stooping as if still shackled. He stumbled out like an ancient troglodyte, twigs and kindling in his hands. 'Men have sheltered here,' he said. 'Many times.'

'How do you know?'

'Piss, I can smell their piss.'

The African lit a fire with some flint, steel and tinder that he had stolen. He then went to the saddlebag and returned with an armful of clothes. He handed them to Gobey and took some himself. They stripped by the firelight and burnt their tatty garments.

They sat in their clean shirts and long jackets, like gentleman convicts, blackguards of the road. You wouldn't trust them with a penny or a daughter. The African spat from the cave and the horses stirred. 'How long were you imprisoned, Tom Gobey?'

'Seven years.'

'For what crime is this?'

'I wrote a pamphlet.'

The African handed him some dry meat. Gobey studied it, turning it in his fingers. He didn't ask what it was and didn't care where it came from. He chewed it as best he could. 'How long have you been a slave?'

'Too many years to remember. Bristol, Liverpool, Manchester, the colonies and back again.'

They sat as free men, but you would never have known it, hunched and frazzled before the fire. They were constantly halting their speech to listen when a branch fell, or a creature called in the woods.

Gobey went to his horse, speaking softly and showing his palm. The creature turned to him, twisting its neck. He kissed its silky nose and gently whispered in its ear. The horse knew his voice, touch, smell, shape, eyes. There was nothing strange between them. Like old lovers, there was no need to converse – they were content with the silence, the close proximity, the abiding comfort of each other's company.

Gobey drifted back to the fire and found Okoye gone. He called for him, but received no reply. His voice sounded strange in the cave's confines – a hint of panic in the tone. Then the African came stooping out of the shadows with a finger to his lips. 'I hear them,' he said. 'The men are coming.'

'From in there?'

'Echo, vibration.'

They stood in silence save for the sound of the rain. Gobey made to speak, but the African raised his finger. They heard a distant cry, hounds yelping, hooves on the move. They thought it was coming from the farm they had passed – voices blowing with the wind, rising and fading, above and behind the clamour of approaching men.

They mounted the horses and edged down the escarpment. Musket fire travelled through the woods, splitting the branches and thudding into tree bark. There were men on foot, on horseback, men with poles, long sticks and rusty pistols. Wild dogs ran among the trees, the men were roaring and cursing, as if going into battle.

Side by side, they travelled through a peat bog. They scrambled out with the shot whistling around them, tearing up the ground. They progressed into a wood of skeletal trees and onto a marshland. They rode with relentless exertion, until they eventually slowed and could not, through will or power, move any faster.

They stopped, and Gobey stood in the saddle to look back on their trail. No one was following, the gunfire had ceased. They were suddenly struck by the silence. The mist came down, swirling over the mud. They walked on, steering the horses around the boggiest patches, on through the mist like men fleeing war. For hours, they trudged in silence, not foreseeing an end, never contemplating turning back. If there were other places in the world like this, they had never seen them – prehistoric ferns and dead trees, mile upon mile of silent bog – not a bird in song, not a bird in sight.

They drifted into woodland with patchy snow on the ground. They weaved through the shrunken shrubbery and bare trees, stopping to kneel at a brook to drink beside the horses. The African handed Gobey a piece of jerky, which he chewed and swallowed without question. They shook hands for the first time – men lost in the world, but still men, despite all they had lost.

They rode onto a track with signs of life before them – felled trees, split logs, turf stacked in layers on the ground. They passed a smouldering fire, grey and pissed upon. They veered in an arc and came upon a muddy road that ran for miles. They hadn't travelled for long on the road when the wind carried the sound of men behind them – galloping horses, loud calls, dogs cutting through the woods.

They came to a forked road, and a pistol fired and zipped over their heads. They veered off into the fields, and through some miscommunication, rode in different directions. Gobey drove the horse over a fence, forcing it through a ragged hedge. He climbed a steep hill and stopped to look back. Okoye was heading for the woods, with men on his trail, driving their horses and travelling on foot. Flaming gunfire flashed among the trees. The dogs tore in and out of the bushes, some howling as they ran.

Gobey splashed on through a brook, the water rising to his ankles. He scrambled up a bank and crossed a field with the sky unfurling behind a canopy of trees. He rode until the Thames came into view. Still locked in a blue glaze of ice, it snaked towards the city and was lost behind the overlapping hills. He pushed on until he came to a crossroads, calling out to an old man shoving a cart. 'Halloa. What day is it, sir?'

The man stopped and scratched his head. 'It's Friday.'

'Friday, you say?'

Yeah, Friday. What's the occasion?'

'I'm meeting me sweetheart.'

'Well, all the best.'

'Much obliged.'

He rode through a town without stopping, passing the rows of coaches and wheeled barrows on the road. The icy rain stung his ears and face. He passed through a coppice and came out upon the river. The ice looked thick enough to traverse and he rode onto it and stood for a moment. There was no vibration, no cracks anywhere. They moved off tentatively, picking up pace, with the horse panting in the cool morning air. At times, they seemed to share a heartbeat, as if the blood passed from one to another in the same circuit.

He hurried the horse across the ice, knowing the river would soon be liquid again. The storm clouds were blowing to the north, leaving a bright sky behind them. The vendors were packing up their goods for the day, and a line of scavengers were scanning the riverbank – for coins, old rope, discarded bottles.

He left the river below Westminster Bridge, where the traders were hollering to the skies. They were stacking fruit and wrapping flowers and slapping red meat in their hands. He watered the horse from a makeshift trough. He rode by the begging children, the shabby tallow-chandlers and bright-eyed sweeps. The mud was splashing everywhere – off the carriage wheels, the horses' hooves, the rolling carts and screeching barrows. The old dandies were splattered up their breeches – their coat-tails trailed in the muck, their wigs were soiled and befouled with brown spots. The road was overrun with swill, scum, froth, clinker, sediment, ditch water. Pools of oily dye gathered in the courtyard corners.

At Covent Garden, he had to slow for those standing in the road – a drunk, a beggar, a peddler blocking his path. He steered around them and rode on. His body ached at the ribs, his chest felt weighted. Stiff and weary, his muscles needed rest, but there was no time to seek it. The clopping rhythm of the horse was shutting his eyes. He could have slept on a rope off the ground.

Up ahead, he saw the bone-setter leave Will's Coffee House, her white hair hanging down her back. He called to her: 'Halloa, Mrs Shapp!' She didn't seem to hear him. He called again, directing his voice with his hand: 'Halloa, there! Mrs Shapp! It's me, Tom Gobey!'

She crossed the road, limping and dragging her feet, kicking through the mud. The line of her shoulder was crooked, one of her arms was stiff and hanging like a dead appendage. He called once more, but she lowered her head and ignored his pleas. She shuffled through a tight passage that was too narrow to enter on horseback. Rounding the corner, he expected to find her leaving the other side, but she didn't appear. When he drew level to the passage, he found her hobbling back towards the Strand. He turned the horse, but was blocked by a carriage that stopped for no apparent reason. He passed the vehicle and stood up in the stirrups, catching sight of her in a downcast stumble towards the river.

He dismounted, patted the horse's neck and stood looking out beyond Westminster Bridge. He watched her plod across the river, a vision beneath the shadowy sky. She went nodding through the mist like some prophet of old Jerusalem, the injured bone-setter in her flowing gown.

She made her way over the ice, a lone figure with no sense of the world around her. He cupped his hands and roared with all he had: 'Hey, Mrs Shapp! Come back! It's all for a-melting, come back!'

He tied the horse and stepped onto the ice. He followed her, calling, but she wouldn't turn for him. He came behind her and spun her round. It took a moment to adjust to her swollen face. She tried to speak through her smashed lips. 'Sorry, sorry,' she mouthed over and over again. 'Sorry, sorry, sorry.'

Under the bridge, Mr Sticks stepped from behind a carriage, tapping the mallet against his thigh. In low grunts, he sauntered towards them, his dark mustardy face glistening. He made a honking sound – half-snigger, half-speech.

Gobey saw him coming and steered the bone-setter away. She shuffled towards the bank, lopsided, her head hanging, her shoulders sloping. 'Sorry, sorry, sorry.' He turned to face the oncoming assailant. There was no fight left in him, no energy for running – weariness rooted him to the spot. He dragged his feet in some kind of preparation, held up his fists, but could hardly clench them.

Mr Sticks paced up and down, showing the gritty stumps of his teeth. He snarled and smiled, tossing the mallet from hand to hand. Whatever way the wind blew, it carried his stench like the emissions of dead cattle. Gobey leaned away from a grazing blow which glanced off his shoulder and struck his cheek, slashing the skin. He sidestepped and shifted, left and right, backing up. The mallet swung again, cracking his jaw and rocking his head.

He sprawled on the ice, looking up at the sky. He had the sense of the current shifting beneath him, the ice creaking all around him. He could still hear the bone-setter as she departed 'Sorry, sorry, sorry.' He lifted his head and was struck another a blow.

Gobey turned away from his assailant. He thought he was close to death and didn't want to see it coming. His cheek pressed against the cool ice, he gazed down the river and saw a figure staggering through the mist. He watched the diminutive form of a boy approaching. As he got closer, he saw it was the young lad, the lad who had sat with him when he was injured; the lad who would not stop talking and asking questions; the lad who was now holding a slender pistol, otherwise known as the bishop. The boy had fallen asleep at the back of the carriage, and had now woken to the commotion on the ice. He moved within shooting range of Mr Sticks.

The boy held the pistol between his knees, using his thumbs to cock the hammer. He approached with the echoing cracks of the ice running downstream. Gobey met his eyes and a fleeting recognition passed between them. How small he looked, with the pistol raised and his arm trembling from the weight of it. The blast was thunderous, a sulphurous cloud of powder filled the air. The boy rocked and regained his footing, dropping the pistol with a clatter. Wild and bewildered, he fled the river sobbing and did not look back on his deed.

Mr Sticks stood with his head in fragments. He swayed and crumpled face down, a vast pouring of blood on the ice. A last breath passed through him and his heart ceased with a shudder.

Gobey crawled and pushed himself up to kneel, staggering as he rose, falling and rising again. He stumbled towards the startled horses, rearing and twisting beneath the bridge. The carriage door shuddered open, Eileen backed out with her arm in a sling, pale and bruised. The clouds were in pandemonium above them. He swayed and she ran to prop him up.

They made a slow, limping exit from the river, over the bank like weary pilgrims. The horses bolted ahead of them, they dragged the carriage over the embankment and clattered along the road into the distance.

They watched the surge of the dark river return. Great sheets of ice were being carried away, they struck the bridge pillars and whirled with the debris of old wood and bobbing barrows. Upstream, the ice cracked from bank to bank, from bridge to bridge, from Tothill fields to the murderous dark Tower.

They made their way to the horse. It was sniffing the air, scenting the aroma of the river. They leaned on a post, victims of too many beatings. Even their eyes were injured, bruised and saddened. 'This man . . .' he said. 'This man you're with.'

'I'm with no man.'

'Then we're free to love?'

She studied the ground, shook her head and swallowed. From the saddlebag, she took a rag and wiped the blood from his forehead. He scrambled onto the horse, leant down and pulled her on behind him. One-armed, she clung to his waist. He thought she was crying – without tears, without a whimper.

They rode into the wind with the trees bending, the houses and people passing in a blur. The boats rocked on the river, the ice slithered downstream in chunks and frozen islands. Onwards, with the rain smelling of coal and the light fading. They rode until a charcoaled sky rolled in from the east, until daylight could barely illume them – silhouettes against the water, two figures quicksilvered on the surface. They rode until the moon rose like a giant head, peering across the landscape.

CHAPTER 24

They rode into a deepening silence. The countryside was silvery in the moonlight, alive with the darkened forms of shadows, the movement of sheep. The river crept over the bank and through the grass, making a marshland of the fields. The sudden illumination of a swan lifted in flight, a slow lumbering departure across the Thames.

The horse went whinnying through the mist, panting in the cold night air. It shook its head, and a silky spume flew from its mouth. Gobey turned to Eileen in the saddle. 'We'll stop at the next inn.'

'Please, no, we must go on.'

'We need to rest.'

'Please, a little further.'

'I'm on the ropes.'

'Please.'

In that squally cold night, they crossed a flooded field, the moon fluid in the grass. They passed through a lowland meadow scattered with large oaks, bulky and indomitable, solid as the pillars of Rome.

Mud spattered, heads down, they rode through the unholy war of the wind. The country before them lay dark and cold, increasingly inhospitable. They took a worn path through a coppice, past the creaking limbs of the trees, the silver glow of the birch. To the north, they spotted a pocket of dispersed lights from household fires and window lanterns. They veered towards the prospect of rest for the night.

They rode into a village, the red lanterns and yellow candles flickering from the houses. Her body was tense at his back, she glanced nervously up at the windows and looked over her shoulder. A sheepdog passed in front of the horse and circled around them, it dropped to its belly and studied their weary progress

They rode on with newspaper blowing over the mud, up against the shop fronts.

They stopped outside a butcher's shop. A pig was hung upside down in the window. Gobey dismounted and limped across the street. From the horse, she studied his movements – a feeble totter with his head down. It was hard to find the old Tom Gobey in that bruised and battered fellow. No spring in his gait, no ease of movement. She thought he was muttering to himself, or over his shoulder to the horse. The colt pricked its ears to listen, as if it understood.

Gobey entered a tavern, stumbling through the entrance, and a few minutes later, he stumbled out. A sack of provisions held to his chest, he looked wildly about to locate Eileen and the horse. She waved and called out, 'Have you found somewhere?'

'Out of the village'

'All the better.'

They rode into the driving rain and followed the arc of the river inland, with the sheep glowing in the fields and the inky sky before them. The flush of water was all around, it travelled through the river gullies and formed ponds that held a shaky promise of the moon.

Drenched, they rode at midnight through the buffeting wind. The horse dipped its head, shook and slobbered disdainfully – it slowed and dragged its hooves in the mud, twisting its neck. It picked up pace when Gobey called, but a few minutes later, slumped again. Twice it stopped for no apparent reason and had to be geed into life.

Upstream, they came to a clearing with the moonlight in the grass. A cottage was set back from the river, the roof was thatched. An old stone well glistened blue in the rain.

They dismounted, dripping like wet dogs. The rain was in their bones, their hearts, their minds. They could barely hear each other speak. He handed her the key and the provisions. 'Go inside! Go inside!'

She entered, knowing that the river had passed through the cottage – a damp invading presence, the ghosts of pike lurking in the corners. The furniture had mildewy spores, brown patches colonized the walls. All the windows were off-centre, every brick, plank and lintel.

She removed her sling and built a fire, lighting lamps and candles on the crumbling windowsill. Once illuminated the room seemed habitable. There was a farmhouse table and stained chairs, and a large grandfather clock with a rusty mechanism. She found an old tub and dragged it across the room with one arm. Back and forth, she ferried the water from the well, heating it in pots on the range.

Gobey led the horse to the barn and watered it from an old bucket. He had never seen the colt lie down, but now it crumpled in the hay and breathed through its nostrils. He pressed his lips to the soft hollow of its nose – that old biscuity aroma.

He entered the cottage and closed the door. She crossed the room and embraced him – his hair smelt of rain, the night air. There were lines on his forehead, etched during their separation. He looked a stone or two lighter than he used to be. She tried to unearth the old Tom – scraps, morsels, tendrils to the past. In the dim light, there was little that remained of the young pamphleteer, the supporter of the French Revolution.

They hugged in their damp clothes, the river ran away with their minds. They couldn't speak. They could hear the tide pooling in the undergrowth, gushing over the bank and crossing the gravel paths into the fields. In the distance, a barrel knocked against a bridge, a drumming cadence to the night's rain. The river passed in its dark melody – blind to their thoughts, dead to their emotions.

They clinched in the firelight, throwing shadows over the wall. He drank her breath, inhaled her scent. He couldn't get enough of her. There would always be a little more that he wanted, a yearning at the heart of him. Her pulse rushed through him, he could hardly stand. All the old memories of her were flooding back – her slender wrists, the thick hair he used to brush with a crackle. The trim rope of her spine where his palm had passed up and down – up and down in the cold snows of winter, the scorched heat of summer.

There was no scope for great exclamations, there was no room for speech. If he tried to speak, it would only amount to gibberish, jumbled talk. So weary – he was almost falling, and if he could find his voice what would he say? I have missed you in the depths of my bones? I have conjured you in all worldly things? I have breathed you as mist, heard you as wind, held you in a shaft of moonlight? I will never stop loving you, no matter what way time spills, I will never stop loving you? *Never . . . stop . . . loving*. But then he found himself falling to the floor, spinning into darkness.

He stirred in the tub and didn't know how he got there. She was somewhere above him in the steam, her dress sleeves rolled above the elbow. With her injured arm still aching, she wrung out a flannel and rubbed a cake of soap over the plateau of his back. He offered his hands like a child, she cleansed them back and front, up his sinewy forearms and over his biceps. She kneaded his shoulders rising up to his neck, pressing with her thumbs, she drove out the knots and deep-settled fatigue. He was a mass of scars and bruises – from lashes, boots, sticks – everywhere a lump or a wound.

She poured water over his face and soaped his hair, gently massaging his scalp. He leaned back in the tub and they laughed – a beautiful echo from bygone days, when laughter seemed free. Sitting up, he took her hand and steered her to the side of the tub. She knelt and he used the flannel to cleanse her hair and scalp. The water trickled down her dress to her navel.

She climbed in the tub with her dress on, the water spilling over the sides. They faced each other, her legs over his. He lifted the dress over her shoulders. Her collarbone was smoky purple, almost bruised black. Their foreheads touched – resting like dead weights they remained, until the water grew cold around them.

They wrapped themselves in a tablecloth and sat by the fire, passing a brandy bottle between them. He boiled some eggs on the range, tore the bread with his hands and spread a creamy cheese with his finger. They ate greedily and talked about the old days as pamphleteers and young lovers. They laughed for no reason, laughed to hear the sound, to experience the sweet joy of nothing in particular. And they were never far from tears, never free enough to shake off the misery of their lost time together. She held his waist, her head on his shoulder, he kissed her nose and blew upon it. They flicked eggshell into the fire and watched it blacken. The rain spat down the chimney and lashed the windows from the side.

They lit the fire in the bedroom, the flames throwing shadows on the ceiling like wavering fingers. They lay on the bed, with the rain crackling on the thatched roof. They spoke in sleepy murmurs. She stiffened, as if she had dreamt of falling and flinched on impact. Her eyes wide open, her voice rang in the silence. 'He'll not let me go, he has me for life.'

'For life?'

'Yes'

'What hold has he over you?'

'A prison chamber, a rope round my neck.'

'You've broke no laws for ropes or prisons.'

'But I have.'

Her voice had a sticky veracity, a sombre and desolate pitch. He felt sick in the stomach, horribly alert to the way she was speaking. She dragged the words, foreboding in tone, sadness in all of them. He stroked her hair, wove the strands with his fingers. He leaned on his elbow to look at her. 'You've something to tell me.'

'I have.'

'Tell me, do.'

Her long hair was tussled on the pillow, splayed like a large fan. The colour of her eyes was lost in the dark, they glistened when she blinked. She sat up and tucked her knees to her chest. Now he could see her eyes, the sea-green flash of them. She held his gaze, then looked away. 'Begod, I don't know where to begin, I honestly don't.'

'Tell me how he holds you.'

'In two ways'

'Give me the first.'

'Saffronetti is a moneylender.'

'And you owe him.'

'I do.'

'That's your bind to him?'

'It is. He kept me prisoner.'

'He stopped you from writing.'

'Yes'

'And blocked me letters from Australia.'

'He has friends in high and low places.'

'Mr Sticks was sent to top me.'

'He worked for Saffronetti, his debt collector.'

Gobey ran a hand over his face, his whiskers rustled under his fingers. He shook his head and went on doing so for some time. Outside, the rain lashed in the trees and they stopped to listen. He left the bed and stood at the window, the black shapeless night came back at him. 'How else does he hold you?'

'I stole his jewellery and gave it to the maid.'

He snatched a breath to clear his thoughts. The walls were blurry in the firelight, a line of sweat ran cold down his spine. He stumbled into bed and drew her beside him. He palmed the hair from her forehead and held it back. 'He might let you go, forget the whole business.'

'They'll string me up at Newgate.'

'Then we'll run, hide. Keep on the move, merge with the country folk. We'll live among the rustics.'

'His confederates are spies, clergy, judges, magistrates. He has affiliations with the Church-and-King associations.'

'Then we'll flee to France, live under the banner of freedom. There's nothing to stop us, nothing at all. We'll lose ourselves in the war and never be found.'

They spoke for hours with the firelight glowing, their speech echoing around the walls of that small room. They spoke until their voices were as one, until their breath merged with the flowing river and the ceaseless squall. Outside, the trees moaned like the ghosts of dead winters. Their thoughts drifted to revolutionary France, but even the spirit of Robespierre could not silence the wind – no guillotine in the hands of man could silence the wind that was surely coming.

CHAPTER 25

The river glistened in the waxy light of dawn, and the day broke with a crack of thunder, a distant farewell to the migrating rain. A flock of geese fanned over the cottage, over the grassland and between the skeletal trees in slanting formation. Gobey woke and lifted his head to the sound of crabby rooks. Eileen embraced him in a tangle of limbs. The horse could be heard whinnying from the barn, shaking its head and demanding attention.

He left a kiss in her hair and staggered from the bed. She drowsily watched him dress with a solemnity she had never seen. Here was a man in internal debate turning things over in his mind. He was still mourning for the loss of her, as if she had not been found. She wondered how long it would take, wondered if he would ever stop mourning in his lifetime.

Pulling on his boots, he could scent her on his hands. He knew she was watching, observing his movements. Her gaze was like a blessing from the heavens. He turned to her in a trance-like stare – her sleepy smile, her milky limbs, his universe in a bed.

He left the cottage and went outside as the river carried a branch downstream like a giant swirling insect. The smell of displaced silt was all around – thick in the grass, soiled on the fence stakes, halfway up the trees. He stood for a moment, dragging the cold air into his lungs. It was the first time he'd felt truly free since landing in London, and he knew beyond all doubt his freedom was founded on Eileen Dineen. There was nothing in his world outside of her, all his aspirations were driven in her direction. For seven years, he had woken to her phantom, bedded down with her ghost. Now he could feel her presence tingling beneath his skin.

He went into the barn and kicked through the straw. The horse was standing, staring right at him – the sapience of its soft eyes, large and placid. The creature clopped slowly over and stood like a supplicant on his command. He ran a hand along its nose and whispered words of affection.

He re-entered the warm-glowing cottage. Eileen's dress was drying on the range. She had baked some potatoes on the fire coals. They ate them with the skin black, spooning out the fluffy meal. After toasted cheese, they were still hungry and shared an apple, taking turns to bite. Draped in a blanket, she made a cradle of herself, rocking on his lap. 'We should get moving,' she said, resting her head on his shoulder. 'They'll come for us.'

'I know.'

'You move first.'

'No, you.'

The fire spat a flaming coal from the range, it smouldered on the floor and burnt out in a spiral of black fumes. From inside the cottage, from inside their bones, they could sense the passing of the river. Dark river on the move, rolling mother of the city – always on its travels and never looking back. Everything was telling them to go, but they couldn't. Weary and bedraggled, they fell into a deep sleep, warm and entwined in a swathe of limbs.

They rode out at midday with the sun behind them. Their shadows made warped shapes on the river. They trotted past the fields with the rooks circling overhead. Approaching a narrow path the horse grew still, raising its head and flaring its nostrils. Upwind a deer was feeding on the track, it looked up with its ears pointing and stood transfixed with marbled eyes.

They rode into the village where they had stopped the night before. The blacksmith came out of his forge to stare at them. Gobey nodded and the man nodded back. They tied the horse to a fence and bought some provisions from a cramped village shop. They returned to the horse and loaded the saddlebags. The man was still staring, as if he had never seen strangers in his life.

Gobey crossed the road, a cart slowing to let him pass. Two old women were on their knees, cleaning the tavern windows. They noted he was a stranger, his handsome bruised face. He entered the tavern to return the keys to the landlord. He came out smiling and calling across to her. 'I've a boat, a boat for France.'

'You have?'

'I have the name of an agent.'

'He'll have us shipped?'

'Let's hope.'

They turned the horse and rode out the way they came in. They passed the baker's with its steamy window, the tannery with the pungent smell of hides. They came by the river with the tide receding. The birds were picking worms in the freshly exposed soil.

They left the river and rose on a track, with the sky dropping down to meet them. The higher they climbed, the tighter she gripped his waist. He leaned back against her, the heat passing through his coat. She kissed the side of his neck, he closed his eyes to relish it.

Over the hill, they came upon a large house, with some of its windows broken. An old man was fixing the panes with his back to them. Gobey called to him, 'Halloa, sir. I'm looking for a fellow by the name of James Canko.'

The old man turned. 'Who be asking?'

'I'm Robert Stools, and this is my wife, Prudence.'

'I be Canko, whatever your name be.'

The old man fixed him with an analytical stare, a cold sagacity in his eyes. His face was lined from introspection, not laughter. He stood upright, lean and intensely focused – every white hair was greased, tamed and restrained, driven backwards over his scalp.

They dismounted from the horse and Gobey turned to face him. 'I've been told, Mr Canko, that you can arrange travel to foreign shores.'

'Maybe.'

'Am I wrong?'

'Nay.'

'Then you can help.'

'*Help* is an ambitious word.'

'You can make arrangements for us.'

'Follow me.' James Canko turned and walked purposefully towards the house. He stopped and pointed at the broken windows. 'Two or three a week, I be always a-mending them.'

Eileen met his eyes. 'May I ask, sir – what causes them to shatter?'

'Birds . . . They rise off the hill with the wind and straight at us.'

They stopped for a moment to consider the windows – there were feathers tangled in the broken glass, blood smudged on the panes. The old man eyed the birds as they flew overhead, charting them in his peripheral vision. Not until they entered the house did his eyes leave the sky.

He bid them sit at the table, they obeyed silently. He left the room and returned with a bottle of gin and one glass. He poured and took a sip, then another before placing the glass down. He licked his thin lips. 'Something to sail the boat out.'

A white stuffed albatross hung over the fireplace. Its wings spanned beyond the length of the hearth, its domed head had been crushed and left that way. There were baskets and nets scattered around the room, bird traps and fishing gut, a heap of tangled rope in the corner. A sludgy alluvial smell drifted from the floor. The floorboards creaked when no one was walking on them.

James Canko raised his glass and took a delicate sip. 'Destination?'

'France,' they said in unison.

He rubbed his chin, stared over their heads as if something fluttered there. 'That could be tricky, most tricky'

'How so?' said Gobey. 'Where's the problem?'

'We be at war with the French buggers.'

'I know it well, an unfortunate affair.'

'You wouldn't be carrying no arms, would you now? Guns and all that?'

'No, sir.'

'You wouldn't be coming back with any aliens, any of those effeminate Frenchies?'

'There's no plans for return.'

'Settling in the land of revolution?'

'That's the scheme.'

James Canko rubbed his chin harder than before, it sounded like wood being sanded. He took a slow, lippy drink and tapped the glass. When finished, in his own good time, he said: 'It will cost you, that it will. Trips to France in times of war will cost. Make no mistake about it, these things cost.'

'It's expected.'

'You'll be wanting a safe crossing, a man to land you all the way?'

'From one shore to the other.'

'Then it will cost.'

'Fair play.'

'One moment.' He mumbled the price and Gobey nodded. The old man retrieved a notebook from a chest of drawers. He flicked the pages and stood looking down. He sat and finished his gin with a single swig. 'A boat sails frequently,' he said. 'Midday from the old dock, every other day or so. The boat be called *Sea Merchant*. The captain goes by the name of McArthur. Arthur McArthur they calls him.'

He lifted his empty glass and tapped it once on the table, the gin coarsely aromatic around him. Gobey paid and they shook on the deal. Canko's hand was dry and husky, inanimate to the touch. He followed them outside and stood in silence as they mounted the horse. His eyes were taking in the birds, surveying their flight patterns.

They descended the hill with the smell rising off the river – silt, fish, carrion. Eileen turned back to Canko – he held her stare, his eyes devoid of emotion. She leaned into Gobey. 'What a man. What could you say about him?'

'Not much to warm the heart.'

'A cold pillar.'

'A barrel of fun.'

'Tight as a drum.'

They cantered across a field with the dew spraying. A hawk hovered in the distance – swooping to pick up a mouse it passed squealing overhead. They clattered over a grey stone bridge and down the other side. They crossed a shallow mush of leaves, with the smell of rot in the air. The sun shone in long-tapered shafts from the sky, like something painted.

Gobey rode slumped in the saddle, his sweetheart clinging behind. Without warning he broke into song, a song he thought he'd forgotten. He hadn't sung since his transportation, all those years ago. The experience made him weep, weep and laugh in the same action, as if all his emotions were beads on a threaded continuum. She hugged him from behind and they sang together, their voices tangled in the wind.

Late afternoon, they drifted into an orchard, the mist coiling around the trees. The sun was sloping behind the hills, an orange fusion upon the horizon. The copper afterglow drew the rising birds into its magnetic rapture, and they glided like saintly converts towards the source of light.

They came upon a gamekeeper, who was leaving the orchard on horseback. They stopped side by side, the horses eyeing each other. 'Halloa there, sir.' Gobey nodded respectfully at the man. 'Do you know the whereabouts of an inn?'

'You're some way off.'

'How far?'

'Ten, fifteen miles as the crow flies.'

'Which way?'

'That way.' The man pointed through the orchard, as if it were possible to pass through trees, a hillside and that great beast of a river. 'You look down-dead weary, me friend.'

'We are, sir. We are.'

'How far have you come?'

'Further than you'll ever know.'

The gamekeeper dwelled on Gobey's words, scratching his cheekbone. It seemed to take an eternity for him to speak. 'Look,' he said, 'You can stay in me hut. I use it for night-watching the poachers. It's not a palace, but it's comfortable. If it suits, you're welcome to stay.'

'Much obliged, sir.'

'Keep going the way you are – keep going and you'll find it. Go right on in and make yourselves at home.'

'You're a saviour.'

'Glad to be so.'

They rode into the orchard, further into the deadening silence of the woods. They passed a large pond, with the sky purple on the water. The light was growing inky, a mist formed on the distant bank. They followed a derelict wall and found the hut among the trees – a crooked jumble of damp timber, knocked together with discarded planks and mossy driftwood.

They tethered the horse and pushed in the rickety door. There were no windows, no furniture. It smelt of apple pulp, fecund soil and skinned rabbits. A straw mattress was on the ground, a tin flue climbed the wall and out of the roof. Blackbird wings, rabbit hides and squirrel tails were pinned to the back of the door.

They carried their provisions inside. Eileen found some lanterns and placed them in each corner. Gobey went to collect some firewood, but she blocked his way, 'Don't you go running off on me now.'

'I never would.'

'I've lost you once, and I'm not for doing that again.'

They fell into a clinch, the old scents reviving memories – days when they had loved in the fields and walked in the rain, days spent in bed with the sun coming up and going down. 'You and me,' she said. 'You and me.' They rocked for some time like the swaying branches of a tree, above a life of known things and senseless exertion. And all the while she was inwardly speaking to her mother. *I have found him. My boy, my sweetheart. My sweetheart has returned.*

Engulfed in her scent, he made his way outside. The silver mist crept over the pond, a duck screeched and the sound ran through the woods. The day was slowly crushing into darkness, the night setting in before his eyes. He made a slow bending effort to gather some logs, grunting as he lifted. He staggered and came through the door backwards, dropping the logs and rolling them with his foot to the fire.

They sat like fakirs on the mattress, cross-legged on the ground. They swigged rum from the bottle and ate a chunk of bread, passing it back and forth. They lay entwined before the fire, pale and exhausted, edging towards sleep. Something splashed in the pond outside. 'A fish,' he said, opening his eyes. 'Only a fish.'

The melancholy hooting of owls could be heard. He struggled to his feet, rolled a log onto the fire and returned to her. They lay with the light spilling around the hut, flames dancing before them. She kissed his forehead and parted his hair. 'I was thinking about Johnny Steadman.' Her voice was slurred, her eyes sleepy. 'What you told me.'

'I'm always thinking about him.'

'He was a fine fellow.'

'He was.'

'And to die in that way, and the old dog too.'

'I can still hear his laughter.'

'Though friends be lost, their laughter shall not.'

They embraced and held a long silence. The next time he looked, she was sleeping, pale and fretful, frowning and furrowing her forehead. One of her eyelids flickered and he calmed it with his finger. He kissed her face, sniffed her hair, neck, hands – all parts of her were delectable. The luminous arc of a falling star passed over their roof, and they lay oblivious to the gaseous spheres of life hurtling around them.

The dawn streamed through the hut in dusty shafts. The birds made sporadic calls from the orchard, a scratchy winter song that was joyless. From miles in the distance, a church bell rang in and out of audibility, a dog's bark travelled with the wind towards them.

They built the fire and sat on the floor staring at it. They ate some dry bread and sipped brandy to enliven their somnolent state. They talked of old times, their plans of changing the world with the humble pamphlet. When the fire grew dim, they gathered their belongings and thanked that small abode for their short stay.

They rode by the pond, the mist hovering on the water. She pressed her lips to his earlobe, he rode with his hand on her thigh. They crossed a field with scattering sheep, and cows with rolling jaws and sorrowful eyes alert to their presence. Down on the river, they followed the boats, their sails smacking in the wind, their masts creaking.

They drifted into an old barn and loved amid the hay, with the horse watching. In the loft with its roaming chickens, they shared a pie and swigged brandy. They lay picking the straw from their hair, picking over the bones of seven lost years.

They rode by the river, laughing, teasing each other, stopping to kiss and riding on. They came upon an old man fishing with a net. He spoke with his back to them, spoke across the river. 'Laugh and live while ya can. The French are coming, invading these shores. Mark me words on that. There'll be no religion then, no laws, no decency. Atheism and fornication will rule the day.'

They stopped to see if he was talking to them, or to some figment in his head. Gobey called to him, 'Good day to you, sir.'

The old man turned to face them. He had no eyes, just pale and sunken sockets. He raised his head to sniff the air. 'Keeps yer loving to wedlock. Don't be bringing the devil upon yer-selves.'

He knocked the laughter out of them, and they rode uneasily past him. There was a lunacy about the old man. 'Ya hear me?' he hollered. 'Leave off the monkey capers, or you'll fry on the hot coals of hell.'

'I hear you,' said Gobey, turning back. 'I hear you.'

The old man spat, the saliva ran off his chin. 'Make way for the second coming! Beware the judgement of the Lord! He shall come to strike thee down!'

They rode on, and Eileen turned to stare at the old man. He was calling to anyone who would listen, but even the ducks had flown. There were men like this all over the country, lunatic soothsayers, the end of the world was always nigh. She turned away, but a residue of his dark prophecy would remain with her.

Early afternoon, they came to a town and stopped at a trough to water the horse. They stabled it across the road from an inn. They entered the inn, the folk merry and hospitable inside, a good fire rising in the hearth. They ate a plate of bacon and cabbage, the steam rising in their faces. They drank tankards of ale and grew flushed, their heads swam.

Some time later, a band of musicians gathered in the corner. There were two bearded men with fiddles, a young girl with a tin whistle and an old seafarer squeezing a concertina. The fire was blazing and people danced and clapped in front of it. Gobey took Eileen's hand and they joined that blissful throng, reeling towards each other and parting among the locals, who were stomping on the boards. In the swaying room, he saw her as others saw her as if for the first time – throwing back her head and laughing, her streaming hair, her soft green eyes. He couldn't imagine a time without her.

When the music halted, they slumped down and raised a toast to love, travel and the finest ale in England. They hired a room above the inn, climbing the stairs with great fatigue. They slumped on the bed. 'Soon to France, Tom Gobey.'

'Not soon enough.'

'And all that's passed won't matter.'

'Under the bridge.'

'And all our life ahead of us.'

'Years of it.'

'Pamphleteers on the run.'

'Long live the Revolution.'

She glanced at him to find him laughing, shoulders trembling, and snorting like a child. He put his hands to his face and the sound came louder. Mumbling incoherently, he lifted his head from the pillow and crashed it down. She removed his hands and kissed his face, over and over. 'Sure, what's wrong with you?'

Still smiling, he gazed up at her. 'Nothing, nothing's wrong with me. That's the thing, nothing's wrong and I'm not used to it. I'm battered to pulp, but I don't care. I don't. We're together, me and you against the world. That's all that matters to me.'

She stroked his hair. 'There's nothing but us, Tom Gobey. Nothing.'

They lay in silence – lay for some time without speaking, without moving. They had dry throats, parched tongues gasping for water, but only had brandy to quench their thirst. He leaned on his elbow to look at her, at those weary eyes – thin lines were making the first irrevocable claims on her skin. He could see how she might age, where the wrinkles would appear on her face. 'I give everything to you,' he said. 'All I have.'

'I know, I give it back.'

'I know.'

He kissed her and went to the window. The horse was peering from the stable across the street. He clicked his tongue and the colt looked up. Gobey winked and thought the creature winked back at him. The day was losing its lustre, the first lanterns were lighting around the town.

They lit the fire and lay on the bed in silence. The mice scurried under the boards and scratched in the corners. They listened to the sounds of the night – a gust of wind bowled a bucket over; a door slammed in the distance; a singer started up in the inn. They thought of Saffronetti, but did not mention his name. They knew the Revolution was over, that too many heads had rolled in the name of freedom, but to France they would travel, with liberty etched into their souls.

CHAPTER 26

These days passed on the road. They stayed at inns, barns and taverns, never parting for more than a few minutes. If one was in another room, the other made sure they could hear them, sense their presence. They always had this feeling that some dreadful form of separation was waiting ahead. They were joyful at their reunion, but fearful it might end. And there would be no peace of mind until they fled this country, landed on foreign shores. They talked at length about the years they'd lost. Let the past be dead and buried they said, but they knew the past was alive in them.

On the morning of their departure, they crossed the marshes in a gale. They rode into a grassy dip, Gobey sat the horse down and they sheltered behind it. A cyclone blew back and forth across the mudflats, spiralling over their heads.

They could see the wind, or something carried in the wind – dust or debris – rolling in a line, moaning and advancing at speed, changing and reforming like a plague of locusts. They watched it whirl and gather, whirl and disperse until it shaped into a twisting cone. The wind made a blur of everything – a shimmering brown river, a black vaulting sky. An uprooted tree was torn from its roots, and sent crashing to the ground. They huddled and petted the horse to calm its fear.

A barn roof appeared in the sky, it had travelled a mile to reach them. They didn't see it coming, or from where it came – it ran a shadow over them like a giant hand, passing judgement on the earth. The roof rolled into the river and was swept away. The horse began to rear and Gobey talked it down, stroking its heaving chest.

Offshore, a prison hulk was rocking with its flags torn – one of the masts had broken and fell crashing into the sails. The rigging was tangled, spraying ropes and chains around the deck in a lashing motion. The screech of wrenching timber ran the length of the vessel.

They could barely hear even by shouting. The wind growled in the distance, and just when they thought it was gone, it returned with a vengeance – savage in its ferocity. They dug in, heads down, and braced themselves against the onslaught. A constant squall surrounded them. 'We'll miss the boat!' she roared, turning from the wind. Her hair was blowing into her mouth, she struggled to remove it. 'We'll miss the crossing!'

He touched her face, kissed her forehead and leaned back to holler. 'It's all right don't worry! We'll catch that boat! Don't worry!'

An hour passed and they were still waiting for the storm to calm. Gradually the howling ceased and the wind began to settle. There were gaps between the gusts, pauses in the blast. The first bird calls could be heard in the distance. Their voices came back and they were surprised at the dead sound of them.

Gobey geed the horse and it sprung to life, it shook its head and stretched its long legs. They crossed the marshes, the gulls moaning above the river, a sliver of sunlight on the horizon. Vast hunks of clouds were shifting from the north, a line of geese passed through them, wheezing and creaking like rusty hinges.

They travelled for a mile, buffeted by the wind, reduced and battered with no capacity for speech. Onwards, across the bleak marshes, exhausted and half-hanging from the horse. The watery slush of mud had a brackish aroma. They rode all morning until they could hear the labour of men in the distance, voices, a line of smoke rose from the docks.

They shambled into the dockyard, among the scattered planks and upturned barrows. They passed the sprawling workshops, the cavernous warehouses, the industrious wood yards alive with sawdust and hollering men. The waft of molten metal steamed from the foundries in a haze of gas. The air was toxic, alive with choking substances, it was hard to breathe and bitter to swallow.

With flushed cheeks and desperate hearts, the hawkers touted their goods. One of their number approached the horse, he was beating a drum strapped to his waist. 'Flowers for the lady, sir. All ladies love flowers.' A goblin man, he had ears like open hands. His long rubbery mouth was upturned, his testicles were hanging out of his trousers.

'No thanks.' Gobey laughed at the sight of him. 'No thanks.'

'Go on, a lovely spray for the lady.'

'Nay, mate.'

'You'll win her heart with flowers.'

'I have her heart and she has mine.'

'Then flowers to seal it.'

'We've no home to put them in.'

'You can carry 'em with ya. Put 'em in your pocket.'

'Nay, nay.'

'How about a pair of drawers?'

'You could do with a pair yourself.' Gobey laughed and his ribs stabbed in different directions. They moved on, the wind blowing grit against their faces. A line of prisoners were set to work outside the barracks, ballast-heaving and driving posts along the embankment. The guards leant against a fence, passing a bottle between them, leering at Eileen on the back of the horse. One of them whistled and called out something that was swept away by the wind.

They rode along the dockside and stopped by an old seafarer. He was wrapping a rope around his arm, grinding his teeth with his nose running. 'Halloa, good day. Where can I find the *Sea Merchant* and captain McArthur?'

The seafarer looked up. He emitted a laugh that wasn't a laugh at all, more an exclamation. He huffed again in the same dismissive way. 'Captain McArthur – now that's a grand title for the man, a grand title indeed. You'll find the *captain* down along the dock. Follow the boats, straight as an arrow and you can't miss him. You'll hear him before you see him – follow the boats.'

Sure enough they did hear McArthur before they saw him. He was below deck, hollering and cursing in a vile temper. They rode alongside the *Sea Merchant* and dismounted. The old vessel was battered, it creaked in a thousand places, a salty aroma wafted from the wood.

They followed the commotion around to the hull. 'Halloa! Captain McArthur! Good day to you, sir! Good day, Captain!'

The gangplank swung down with a crash, and a huge man stood with his thumbs behind a frayed belt. He had one eye closed, a long hennaed beard, and his face was battered by the wind, reddened by strong liquor.

'Are you Captain Arthur McArthur?'

'Him I am.'

Gobey observed this huge man. 'My name's Robert Stools. I'm here with me wife on a trip to France. James Canko sent us. He said you were sailing today and would be kind enough to take us.'

'Who sent ya?'

'James Canko.'

'Who?'

'Mr James Canko.'

'Never heard of him.'

'Tall old fellow, lean, upright. An icy disposition.'

'Him I never spied.'

Gobey ruffled his hair to think for a moment. Then he turned back to McArthur, 'He said he was an agent for you, sir.'

'I work with no agents.'

'No?'

'Never have, never will. The only agent I know is God above. And he takes no commission, not a bribe or a penny.'

'Look, if this is some kind of swindle –'

'There's no swindle and no nothing. I know no agents old or young, tall or short, warm or cold. I work alone, and I only answer to him upstairs. Now if you're going to waste me time –'

'No, I'm sorry. It's some kind of mix-up, some mistake. This Canko fellow has rolled us over. He's had our money on a false promise. It's no matter for you and we must travel.'

'To France, is it?'

'Yes, sir.'

'The land of Buggerantoes?'

'If that's what you call it.'

'I do.'

'Will you take us?'

'Aye.' McArthur scratched roughly at his beard. 'I'll take ya. For a small cost, I'll take ya.'

'But I've already paid.'

'Not to me you ain't.'

Gobey took a deep breath and exhaled. McArthur came down the plank with the wood straining beneath him. Tall and blocky, he was the width of two men. 'I'll not rob ya,' he said. 'I'm sailing with or without ya. It's no skin off my nose. A small fee is all I ask, something for a bit of food and ale.'

'Name your price.'

'Call it two shillings. I can't say fairer than that.'

'Fair enough.'

McArthur held out his thick hand, black and rubbery like a bear's paw. His palm had a large hole where a stake had passed through it. There was nowhere to place the coins, so Gobey dropped them on his fingers. The captain rolled them tight and ran them into his pocket. 'The weather's against us,' he said, half-grimacing and narrowing his eyes. 'Cutting up rough. We'll not sail till late afternoon, early evening. Get yourself back here for then.'

'Will you take me horse?'

'Aye – horses, goats, pigs and cows. Anything you like, bad spirits and old songs.'

McArthur turned without salute or valediction and clattered below deck. They mounted the horse and rode out with the men roaring on the docks, hammering down planks, pulling on ropes and pushing up barrels. Handling rusty chains, they swigged from bottles and spat. They were soiled by the river, bludgeoned by the tide, they clicked through their teeth and stared lasciviously at Eileen. She turned away to the smouldering ranges, the taste of alloy bitter on her tongue.

They followed the slurry river to the smoking chimneys of the city. The beggars picked stray fruit from the ground, a gang of sweeps were clearing the road of storm debris – roof slates, fallen signs, tree branches, toppled barrows. The waft from the opium dens made a coiling passage through the rookeries. Every corner had a band of peddlers trading in whooping cries.

They steered into Cheapside, the horse nodding in a gentle sway. The crowds were pouring out of Newgate, filtering towards Smithfield and Bedlam. Leaving an execution in carnival mood, they were jeering with explosive hearts, the air full of bloodlust and bitter-charged song.

Gobey turned the horse into an alley, where the destitute were seated on the cobbles. He waited for the crowds to thin and rode out behind a carriage towards Newgate. Down the street, a body was hanging on the scaffold, the hanged man's face twisted away from them. They made a slow clopping approach, but refused to look at that grim spectacle.

Gobey roared and drove the horse on, they steered around a barrow and scattered a group of women in shawls. Some soldiers tried to block him, but he ran them aside. He rode headlong into the Strand, turning heads and provoking curses. On the open road, they leapt a fallen tree and splashed down in the mud. They thundered through a puddle, the horse galloping wildly.

They took a path where the dark forms of cattle roamed. They dismounted and sat upon the roots of an oak tree. They embraced and wept for the years they had lost together, wept until their faces grew taut, their spirits fell calm. The river ran their sorrow upstream, they followed the line of its departure through the city and beyond to the endless swathes of water. The horse stared at Gobey, stared in the way that animals do when acknowledging sadness. He stood up, kissed its long neck and whispered in its ear.

Gobey took the brandy from the saddlebag, and they sat with their backs against the trunk without speaking. They drank in silence – a wood pigeon cooed from the tree hollow, vibrating through them. She sang an Irish ballad and he wept openly, wept and laughed and wiped his eyes with the back of his hand. They could not move, they sat and drank and could not move for the overpowering weariness.

They rode through the city as the wind was picking up. An old gent had his wig blown off and carried down the road. The windows of the taverns rattled as they passed, great gusts blustered through the alleys, clattering a bucket and tearing down a fence. From the rookeries the wind rumbled like some stirring beast, forever disgruntled in its restless roaming.

A gust hit them from the side and they almost toppled. They dismounted and led the horse by the reins. A beggar without a nose begged from them – an aged man thin as a stick with desiccated skin. Eileen gave him an apple and he blew away like a crumpled newspaper, clambering along the shop windows to keep upright.

They entered an inn with lanterns that flickered on the walls. At a fireside bench, they slumped themselves down. They supped ale and crashed tankards to bid farewell to England, land of the not-so-free speech. They drank heartily, the ale running off their chins, and they kissed, anointing and blessing each other for the life ahead. They spent the day in the manner of the liberated – ecstatic in the drunken hour and not thinking beyond the moment.

They rode into the wind, steering around collapsed walls, strewn branches and sparkling glass shards. Lost hats and sheets of newspaper collected in the trees, windows were smashed, roofs carried off and dumped as splintered wood in the road. There were slate fragments all around, in every direction roadside wreckage.

In that hazy afternoon, they rose on a trail strewn with rubble. The day was pale and colourless, as if the wind had torn its guts out. Reefs of mist gathered on the road, forming and dispersing in the cool air. The path rose on a hill and they followed an old cart track, where the wheels had churned up the mud. They looked back on the city – it might have been burning, if judged by the vast clouds of black smoke in the sky.

They followed the curve of the river, past the grubby fishermen flinging out their nets. The boats were sailing in all directions, sails smacking and oars heaving and the voices of men, always more mysterious when travelling across water. They reached the smoky docks, the workers hollering in the wind.

They passed a group of soldiers who were staring at them, leaning on their muskets and fiddling with their belts. One of them flicked a toothpick that hit the horse, and shouted something obscene at Eileen. 'Ignore them,' she said to Gobey. 'We'll be away soon enough.'

'Don't worry.'

They clopped along the dock and dismounted at the *Sea Merchant*. The gangplank was down and the men were loading the boat with a winch. McArthur saw them approach and beckoned them aboard. They led the horse on deck, its hoofs clattering over the planks. The captain was in good cheer, drinking from a bottle and happy to pass it around. They declined the offer, having supped all they could for that day.

They led the horse to the stern and prepared to leave. They made their way to the front of the boat and stood looking out – the sun was going down in a blazing disc, reddening the atmosphere. Gobey leaned into Eileen and she supported his weight – one life against another they balanced a world, the motion of the planets, the drag of the sea.

The *Sea Merchant* left the dockside with the wind in its sails. A flock of gulls followed the vessel, circling overhead and wheeling against the current. They sailed into the sun with their shadows on the deck. They followed the river as devotees, bending to its will, listening to the ghostly hymns of the water.

WHY I WROTE *DARK RIVER MELODY*

The germ of *Dark River Melody* probably started at the British Library while researching for my PhD. I was writing a thesis on the radicalism of Samuel Taylor Coleridge in the 1790s, a turbulent period in England's political history. Working my way through a mountain of old newspapers, pamphlets and various publications, I found myself being drawn into a world that was both captivating and abhorrent. I recall being struck by the brutality and oppressive mechanisms of the state against those who dared to speak out against the Church, Monarchy and Government. I was also stunned by the brutal way that the urban poor were punished for petty crimes. I was supposed to be concentrating on my thesis but was constantly distracted by the moving human stories I encountered. I found myself frequently sidetracked to read a newspaper report or trial proceedings about a hanged thief, a transported prostitute, a drunk in the pillory. None of this was getting my PhD finished, but it was compulsive and impossible to ignore. Unconsciously, I had started to write *Dark River Melody* without putting ink to paper.

Some years after finishing my PhD, I began to write my novel. I chose Georgian London, not because the market was awash with Victorian novels and needed a refreshing change, but because I was passionate about the period and location. Much of the research for the novel was established from my previous studies, and I was born and lived in London for the first 38 years of my life. London in the 1790s then, seemed the obvious place to start.

My experiences from childhood and beyond told me that London was the best and worst place on earth. It *was* and *is* a place of extremes where the bewildering variety of life still thrills me. The polarity